Of
Metal
And
Earth

Jennifer M. Lane

Cover art by Leigh M. Morrow – plotbunnies.net

ISBN-13: 978-1-7334068-7-1

ACKNOWLEDGEMENTS

Thanks to Kendra, Michelle, Rick, and David.
Special huge thanks to Babs, Leslie, Darby, and Nick.
Especially huge thanks to Sunyi Dean, Alia Hess, Essa Hanson,
Leigh M. Morrow, and my editor, Cheryl Murphy.

DEDICATION

To my grandmother Bette for the voice. You've been with me all along.
To my grandmother Lily for the rainy night spent creating drivers for the
passing cars.

To Matthew for the love, support, and for sharing your dreams with me.
Without yours, this one of mine wouldn't exist.

And to Murphy... Wherever you are, whoever you're with.

CHAPTER ONE

Dirt. Bullets of rock. Tree and plant and bone showered James in a hailstorm of earth. It smelled like hot metal. They'd prepared him for a lot before they shipped him off to Vietnam, but nothing prepares you for that much blood.

He wiped his face with the back of his hand, the copper taste of flesh and gore washing over his tongue. Not his. Someone else's. There wasn't time for his stomach to lurch, to give in to the question of which flesh. Whose blood.

James ran for the Jeep, one hand on his helmet, hot from the sun and pitted by the enemy. The other clutched a gun that was no match for artillery. He rolled beneath the Jeep.

Squinting through smoke and dirt, trying to focus while the sky settled, all he saw was earth, strewn red with flesh in strips and slabs. A foot. A finger. Andrew. Norman. David. Indistinguishable.

They weren't supposed to be here. Four friends volunteered. Three followed. Tom stayed home to work at the bar with his dad. James should have stayed. They all should have stayed. If only he could close his eyes and wish Elk River into focus, but he needed to see, to make out the forms of his friends, what was left of them. Thirty men. Seven childhood friends. No one could have survived this.

Calling out to check would give him away. He wouldn't hear their reply, anyway. His hearing had dropped out when the shells fell, heightening his sense of smell. Bile and blood. James buried his face in the grass, playing at death as it gripped his company. He waited for salvation. He didn't care what kind.

* * *

James wore his fatigues home from Vietnam, more a habit than a choice. The bus rocked from side to side. Beside him, a woman tucked one magazine into her bag and pulled out another. Premier Khánh from South Vietnam painted on the cover of *Life*. Her hands moved constantly, thumbing through pages and digging through her giant bag for hard candies and mints, which she offered to James with a running commentary on the state of the world.

The motion of the bus should have been calming, but there was nothing to calm. The closer James got to home, the more aware he became of the things that should bother him but didn't. His chest was an empty pocket where sadness and pain should have been. He focused on the back of the seat in front of him, concentrating on the ripples in the leather. Little rivers, black with dirt. Maybe fifteen miles to Elk River? With the exception of the trip to Vietnam, James had never been so far from town. He was tempted to ask the lady next to him, but she'd only spoken at him, not to him, and James wasn't ready to open the door that he'd closed between himself and the rest of the world. At least she wasn't a war protester.

"Did you see this? John Glenn wants to be a senator." She flipped through the pages. "There are protests everywhere. Segregation. I read that a group of boys in New York burned their draft cards. Where did you say you were heading?"

James craved quiet, but he didn't want to be rude or invite sympathy.

"Just heading home." His mouth was dry, and his voice sounded foreign and distant.

She paused, turning up her nose at an ad for Hamm's beer and playing with her cocktail ring, a chunk of turquoise surrounded by little blue and clear stones. She reminded him of someone's grandmother with a pillbox hat and an oversized blue dress that looked like curtains. She smelled like mothballs and cheap perfume. "A few minutes ahead here is tiny little Elk River. It was on the national news for losing all those boys. Such a rare thing for so many who knew each other to end up in the same platoon and then to lose so many at one time? Tragedy. They're talking about ending the Buddy Program."

James pulled in his elbows, a protective measure. "National news, huh? Tom Brokaw?"

She chewed her lip, flipping past ads in the magazine. "And Walter Cronkite. All of them. I know a man in Elk River. He owns a hardware store. Actually, I knew his wife, but she passed away ten years ago. Goodness, he must be ninety years old by now. I think it's next to the diner." She pursed her lips and shook her head. "I've eaten there so many times, and now I can't remember the name of the lady who runs the place. Anna, maybe. Or Amber."

"Angie. It's down the street from the hardware store, but yeah. Angie." James kept his eyes trained on the wooded horizon. He'd heard little from Elk River. Just a letter from Tom offering him a place to stay, saying that his mail was at the bar and how hard it had all been on the town. Tom hadn't mentioned anything about the national news. James didn't want to ask about the town, to invite questions he'd have to answer or sympathy he'd have to assuage, but he needed to know what was on that horizon. "What's it like there? Media camped out downtown?"

She wrinkled her nose and fumbled for words, which she offered in sing-song sympathy. "Um…It's been a tough time for that little town. Our church went down to offer some support. There's a lot of pain. I think most of that town lost someone." She offered a sad smile to her magazine. "They'll be glad to have you back."

James took in a long slow breath, letting air fill so much of him that there was no room for emotion—if any decided to show up.

Someone at the back of the bus sneezed. Another offered a blessing. Both felt like the spread of disease to James. He shifted in his seat, searching for elusive comfort for his weary bones. "It's been a long trip. Do you mind if I tune out for the last leg?"

"Of course. Listen to me, prattling on. You've had quite the experience. I have a whole pile of magazines here. I'll just let you be." She lifted her hand and patted his knee with her painted nails and giant ring.

James leaned away and held his breath for as long as he could to keep from fogging up the window. There should be fear in there somewhere, but a numbness kept the world outside from coming into tune, like radio static. What would he say to them? What would they want from him? Would they want to know what he saw? Would they want to hear the last words? There weren't any. What would they expect from him? Sadness? He didn't have enough for himself, and he certainly didn't have any to spare. Their questions, what he expected they'd ask, came at him fast. He tried to prepare answers, create a procedure for handling them.

He stopped trying. He didn't plan to talk to anyone, anyway.

Rolling hills melted into farmland, into patchwork quilts of corn and soy. Valleys dotted with sheep and cows. The houses crept closer to the street and each other until they were closely packed.

Everyone who lived there was touched by the loss of someone in the war.

Downtown appeared in the windshield. The bus passed his father's house, and he looked away. The faintest shadow of loss passed over him, but he couldn't grasp it.

Not ready for that yet, he thought. The smell of the house, of sawdust and varnish. Of a future and a family he expected to come home to, if only his father's heart hadn't given up. Unexpected shrapnel from home.

Let's just hope that Tom has a comfortable sofa. Something better than that cot he'd slept on at Tom's when they were kids.

The brakes squealed at the only red light in town and the bus gave a gentle lurch forward. The Methodist Church sat adjacent to the Baptist Church. James had never been inside either. A carefree group of boys dashed out of the five-and-dime store, ricocheting off adults on the sidewalk like pinballs, clutching hauls of penny candy and toys. He and his friends had been carefree once, but that was a long time ago.

Almost home. He tapped his heel against the floor and ran his fingernail along the seam of his pant leg, counting the stitches, a habit he used to keep it together, though lately he was so numb and distant he wished he could fall apart. Another squeal from the brakes, another lurch, and the bus threw open its doors. The chatty woman stood and allowed James to pass.

"You take care now," she said. "Welcome home."

"Thanks for the company." James offered a weak grin and gratitude that he couldn't feel. "Enjoy the rest of your trip."

Heat rose from the sidewalk, and humidity hugged the town. An air conditioner buzzed and dripped water into a pool on the sidewalk. James stumbled onto the pavement and slung his bag over his shoulder. His boots were heavy. Running his hand along the brick wall that led to the door of the bar, he traced the mortar with his finger. He wondered how many years it would take to wear away that mortar if he ran his finger along the sandy trench every day.

CHAPTER TWO

James faced the door to the bar. The door was a landmark. Opening it with ease was a rite of passage for the men of the town, and James and his friends learned young. It was swollen in the humidity but gave way when he pressed the latch of the wrought iron handle and lifted a little while he pushed it open.

Thick-bottomed glasses thudded against the bar and voices faded into the hum of the air conditioner. The room fell silent.

All eyes turned to James. He let his bag fall.

His boots scraped the floorboards as he stepped behind the bar and took a glass from the shelf. He let the corner of his mouth lift into the hint of a smile, feeling like the sheriff in a western, grateful for the role to play.

"Stranger. Beam?" The bartender took a bottle from the shelf and filled the glass halfway when James nodded his approval.

"Tom." James nodded his thanks.

"You're not supposed to be behind the bar, ya know."

"Place is packed. Figured I'd wait forever if I didn't help myself."

Sound returned to the room. Tom took a beer from the cooler for himself. "You just get here?"

"Yup. The one fifteen bus was on time for a change."

Tom inspected him like a used car dealer sizing up a trade-in. James expected as much but wasn't going to hang around for it. He ran a finger along his hairline. A week ago, maybe two, he'd washed bits of their childhood friends down the drain in a cold shower. James nodded toward a door behind the bar. It led to a narrow flight of stairs. "Am I staying upstairs?"

Tom nodded. He threw his apron on the counter and led the way up the stairs. The sounds of the bar faded and muffled behind them. James's boots fell heavy on the stairs, a hollow sound, and his bag brushed the wood-panelled walls. A brass doorknob rattled. Tom reached inside and flipped a light switch. His small apartment smelled like wood and old books. A narrow hallway led to a bathroom and a small room better suited for storage than sleeping. The walls were closing in.

"It's not much. I mean, this is where my dad kept giant cans of God knows what until I moved up here. Sorry it's not bigger. You could fit a dresser in here, I bet. We can borrow a truck from one of the guys at the bar."

"I'll figure it out." James threw his duffel bag into the far corner and gave an empty grin to the bed. "Did you get this for me?"

"Yeah. I didn't want you to come back here to nothing. Thought you deserved somewhere to sleep after all that." The trim around the door was loose. It squeaked when Tom leaned against it.

A stack of envelopes at the end of the bed slid when James sat next to them. "Thanks for getting my mail."

"No problem. Small town. They figured we'd be in touch. Brought it by the bar."

James scattered the envelopes. Letters and cards. Probably condolences and unwanted sympathies. He pulled an official-looking notice from the bank to the top of the stack. "I need to head out there to sort out Dad's money, I guess. Do you know what they did with his stuff?"

"I don't know details but from around town? I saw ads for furniture in the paper."

"The tools?"

"Clarence said everything—his truck and everything—was sold to a guy out in Elmwood. Said they got a good amount for it. Looks like you have a chunk of change coming your way."

"Clarence. Busybody." James gritted his teeth. "What are they saying about me?"

"Honest to God, nothing. Other than saying that they're glad you're back, no one's really focused on anything but picking up the pieces around here."

James grabbed the vinyl strap of his duffel bag and gave it a swift yank. It slid toward him across the hardwood floor. "I gotta unpack this stuff. Take a nap. Thanks for letting me stay here."

"You'd do the same for me." Tom turned to leave. "Hey, you got anything you wanna talk about?"

"There's nothing to say." James pulled white T-shirts and one pair of green pants from his bag. The bag was lighter on the return trip. Eager to leave the war behind, he'd left most of the contents in a trash can in Rhode Island.

* * *

James tilted his drink, watching little beads of condensation join forces as they made their way down the glass. The larger and heavier the drops became, the faster they'd move, forming little streams and rivers. For months he'd spent each night wishing those rivers would carry him away.

Tom cleaned, and James let the last of the laughter and scraping chairs fade from his short-term memory. He did a quick scan to see if long-term memory had anything to offer. It rarely did. Only fragments of scenes and hints of voices. Playing jacks at the bar, his feet dangling above the floor, while Tom's father served cheap beer. The high-pitched voices of boys, before the vocal cords stretched, fading in and out like ghosts playing games with his mind. Riding bikes to the five-and-dime. Playing cops and robbers in the alleys. Pointing wooden guns at each other and yelling. *Bang. Bang.*

Tom's voice broke through, running a rag over the bar and collecting money as he went. "I'm not criticizing you. I don't know what it's like to be where you've been, but I know it was hard to be here. Every time that door opened, it got quiet in here. The news was never good. A whole week of funerals. Every guy I grew up with except you."

"You were lucky." It was the only thing James could think of to say. He sat his drink on the wet bar and stared down into the golden amber liquid. It smelled like wood and ash.

"I don't feel lucky. I feel guilty. I feel like a coward, 'cause I didn't volunteer with you guys. 'Cause I wasn't there. And I'm sad 'cause I lost most of my friends. Now I feel like I'm losing you, too. You've spent months doing nothing but drinking. Months."

"You wish you were there? What were you gonna do that I couldn't? It wasn't a summer at the beach. It was a gruesome, bloody disaster. If you're expecting me to apply a bandage to your wounds because you were here instead of there, you're asking the wrong guy."

"That's not what I was sayin'." Tom ran a hand through his shaggy brown hair, pulled the tray from the register, and counted down his drawer. "I'm doing a bad job of saying that I want you to be happy. We grew up together, man. We played darts in that corner over there while my dad sold drinks to all those losers from town. We watched them stumble out of here, miserable, every night. Going back to their run-down houses and their angry women. We don't have to be like that. You've been sitting at this bar for months and you can keep sitting here for as long as you need to but at some point, I just want you to be happy and have a great life. They'd want that, too. The whole town. Seeing you do well and be okay. Everybody wants that."

"Yeah, except it isn't everybody's business."

"I guess you're right. It is your business. If you are totally fine with the whole town watching you become an angry, bitter drunk then I guess that is your business."

What more does the world want from me? The back of the chair creaked when James pushed away from the bar. "Angry, huh? That's what they're saying?"

"Not in so many words. It's not like people sit around and talk about you. They don't. Nobody pities you. They just want more for you than..." Tom trailed off, zipping cash into a pouch.

Sure. Nobody sat around and talked about how he spent his money or how he drank his time. Not in this small town. "Want more for me than what?"

"Maybe they're looking for a little bit of hope after so much sadness around here. And watching you search for rock bottom hurts a little bit. People want to help you find a job, see you doing something with your life. But you're just slinking around town. You don't talk to anybody. You don't even talk to me. It's just...I'm sorry if I sound mad. I'm not. Just don't wait until it's too late before you let people help you."

They trained me to be a killer, and now they want me to be their cure? He took a sip of whiskey and let it wash over his teeth, numbing his gums. "What do you want, exactly? You want to know what it looked like? What it smelled like? You want to know what it was like when I picked up Andy's arm? Maybe it wasn't his. Shit. It was hard to tell." It wasn't often that the door to those memories opened, but when it did, a gust of images would blow in, vying for attention before fading away. It was frustrating, trying to grab

11

them and make them stay while fearing what he would remember. "It wasn't a family vacation, and I don't have a photo album. I'm not a hero, okay? I'm just a guy who came home. I don't want to seem ungrateful, 'cause you're the closest thing to family I've got. I just don't have anything to tell you."

Tom took a toothpick from a shot glass on the bar and stuck it between his teeth. "I don't think anybody wants to make you go through that. I don't. That's not what I meant. But if you ever wanted to talk about it…"

"What? You're here for me?" It would take a time traveler to undo the things he'd seen, the things he smelled. To bring back what he lost of himself when he lost his brothers in arms. No amount of goodwill on Tom's part could fix James. "We've been friends since we were…two? I know. I wish I had something to say. I wish I *felt* something, but there's nothing. Everybody wants something from me. Sadness, anger, hope. I've got nothing to give 'em. I don't feel anything at all."

"Pleasing them isn't your responsibility. You are your responsibility. I don't know anything about going through a war or putting the pieces together after everything falls apart, but I know you can't climb outta this hole unless you pull yourself up. There's gotta be some hope for the future. A job? A car? A girl? Not to live in my closet for the rest of your life?"

James pushed his fingernail into the bar. The old varnish had given up and become gummy and glutinous. "Look at me. Look at what I am. You think I don't see the way they look at me? Half of them resent me because I'm here. The other half are afraid of me. Who's gonna give me a job? I'm either waiting for people to treat me like I'm normal or marking time before I leave, and this place is all I know." James finished off his Beam and walked his glass behind the bar to the dishwasher. "I'll pack up and leave if that's what you want."

"That's not what I want. I feel like I'm watching you fight for your life. I just want to help, and I don't know how."

"Funny. That's the last feeling I remember having." James closed the dishwasher door with a click.

James's boots thumped up the stairs. He held the knob while he turned the key and walked gently through the apartment. He hated the sound the drinking glasses made when they rattled against each other on the shelf above the sink. He closed the door to the closet where he slept, unlaced his boots, and watched the room spin.

He searched his mind, digging through fragments. A flicker of a memory. The ghost of a voice. The faintest hint of a smell. He picked at the scabs and poked at the scars, but they wouldn't bleed.

Flat on his back, drunk, his knuckles rested against the cold hardwood floor, and he watched the ceiling. Spinning. Falling back into place. Spinning again. His breath reeked of whiskey. He breathed deep, letting his chest rise and offering up his spirit like a prayer, but there was no savior to accept it. He wanted to rise like a song from a choir. He yearned for something to hold onto. A grudge. Vengeance. For something to clamp down on his heart and squeeze until he could feel.

He put his hands over his eyes, peered through his fingers like prison bars, and listened to the wind against the window, to the curtain scrape against the floor. Groping, he found the toe of a shoe, the thick sole, the ripple of the rubber etched by miles that meant nothing, that were marched by someone else in another life.

He sat up, laced his boots, left the apartment, and started to run.

Street lights made yellow pools in the road. He dodged them, staying in the darkness. It began to rain. A cold rain that dripped from his hair into his eyes. It soaked his shirt. It ran down the back of his neck, down his legs, and into his boots. He ran to the door of the house that was once his father's.

It was supposed to be easy, the leaving and returning home. He should have been mending people's porches, not hiding from their opinions of who he ought to be and how he ought to feel. Taking shelter on the porch—on his knees—he cried for the boy he used to be and for the man his father would never know.

Day arrived as a pink glow. It seeped between the houses and around their rooftops, painting the street, but it was a newspaper that woke James. It landed by his feet, on the porch where he slept on a metal glider, rusted from years of neglect. He swung his feet to the floor and picked up the paper, rolled tight with a rubber band and wrapped in an ad for Jenkin's Jeeps.

James knew that he couldn't live in the darkness forever, waiting for dawn. He had to pick up that darkness and carry it with him into the light. It wouldn't be easy, but he only had one chance. A chance his friends had lost.

CHAPTER THREE

The key was small, no bigger than the one he still carried that locked his father's old filing cabinet. James slipped it into the ignition and turned it until he felt resistance and the engine fired, its idle high. He shifted his weight in the driver's seat and adjusted his wallet in his back pocket. It was lighter. He felt no remorse.

He inched the Jeep through the dealership parking lot, stopping where the curb sloped toward the street and waited, not for passing cars but for direction. To the right, Route 62 would drop him in front of the bar. It was tempting but not as tempting as the mountains and streams to the left.

He drove past fields bordered by lines of trees, property lines and crop divisions untended by man and sustained by nature. The fields grew smaller and the trees more dense. He filled his lungs with the crisp, damp, cool air that hung in the shadows. Pine and decay. Water and rock. A gravel shoulder with deep wheel grooves gave away the fishermen's secrets but James already knew. He'd met with nature there as a child. Slipping down the spongy hill, thick with needles and damp leaves, he landed by the stream where he first learned to pray the way boys without religion do. Nature always called to James. It knew when he had something to say.

He rested on a flat rock at a curve in the creek where water churned in an eternal babble. Two sticks with strings lay in a tangle, the makeshift tools of boys who fished for sunnies. Some things never changed. He hugged his knees, his boots leaving wet prints on the rock. Thick and clunky. They looked three sizes bigger than he felt.

James watched the path of leaves carried by the stream and felt small but connected. Made of the same stuff as the leaves and twigs that floated downstream and moved by the same force that pushed the water to the ocean. He picked pebbles and mud from the sole of his boot and decided he needed new ones. Something he chose that wasn't assigned to him by rank.

He remembered something his father told him about being humble in defeat, but the voice was drowned out by laughter across the creek. The boys, perhaps, returning to their fishing. The shadows had started to change direction, anyway. James rose to his feet, brushed off his jeans, and climbed up the hill to his Jeep.

He drove toward town, retracing the route of the bus that delivered him home to Elk River. Past the bar and the Five-and-Dime store. Past the diner and the church. He aimed toward the feed store for a new pair of boots. A different color. A whole new path.

But the horizon listed to the right, and the *thud, thud, thud* of a flat tire pulled him to the shoulder. He came to rest at the foot of a driveway.

James turned in his seat and dropped to the ground. The soft doors and top were options he'd ordered. They would arrive in their own time. Without them, the ground was merely a step away. He ran his hand along the curved hood, its headlights large and round like bug eyes peering from the black grill. He placed a hand on the fender, wide and flat with a curved edge that sloped toward the tires and dropped to one knee.

A nail. At least he had a spare.

"This one of those new CJ-5s?" A sun-soaked man in his late seventies stood where the driveway met the street.

"Yup." James stood, brushing dirt from his hand.

The man took a sip of tea. "Looks like you got yourself a flat tire."

"It's always something."

"You'll have to come up to the house then and get yourself some tools." The man turned and walked up the driveway to a red barn. James followed him inside, the hot air thick with pine and cedar. "There was a time I'd have fixed it for you, but my knees are older than yours." He gestured to a tool box. "Take what you need. Third drawer down."

James gathered sockets in his left hand and held out his right. "Name's James. Thanks. I appreciate the tools."

"John." The man introduced himself with a drawl. He had a slouch that gave him a calming demeanor that James found approachable. "I know who you are."

"You know who I am?"

"You've done work for me before. With your father. Chest of drawers for my wife."

"Painted green. I remember." James remembered the rare paint color and learning to make classic dovetail joints.

John gave a slow nod. "Your father was a good man."

"Yes, sir. Thank you." James shuffled the sockets in his hand and grabbed a ratchet from the drawer, holding it tight in his fist. The sooner he could get back on the road and away from the small talk, the better. "If you don't mind, I'll change this tire and get out of your way."

James stepped through the barn, across the threshold. His boot landed in the sun.

"I need help around here," John called after him. "If you know anybody."

James lifted his chin and ran through the possibilities. He'd never worked on a farm but he wasn't afraid of hard work. Distance from the town, from the chatter, and the scrutiny were appealing. "What kind of help?"

"Simon retired a few weeks ago. He was our odd jobs man. We've been looking for the right person to take over the work ever since. Run equipment during harvests, move cattle around in the fields, fix broken things. Car tires, doors, shutters. Fences. Lots of fences. Something's always falling apart out here. There's plenty of work to do. Only thing is, we're a small farm. Simon used his own truck, and we can't afford to buy one right now."

"I got that Jeep. I don't have much experience, but I can learn. Are you offering me a job? You don't even know me."

One corner of John's mouth curled, and his eyes narrowed. He looked like a man with a secret he'd never share. "Son, I've been around for a long time. I know what I need to know."

James adjusted his grip on the ratchet. "What about me? What would I need to know?"

The old man stepped into the sun and stood next to him, looking past the two-story gothic farmhouse, toward the rolling hills beyond. They were cut into squares of crops and fields, bordered by dirt paths and wood fences.

"It's not glamorous. It can get dirty out here. We're a small farm. We do the best we can with what's on hand, but we pay well enough. Your father was out here a few times. He did good work, and that's all I need to know. We don't expect perfection, but we like loyalty. Fit is important. We're a family."

Family. James didn't need family. "I don't know if I'm cut out for..."

"Don't get me wrong. This is a pretty solitary job. All those fences haven't been touched for years. They're rotting from the inside out. It could

OF METAL AND EARTH

take you months, years, to replace the broken parts. I don't care where you start or how long it takes, as long as it gets done. You show up and work, we'll pay you to do it. Tomorrow then?"

James looked out across the hills at a landscape made by the same forces that moved the streams and rivers. He might not find salvation at the farm, but solitude and connection were the next best things. "Tomorrow."

"A'right. I'll see you in the morning." John stepped toward the house. "Come on up to the porch after dawn, and I'll get you started. My wife, Lily, serves lunch inside. She rings the bell at noon."

* * *

James spent weeks pulling fence posts from the back of his Jeep and sinking them in the ground. He was far from the farmhouse in a distant field when Lily rang the bell on the porch and it pealed across the farm. He took a sandwich from his toolbox and let the lid close with a bang. From the passenger seat of the little green car, he watched a dozen men emerge from barns and tractors, from tall grasses and low crops, making their way toward the house. Crows landed and took off again, cawing at his unwanted presence. James turned his back to the house and slid into the passenger seat as he'd done for weeks, peeling the parchment from his sandwich and biting into it while watching the sheep graze. A wound on his hand throbbed when he sat still long enough to notice.

It was a cut from the edge of his toolbox, deep, and sliced into the side of his hand below his pinky finger. Probably needed stitches. Nothing fatal. Blood seeped through the bandage, leaving a dark stain. With his teeth, he tugged at the knot and let the rag fall to the floor. He tied a new rag from the glovebox around his hand and used his teeth again to secure the knot.

"James." He jumped when Lily dropped a basket into the back of his Jeep with a hollow thud.

"Miss Lily? Is everything all right? Do you need help at the house?"

She was larger than her age and fragile frame suggested, hands on hips and feet firmly planted. "Not really. What I need is for you to go up the house to wash your hands before you eat. Of course, I'd like it best if you ate at the house because I cook enough for everybody, and I hate to see it go to waste, but if you insist on eating outside, you at least need to come in and wash your hands before you acquire some strange disease."

"Yes, ma'am. I enjoy the quiet out here, and I like to eat and get right back to work. I don't mean to seem ungrateful…"

Lily waved a hand. She slumped her shoulders at the sight of the half-eaten sandwich. "Do you keep your lunch in your toolbox? You can't eat food you store in a toolbox. And you need more to eat than that. I will not have you starving to death out here in a field."

James started to protest to secure his privacy without offending her, but she didn't give him room. "Your lunch is in that basket. If you're not going to eat at my table for lunch, you'll have to take it home for dinner, so I know you're eating something other than those thin, floppy sandwiches. You can bring the basket back to me tomorrow morning." She patted his arm, turned on her heel, and stomped a few steps across the field. "And if you cut your hand on something rusty, get a tetanus shot. Don't want to live with that in your veins forever."

CHAPTER FOUR

Fall faded into winter in 1967. James moved from the closet above Tom's bar and into an apartment above the newsstand. He descended the stairs into a dusting of snow. The air was thick. More snow would fall. The Jeep's metal door pull froze. He pushed until it gave way, opened the choke, and started the car, blowing air into his hands while he waited for the engine to warm. He knew exactly how long it would take. He counted.

Fifty. Fifty-one. Fifty-two.

The car was his constant companion, a soundtrack to his life. Clanging tailgate chains. Creaking body panels. The idle of the engine. He knew how it ran in the winter and how it smelled when the warmth of summer's hottest days released the scents of rubber and oils and grease. He knew the feel of the thin steering wheel warmed by the sun, and the cold seats on a brisk autumn morning. James was alone, but he wasn't lonely.

Snow swirled into the barn and across the concrete floor in the wake of his Jeep. It was too cold to face the wind in the fields but not too frigid to work in the barn, the perfect day to fix the doors to the cabinets that lined the wall. He knelt on an old horse blanket to insulate his knees from the floor.

"Good morning." Lily loomed over his shoulder as he removed the hinges that held a cabinet door in place. "What are your New Year's Eve plans?"

"New Year's Eve? Sleep?" He didn't look up at her. He knew what she was up to.

"John bought funny party hats, and I'm cooking a goose. Most of the men are bringing their wives and kids. It'll be fun. You could bring someone with you, if you want."

He removed the last screw, pulled the cabinet door from its frame, and stood. Lily could be relentless in her search for his happiness, as if it must be on her terms. "Like who?"

"Like, a girl?"

"Miss Lily. I keep telling you. I like a simple life. Just me and my Jeep."

"It'll change one day. You let me know if you change your mind. There's always enough food to go around."

James brushed sawdust and shards of old paint from the knees of his pants. Three years. Lily wasn't ever going to give up. He returned the tools to the box in the back of his Jeep and raised the tailgate, giving it a friendly pat. He would eat at her table, but he didn't need the complications of people and the transient nature of life. The inevitable rust and rot and decay of his Jeep, he could predict. Metal he could mend. Flesh was fleeting.

* * *

Spring teased at the edges of March. Patches of melting ice and snow floated on the fields like icebergs, and James drove his Jeep among them, making his way back to the house. Mud splattered his pant leg and the sides of the CJ-5. At the side of the barn, the car came to a creaking halt, and James lowered one foot at a time to the wet earth, mud oozing around his boots.

He slogged through sludge and stopped at the bottom of the porch steps to kick his feet against the post. Piles of mud formed in the gravel.

James called up to John, who rested against the house, next to the screen door, blowing warm air into his hands. "The fields are so wet you could sink halfway to your knees if you stand still too long." The bottom step was heavy with water, its planks swelled. He pushed at one with the toe of his boot and water bled from the grain of the wood. "This porch isn't doing much better. Some of these planks need replaced and all these rusty nails keep popping up."

"Too much going on to worry about that." John fixed his eyes on a spot beyond the tree line.

"I'll take care of it. Won't take a day or two." James climbed the stairs and followed John's gaze toward nothingness.

"She'll never be the same. The bones don't heal the same. And at her age, she probably broke her hip before she fell, which means that her bones aren't as strong as they used to be. Best case scenario, she'll need a cane. Either way, she won't be getting up those stairs."

Everything about John looked tired. His skin was loose on his arms, papery and thin. His face was gaunt from the hunger strike. In a way, James envied his broken heart and the courage it took to spend a lifetime with someone, knowing it would end. But if that was the toll a man would pay, James could do without it.

"I can take on some of this. Let me turn that sitting room behind the kitchen into a permanent bedroom. I'll get the guys to help move the furniture down there. We'll work it out."

"It's going to take more than that, James. She can't be left alone, and I'm not putting her in some hospital."

James chewed on his chapped lower lip and shoved his hands deeper in his pockets. John would have to accept his sweat equity, because his brand of emotional support would barely qualify as scaffolding. "I can drag out every little project so she's never alone in the house and you don't have to worry. There's a long list of stuff inside we could tackle. Fix up the kitchen. Get that wallpaper out of the bathroom."

"That'd be a big help. That stuff needs to be done anyway." When John sighed, the farm seemed to swell and sink with him. "You know how much we appreciate you. Everything you do here. You're like a son to me." James watched John's weak smile deflate, and his eyes refocus to the wooded horizon. "I'm not going to be able to run this farm by myself anymore. There's too much to it. There's too much land to keep up with, and the business stuff takes up a lot of my time. I'm not young anymore. I need her more than I need this farm, but I can't let it fail. It's time I start teaching you how I run it."

"Me? Isn't there someone more qualified than me?"

"Who would you pick? Martin can barely read. Half those guys don't know enough math. They do one set of tasks and that's it. You got your hands in every bit of this farm but the checkbook. I know you got it in you."

James chewed the ragged end of a thumbnail. "Things'll settle down. It'll take some adjustment but—"

"I've been at this my whole life, son. This is the only thing I've ever known. I was born in this house. Lily and I got married in the yard here. Our son doesn't want this place, and if we don't start delegating some of the heavy lifting around here, it won't last."

James couldn't offer much in the way of comfort. He had no relative tale to tell. Neither the emotion nor the words were in his vocabulary. Following John's stare past the farm, toward the woods, the best he could do was hope.

* * *

James closed the bank ledger and added it to the stack of invoices and account statements piled on the small kitchen table. He looked to John, waiting for more instruction on managing the books but the weary man rubbed his eyes with the heels of his hands and ran his bony fingers through his thinning hair.

"That's all there is to know," John said.

"Seems easy enough. Just paperwork." More money went out than came in most months. Looking at the numbers required strength, and that was the hardest lesson to learn.

"Thanks for agreeing to take this on." John traced one gray eyebrow and moved to the fridge. Glass jars of milk and moonshine clanged together when he opened the door. "Listen, before you run off. We've got some business people coming to the house, and you'll probably be meeting a few of them. You can't say anything about them to anyone."

Business people. Probably with their hands out. "Like who? And who would I tell?"

"I know. You never talk to no one." John poured orange juice into a glass for himself, and offered some to James, who declined with the wave of a hand. "There'll be lawyers and real estate agents and banking people around from time to time. Just pretend you don't know anything."

"Bankers and lawyers and real estate agents are only good for one thing. Are you selling the farm?"

John lowered himself into his chair at the table and pushed aside a stack of papers, making room for his glass. "Not the whole farm. Part of it. Taxes keep going up and profits don't. We have more land than we use. You know there's more than a thousand acres behind those woods? The government wants to buy some of it so they can put a highway back there. The timing is right to sell the rest to a developer. It'll give us the money to secure the future of the farm while Claire decides what she wants to do."

"Claire?" Life at the farm seemed to be changing so quickly, yet getting the information from John seemed to take so much time.

"Granddaughter. Our son never cared about life on a farm, and I can't blame him. He married a fancy city girl, and they live outside Philadelphia now. Claire is a veterinarian, and she has it in her head that she might want to run the farm after Lily and I are fertilizer. Hasn't been here since she was a kid, though. Her father's trying to convince her not to, but she thinks it sounds romantic, getting away from the suburbs and running a farm."

James took his glass to the sink and hoisted his coat onto his shoulders. John was asking a lot of him, to carry the worries of the farm. The peaceful days of mending fences were over. From here on out, he'd be holding the place together by the seams.

* * *

Men arrived in fancy cars, straightening their ties and carrying briefcases to and from the house. Rumors and unease blew across the farm. John stepped outdoors at intervals for welcomes and farewells.

Late spring sun warmed the earth and slid down the sky toward the horizon. The tan and brown fields of winter were splattered with growing green crops of soy and corn. A breeze pushed across the porch where John dropped a case of cold beer and stood, his feet firmly planted, watching the sun set on the men who worked the land. They were the latest custodians in a timeless chain of farmers who cared for the earth, for a plot of land that was equal parts heritage and home. He had no regrets for selling what he no longer needed. As far as John was concerned, he had no choice but to trade his youth, and he was happy to do it, as long as the legacy remained. With the rope held tightly in one strong but tired hand, he rang the bell and called the men to the porch.

The red-orange sky faded to purple. Men leaned on railings and sat on stairs. Sweat dripped from bottles of beer, falling in heavy drops to the planks of the floor. John reached inside and turned on the porch lights, silencing the nervous chatter. He let the screen door slam to a close and cleared his throat.

"Boys, we all have a reason to celebrate tonight." John sipped his beer and let himself fall back against the wall. He rubbed an eyebrow. "I know you've all been uneasy lately. Asking questions about the people coming and going and us turning so much over to James. Some things around here have to change. We have to prepare for a time when Lily and I can't run this farm anymore."

John wiped condensation from his beer onto his pant leg and took a sip from the bottle. He held it in his mouth and searched the rafters for the right words. "We sold all that land behind the tree line for that highway they're putting in, and a developer is gonna build a bunch of houses on the rest. We won't miss it. Hasn't been farmed since my grandfather's day. But it gave us some money for our future. And yours."

The men picked at rolled-up beer labels and let them fall to the floor. The porch creaked and sagged under the discomfort. "The good news, then. We've never made enough for profit sharing or bonuses, and God knows you don't get a pension working on a farm, but you've stuck with us anyway. Part of taking care of our family means taking care of you, and we worked it out so each of you get a little lot back there with a house. The lawyer guy and someone from the developer will be here in a few weeks to talk to you about it. You can keep it or sell it. Either way it's yours."

The sun had set. The first moths of the year found the porch lights, casting shadows on the floor and walls. Gratitude filled the silence.

"One more thing." John raised his hand and cleared his throat. "Some of you remember our son. He has no interest in running this farm, but our granddaughter thinks she might. She's a veterinarian now. She called today. She'll be moving in here soon to take over animal care. She'll be learning how this place operates. Maybe open a practice in town to treat cats and parakeets. It'll be nice to have an extra set of hands to help out around here.

Make her feel welcome."

John swallowed a sip of beer and swatted at a mosquito. "That's all. All good news. We still have the farm to run, and you all still have jobs. Tomorrow is just another day."

His eyes scanned the porch and found James in a dark corner. He nodded a request to linger.

The men offered their thanks, and John shook their hands, painting a reassuring smile for the workers he considered his brothers and sons. One by one, men launched off the porch, tossing bottles into a metal trash can by the barn. Breaking glass echoed against the house. Heavy car doors slammed, and engines roared to life until all that remained were the crickets and the sound of chairs against the floor as James pushed them back into place.

"We've got a lot to do before Claire gets here," John said. "The whole upstairs needs work. The bedroom smells like Ben-Gay and mothballs, and there's that creepy wallpaper with birds on it. Everything needs paint. You know Lily will have ideas. Maybe we could turn that old sewing room into a sitting room. Fit a little kitchen up there so Claire can be independent."

James pushed the last chair against the wall. "I can get started on it in the morning."

"Thanks." John paused with his hand on the handle of the screen door. "We really want her to be comfortable up there. Anything you can do to make it livable for someone your age."

* * *

James straightened one of Lily's old dish towels on the handle of the stove, but a hot summer breeze pushed through the open window, and it fluttered to the floor again. He stopped fighting with it and left it in a ball on the counter, waiting for John to finish his tour of Claire's new home on the second floor.

"You've done a lot of work up here." John glanced around the kitchenette.

"All the wallpaper is gone, everything's been repainted. Tore the carpet out, cleaned up these old floors by hand."

"Lily's old sewing room makes a nicer bedroom. Don't know why we never thought of that. The sun doesn't hit you right in the face in the morning."

"It just worked out that way. I followed the water line and put the sink on the other side of the wall from the bathroom, where your old bedroom was. Then I turned the other room into a living room."

John patted the counter top. "These came out nice. And that table? That's new."

"I made that. It's an odd size space, so I made one to fit right under the .window."

"She'll love it. It's much nicer without all the busy wallpaper and peeling paint."

"Thanks. It still needs some things. Some rugs, I guess. Curtains. A trash can. But that's the kind of stuff she'll want to pick out on her own."

"I'm sure the two of you will be running all over town once she gets here."

James inched toward the stairs, eager to put distance between himself and the idea of spending time with John's granddaughter. "I'm happy to do it. I really am. But don't you and Lily want to help her get settled? I can hold down the fort here for a day while you take her into town."

When John's shoulders fell, James saw him as he was—an exhausted, frail man who was grasping at the loose threads of his unraveling security blanket. "I would love to, but I've got my hands full around here, and my back's too weak for heavy lifting. I have plenty of time to catch up with Claire. Besides, she's going to want to know some people her own age. No one wants to hang around with us old folks all the time."

"I don't complain."

John laughed. "No, you don't. But you should definitely get out more. It would get Lily off your back, at least."

"I hear my name." Lily's voice resounded up the stairs as James turned to walk down them. "Stay there, you two. I'm coming up. I want to see this penthouse suite you've built."

"I wish she'd stay in that wheelchair. Persistent woman." John rolled his eyes. "Soon, we'll have two of them."

James held in a breath to suffocate the anxiety. It looked increasingly likely Claire would be inserted into his world, if not for work than to satisfy Lily's goal of seeing him match her definition of happy. He'd built a comfortable routine, and now he had to alter it before Claire did.

He met Lily on the stairs to lend his shoulder and supported her as she inspected each room, coming to rest in a velvet channel-back chair that James had borrowed from downstairs for Claire's sitting room.

"She'll like this very much, James. You do nice work, and I think she'll be cozy here." Lily supported her weight on her cane and lifted her chin, scanning the room. "All the years I spent up here, knitting baby blankets and mending the clothes John tore to shreds in those fields. I never imagined my little grandbaby would be living up here. James, have we told you about Claire?"

James didn't need to know about Claire. He didn't need to know what furniture she liked, what she planned to do at the farm, or even how she took her coffee. The only thing he needed to know was how to avoid her, but he couldn't avoid Lily. "I know she's a veterinarian."

"She's smart as a whip. She gets what she wants. She grew up in the suburbs, and she doesn't know a thing about life on a farm, but she's a determined little thing. Don't underestimate her. Claire is a healer. The rest is up to you to find out. I think the two of you will get along just fine."

James said nothing. He watched as she rose from the chair. "Now help my old bones downstairs, James. It's time for tea."

CHAPTER FIVE

James folded the newspaper over his knee and let it fall to the porch beside his slat-back chair. Memories stirred at news from the Quế Sơn Valley. His eyes scanned the tree line, and he shook himself free, grounded by the sound of the creaking porch swing. Lily rocked, tea in one hand and her cane in the other. The faint smell of gasoline grew stronger, preceding Claire's arrival.

Mud and sludge sprayed from the tires of her Wagoneer as she careened toward the barn, her brakes squealing. James winced, afraid she would plow into the back of his Jeep or right through the barn and into the fields beyond. The car rolled on its chassis when she came to a stop next to his CJ-5. Claire failed at slamming her car door, and it bounced open as she bolted for the porch, dodging puddles like a ballerina in battle.

John and James rose to greet her, but James only had eyes for the car, passing Claire in the driveway to inspect it. He closed her door, opened the hood, and peered into the pile of smoking mechanics as the family finished their hellos.

Cars, he thought. *They must have a mind of their own. Only willpower could have propelled this one halfway across the country.* He knelt on wet rocks to inspect the brakes.

From the porch, Lily made her introductions. "That down there is James. He's not much of a people person, but if it's broke, he can fix it. If you need anything, he's the one to ask. When you have a list of things you want, he can take you into town and show you around. You'll have much more fun with him than you will waiting for our old bones. John." Lily nudged her husband's foot with the tip of her cane. "John, call James up here to meet our granddaughter."

But James was there, facing Claire who extended her hand in greeting. "I feel like I'm meeting a local celebrity."

"Nice to meet you," he mumbled. He glanced down at his palm, wet from the rain, covered in fuel and grease. His nails were broken, jagged, and stained. One was purple, smashed between two planks of wood. He held up a hand, declining the offer. He didn't want touch her anyway. But she extended her reach, insisting on the shake, and his ears grew warm when he took her hand.

She had long brown hair the color of pine bark, flecked with red and gold. There were hints of green to her amber brown eyes. She looked fragile but smelled like fuel and exhaust fumes. A pleasant smell. In her bell bottom jeans and knit top, she looked like Peggy Lipton. More flower child than farm worker. James looked down at their hands, his watch band, held together with a piece of black tape. After a morning installing new gates on the stalls, he smelled like the barn. The hem of his old gray T-shirt was coming unsewn. Conscious of the contrast between them, he released her hand.

Claire tucked hers into her back pocket. "It is a pleasure to meet you, finally. My grandmother's told me a lot about you."

Of course, Lily had her own motives. "Hopefully not too much. They know me pretty well, but they're optimistic."

Lily gestured in the direction of Claire's car. "John, I don't think this rain is going to let up. Maybe we should back the car up to the house to get this stuff inside?"

James was grateful for the escape hatch and launched in front of John and toward the car. He took his time on the way there, his hair and clothes soaking up rain. The discomfort of nature was temporary. Something told him Claire was not. He grabbed two suitcases and rushed them to the porch, dropping them at her feet.

"I owe you for running out there in this weather. I wasn't looking forward to it, myself." Claire looked across the fields, toward sheets of blowing rain. Without looking, she reached out and grabbed James's forearm as he stepped off the porch. "Don't you dare. I can get everything else tomorrow. It's just a bunch of books. It'll stay dry in the car." She turned to her grandmother. "What I could really use is a cup of coffee. Is there any coffee, Grandma?"

"Oh, yes. We have coffee." Lily rose from the porch swing and steadied herself on her cane. "But I'm afraid James will have to make it for you, because I'm just not as nimble as I used to be, and John really needs to get back to work. I'll be in the living room, if you care to join me. I want to hear all about your trip." She nudged her husband down the stairs before teetering into the house.

Alone on the porch with Claire and her luggage, James was tense, afraid to breathe. He watched Claire as if she were an unpredictable wild animal. Breaking the uncomfortable silence, she stood with her hands on her hips and a thin, shaky smile that did nothing to put him at ease. "Thank God for you or there'd be no welcoming committee at all."

"Don't let 'em fool you. They've talked about nothing but you for weeks."

"I hear you did some renovations."

Claire searched for a place to settle her hands. Hips. Arms folded. Back pockets. He took a step back. For both of them. "Just a few. You have your own kitchen."

"I can't imagine trying to get appliances up those stairs. I haven't seen them for a few years, but I remember them being narrow."

"Wasn't easy."

"I bet."

In the heartbeat that followed, Claire looked down at her muddy sneakers, and James took a deep breath, trying to shake the stiffness from his shoulders.

"You wanted coffee? We could go make some." James nodded toward the screen door.

"We should, probably."

"Right, I'll just carry these—"

"One second, though." Claire crossed her arms across her stomach and hunched forward. "I just wanted to say that I really hope there won't be any tension between us."

James straightened his back, eyes narrowed. "Why would there be tension?"

"I don't know. I've been nervous about meeting you. My grandmother talks about you all the time. I know my grandfather's been teaching you to run the farm. Then here I come. I don't know anything about this place. I don't want to walk into a conflict."

Claire had been described by her Grandfather as straightforward. James might add, high-strung. "What kind of conflict?"

"That you might think I'm trying to take your job or something."

"Unless you plan on taking up carpentry, I'm not worried. We don't do the same things. Look, I do odd jobs around here. Helping out is what I do. When you're up and running, I'll have more time to fix broken things."

"Fix broken things," Claire repeated in a whisper, looking at her shoes. "Okay. I just want to start off on the right foot."

James looked straight through her to the field beyond. He didn't know what the right foot looked like, either, but he knew that it didn't look like them spending time together, and it didn't involve small talk.

"You're the keeper of the coffee?"

Claire grasped the handle of the larger suitcase and lifted it two inches off the porch, hunching to one side. The suitcase banged into her leg when she took a step. Without thinking, he reached out and took the handle from her. "You're going to hurt yourself before you even get in the house. What good will you be around here then?"

CHAPTER SIX

James brushed his teeth and walked through his threadbare apartment. What counted as comfort for most, pillows and blankets and trinkets, offered nothing to James. Instead, he surrounded himself with books that offered shelter from the storms he feared would come if those storms found room in his mind to rage. He placed the book he'd finished the night before on the shelf, tossed a new one in his work bag, and spit in the kitchen sink.

The clock on the kitchen wall was four minutes slower than his watch. The battery was dying. He adjusted the time and knew he was wasting it. Procrastinating. Proximity to nature and years of long hours and hard work had kept the nightmares at bay. Changing his routine could be devastating. Claire gave him plenty to worry about and being late for work would only delay the inevitable.

The drive to the farm seemed shorter than usual. Hardly long enough to invent new ways to avoid the house. To avoid Claire. He pulled on his armor as he pulled in the driveway and parked next to her Wagoneer. He felt drawn to it, a wounded machine in need of regard. Circling the car on his way to the farmhouse, he wondered how to repair it without inviting a connection with its owner, but the thought evaporated when he reached the back door of the house. For years, he had been the first person to open it in the morning but not that day. The door stood open, the smell of coffee passing through the screen. Inside, he found Claire adding milk to two mugs.

"Light milk, no sugar, right?"

"Thanks. You remembered." The morning newspaper sat on the table, unfolded, its sections scattered.

Claire leaned back against the counter and cradled the cup in her hands. "My grandfather told me that the two of you have a morning coffee ritual. I figured if there's a ritual that involves coffee, I want in on that."

"I never thought of it as a ritual, but I suppose it is. Mostly a meeting, though."

"Whatever it is, at least there's coffee."

James welcomed the silence that followed and tried to ignore Claire's nervous fidgeting. It wasn't his job to make her feel at ease around him.

"My grandfather also said that following the two of you around is the best way to learn how to run a farm. I hope you don't mind my tagging along."

James dug a hole through the black and white floor tiles with his stare. "Not at all. That's how I learned, following John around."

"I have no idea how to run a farm. Sick sheep I can do. Running a business and growing crops is foreign territory." Claire grasped the back of the chair and pulled it across the floor. She picked at a chip in the handle of her mug with a clean and filed fingernail. "Listen, can I apologize for yesterday? I feel like I should."

James focused on the wall behind her, wishing he could crawl through it and get back to work in the fields. "What? Apologize for what?"

"For assuming that you might be unwelcoming or that things might be awkward between us."

"Oh, I don't care about that. Don't apologize."

"I feel like there's a lot of pressure to start things off the right way, and I don't know what the right way is. I'm here to learn, not to bark orders at people, but I'm afraid no one will know what to make of me, you know? That I won't fit in here. Some city girl moving in with her station wagon and telling all the farmers what to do. I don't want to come across that way."

Beyond Claire, beyond the kitchen counter with the black cookie jar shaped like a tea kettle, beyond the wall and across the drive sat James's Jeep. He wanted to get into it and drive far away. "Honestly, I don't think anybody puts that much thought into it. We're not that uptight around here."

"I was wondering, maybe instead of my grandfather introducing me, maybe you would be willing to do it? Only if you want to. I thought it might make it easier. So it's not the boss's granddaughter. I just want to be the new set of hands around here. You know?"

James slowly shook his head before tearing his eyes from the cookie jar and transferring his gaze to Claire. "Nope. I'm not the right person for that."

The tips of Claire's ears turned red, and she tucked her feet under her chair. "Oh. Of course. My grandfather should do it."

"It's not personal. Trust me. I'm just. I'm not the right person for that. Sorry." James pawed at the unfolded newspaper sections, pulling them toward him one by one, wishing he could build a wall from them. He pulled the morning news close.

"Please. Don't apologize. You're right. Actually, I'm the one who should be sorry. I didn't fold the newspaper when I was done with it."

James waved a hand and scanned the headlines. "You apologize a lot. You don't have to. I only read it to pass the time until John gets moving. I mean, I like the news. That's not the only reason I read it."

Claire laughed. She had Lily's eyes. "Listen to us. I'm the most socially awkward person. You're just a quiet guy, here to do a job, and I'm being needy."

James stacked the sections of newspaper, lining up their corners. With his forearms on the edge of the table, he leaned forward, his eyes fixed on a headline. The post office was changing its hours. "I'm just private, that's all. Very private. I don't have anything against anybody. But I work alone. I'm not trying to be anti-social."

"No, I get it. It's okay. I like to work alone, too. I had a lot of friends at home, but I do like my peace and quiet. And I know that you're a bit of a loner. At least that's what my grandma says. I didn't mean to…"

James reclined and rolled his eyes, offering the faintest smile. "So much for privacy. I really do like your grandparents. I appreciate they took a chance on me but…"

"What do you mean, they took a chance on you?"

"Well, I'm sure there were more qualified people out there. I probably wouldn't have hired me. We all learn on the job to some extent, but I didn't have any experience working on a farm either."

"I'm sure you were qualified, or my grandfather wouldn't have hired you. You know, they only invade your privacy because they like you. They talk about you all the time. I know my dad feels better that you're here." She lowered her voice. "I think you're like a security blanket for my grandparents. They're getting older, and the house needs work. The way my grandma talks about you, it's like…like everything is fine because you're around. It definitely makes my dad feel better, since he can't get down here."

"I'd expect him to feel the opposite. Isn't he worried about this stranger that his mother talks about all the time?"

"You're not as much of a stranger as you think. My dad knew your dad. They grew up together. My dad moved before either of us were born, but they were friends when they were kids."

"Of course. I should have put that together, that'd they'd have known each other." James dog-eared a corner of the sports section. "But no one here would let your grandparents sink. It's one big family."

"No. No, they're all loyal employees, and it's a family, yeah, but they don't think of the rest of the guys the way they think of you. You're like another grandkid to them. I know my grandma hopes we can be friends. I do, too."

James rose from the table to refill his coffee. A friendship with Claire was not an option. A professional working relationship, maybe, but friendship was off the table. He couldn't risk even a glimpse of what life would be like if he had to start talking about himself. Explaining himself to other people. To be responsible for someone else's emotions. "I'm grateful for them. Especially your grandmother. Her cooking probably saved my life."

Behind him, Claire turned in her chair and held out her cup. "You can repay the favor and save mine. Refill?"

* * *

Rivers of water rushed along the street, waves curling from the Jeep's wheels. James made his way to the farm through a late September storm. He pulled into the barn and worked quickly, removing the canvas top, lowering the tailgate, and spreading an old horse blanket in the back for a cushion. With the barn's bay doors open, he watched the rain come down in walls of water pushed by squalls of wind. Water pounded the earth and beat on the roof, a pummeling that echoed through the barn. He fixed his eyes on the dark horizon where lightning bounced between the clouds and the distant hills. The storm denied the sunrise, and James lost track of time, breathing deep, taking in the smell of the rain. It cleared the fog that had suffocated him since Claire started pushing her way in.

She appeared at the corner of the Jeep with a thermos, a glass jar of milk, and two empty cups. Beads of rainwater dripped from her hair and her sneakers were covered in mud. "I saw the barn door was open and figured it was you. I brought coffee, but you look peaceful. It's like a hurricane out here. How can you be calm in this?"

"Lots of practice." He couldn't turn her away. He didn't really want to. With Claire, he didn't always need to wear armor. Sometimes she just let him be. He raised himself up and sat on the wheel well, patting the one opposite. "Hop on up here."

She lifted her eyebrows in mock surprise. "You'd let me sit in your Jeep?"

"Best seat in the house. Just wipe your feet. You don't want to get this old horse blanket dirty." James watched as she took off her muddy canvas sneakers. "I can't believe you wore those outside in all this. You need decent rain boots."

The Jeep rocked on its leaf springs when she climbed into the back. Once it settled, she poured coffee into mugs. He was careful not to touch her hand when he took it from her. She wasn't so bad. She wasn't as disruptive as he thought she'd be, to the farm or to his psyche. Things usually turned out better than he figured they would. It was a lesson from nature he often forgot, to let things be. They work out in their own way, in their own time.

"I need more than rain boots. I need real boots, jeans. I have practical clothes. It's not like my closet's full of evening gowns, but I need more outdoor clothing. Farm appropriate stuff."

"You're going to need a decent work jacket, too. It gets real cold out here in the winter. There's a supply store about twenty minutes away. I have to run out there anyway when this clears out. I can take you, if you want."

"Wait. You're offering to chaperone me on a clothes shopping trip? I didn't think men had the patience for that kind of thing."

"Not every man gets to accompany a nice girl to a feed store to buy some rain boots. Woman, I should say. You're not a girl. Sorry."

"I'm only three years younger than you."

"Let me guess. That information came in the Lily Elmer welcome packet, along with my social security number and a list of my favorite foods."

Claire looked into her coffee cup and smiled. "Fried chicken. I know you love her fried chicken. And hamburgers. But you hate hot dogs and anything with Jell-O."

James stopped trying to keep things from Lily once he realized that having someone keep tabs on him wasn't so bad. Her meddling was harmless. He shook his head and shrugged.

"Come on. She must have said something embarrassing about me? Told you the story about the time I got lost in the corn when I was four years old, and I sat down and cried, and no one could find me? How about when I was twelve and Granddad tried to teach me to drive a tractor? I almost crashed through the barn door because he forgot to show me how to stop."

"She didn't tell me anything like that. But she did tell me a little. Enough." James still deserved to keep some secrets. He kept his eyes trained on the horizon, waiting for a hint of blue to push through the storm and a sign that the worst was over.

They watched the sky in silence, flashes of light moving closer to the claps of thunder. James welcomed the interruption. He didn't like to think about things in the past any more than he liked to consider the future. As the winds started to shift, the rain began to creep across the threshold of the barn door, closer to the Jeep.

Claire watched the line of water move closer. "Should we close the door?"

"Not yet." James wasn't ready to move. He was comfortable. "I like the smell."

"Petrichor." Claire looked out into the fields, huddled over her cup of coffee.

"Petra-what?"

"Petrichor. It's what they call the smell after it rains. It was in a nature journal I read. When it's dry out for a while, and then it rains, oils from the plants wash into the soil, and then the dry soil gets wet, the stuff in the soil mixes with the oils from the plants, and you get this smell of…" she paused, looking for the right word. "Earth, I guess. It smells like earth to me."

"I had no idea there was a word for that smell. That might take some of the fun out of it."

"Really? Why's that?"

"Sometimes when you unravel a mystery and give it a name it makes it…official. It has a definition. So the next time you experience it, it has to live up to it. Some things are better when you don't know why they are the way they are."

"Now I feel bad. I ruined the smell of rain for you."

"Oh, you didn't. It's nice to know why, I guess. That explains why it smells different out here than it does at home."

"Home," Claire repeated. James hoped she was thinking about her own and wouldn't ask about his. "Different plants, different soil, maybe. But you have a good point. It is magic. The smell of rain is one of those things that makes the world slow down, like snow."

"Especially on a farm. Sometimes there are things you can do inside and other times, like now, there's nothing you can do but wait. Some of my favorite times are sitting out here, watching a storm. It's like, no matter what you're doing with your life, no matter who you are or where you've been, none of us are any match for nature. It's powerful, the way it rolls across the hills like that. You can't see that from town."

He'd said too much. Her narrowed eyes, her knowing smile. Like she thought she knew him.

"You drove here just to sit in the back of your Jeep and watch the rain?"

James felt his chest tighten, and the familiar need to run spread through his nerve endings. He inched away, putting more space between them. "That's exactly it."

"I can see why. I have so much to do, but I don't want to do any of it."

"Then don't. The weather will change. The work can sit there."

"True. It is beautiful out there." Claire looked down at her feet and wiggled her toes inside her white socks. James wished he had her stillness, her calm. It looked so easy for her to sit and talk to him, but he fought a battle against his clenched jaw and a ringing in his ears. His breath was shallow. The Jeep creaked as she shifted her weight. "So, James, what do I need to know about life on the farm that my grandparents haven't taught me yet?"

James swallowed the last drop of his coffee and leaned forward. The first hint of deep blue appeared on the horizon as the lightning pushed across the hills. "Everything is cyclical out here. Time. Weather. Hot and cold. Birth and death. Even so, nature can throw you curve balls, and it always has the upper hand. Knowing that, understanding it, is one thing, but living it is something else."

"What do you mean?"

Harmless, he told himself. *She's harmless. Nothing bad can come from stringing words into sentences. She isn't half as dangerous as that storm.* "Nature is always in control. Always. You can lose a whole field of crops. Nothing you can do to change it. Disease can wipe out an entire flock of sheep. You just have to roll with it. Harvest is ready when it's ready. Nature has all the power. It can make you jump and run to clean up a mess, but it also tells you when to sit down and relax."

"I don't think I've ever really relaxed. Not the way you do. You just seem to turn off. I've got a million things on my mind." Claire looked into her cup and scowled. "You're not worried about storm damage or flooding?"

"I can't do anything about it. Worrying isn't going to stop it from happening or change how I deal with it. Getting worked up about imaginary consequences only makes it harder to deal with the problem when it gets here. Plan for what you can, deal with everything else when the time comes."

"Sage advice, James. I only wish I could follow it."

James brushed rust from his pant leg, and it stained his hand red. He wiped it on the horse blanket at his feet. "So what's on your list of things to worry about?"

"I am so overwhelmed that I haven't even made a list yet. That's saying something for me."

"Well, it looks like this storm is going to blow out of here soon, and we can leave the barn without drowning. There's paper on the workbench over there and pencils in the toolbox if you want to make a shopping list."

Claire rested her elbows on her knees and watched daytime win the battle against the storm. "You know, I think I'll just wing it."

* * *

Claire dodged the last of the thick raindrops and leapt over puddles on her way toward the house. Behind her, James stepped over pools of mud. They stopped to wipe their feet on the porch, and through the open kitchen window they heard John say, "You might get your wish."

"As long as nothing stands in their way." Lily's voice was distant, echoing from the living room. "Stop peering out the window. They'll think you were spying."

Claire flung open the screen door and kicked her shoes off onto the mat. "I'm going to the feed store with James."

At the sink, she fumbled with the thermos lid, her ears burning. She tried to read James, wondering if he would be more comfortable facing the firing squad alone. She could almost feel the moment he detached from the scene, the machine version of James taking over from the one who had spoken so openly in the barn. He grabbed a towel and dried the thermos, unfazed, as if he could hear nothing at all.

"Do you need anything?" Claire asked.

Her grandfather opened his mouth to speak, but Lily beat him to it. "Nope. Can't think of anything. You two have fun and take your time."

Claire followed James back to the barn, giving him a wide, comfortable berth. He moved deliberately, tossing the horse blanket over a rail, closing one set of barn doors and opening another. Standing over the canvas top, Claire looked down at the confusing tangle of plastic windows, snaps, and zippers. "Do you want to put the roof back on?"

"No way. I love the air, the way it moves through the Jeep. You might get wet, but you'll get used to it. Let's live dangerously."

Claire wasn't sure how much danger with James she could take. She found a spool of leather cord on a table and cut off a small strip, tying her hair back as she climbed into the Jeep. The high idle slowly settled into a rumble and they bounced down the gravel drive, crunching over rocks and splashing through puddles. When they turned onto the main road, she listed toward the center of the car to avoid the road spray and watched the landscape change as they passed. The farmland gave way to wildflowers and grasses where little drops of opalescent water hung, refracting the sun.

Humidity began to rise like a dome had been placed over the countryside.

James pulled into a service station about ten minutes from the farm. "I just need a can of engine oil. Want anything?" he asked.

A hand truck clattered as a delivery driver pulled ice cream into the store. Her tummy grumbled. "I do, actually. I'll come in. I just realized we missed breakfast. Are you hungry?"

"I had cereal before I left home, but I could eat."

"Ice cream."

"For breakfast?"

"You're the one who suggested we live dangerously. What's your favorite kind?"

"Surprise me."

Claire met him at the register with two cones of peach ice cream. "My treat."

"You don't have to do that."

"Oh, please. It's just a container of oil. It hardly covers the cost of the gas to get here." They walked side-by-side back to the car. The tailgate was splattered with mud and grime kicked up in their wake. She didn't care, leaning against it and watching rain shower down from tree branches as birds returned to their search for bugs in the wake of the storm.

"Good choice." James propped himself next to her against the tailgate. "Peach is my favorite."

"I figured."

"Did your grandmother tell you that?"

Claire blinked at him. "No. I just figured you would like it."

CHAPTER SEVEN

The porch swing creaked and swayed when Claire dropped her notebook to the floor. It landed next to her coffee cup. Months of unfinished business in an all-caps list demanded her attention. Was the knot in her stomach the flu or a symptom of her disorganized mind? She brushed at a coffee stain on her shirt, another reminder that she couldn't get it together.

Painting. Bookshelves. Unpacking. Finding a job or building an office? Her veterinary license. She missed her friends. Her car was broken. And James. Friendly but inconsistent. One minute, chatting like an old friend, and the next, hiding behind a wall of vacant stares and detachment that she couldn't scale. At first she thought it was her fault, something she had said or done, but as months wore on she was convinced he was trying to keep her out. He wasn't the type of guy you'd ask, though.

James was the closest thing to a friend that Claire had in Elk River, and the best part of her day was the morning coffee they shared, until he turned away or looked straight through her. Claire rested her head on the arm of the porch swing and stared at the rafters, replaying conversations and encounters, searching for clues.

The familiar sound of Jeep tires kicking up gravel on the driveway sent her into the kitchen. The floor creaked as she paced, a full cup of coffee in one hand, the other rubbing a spot at the base of her neck. She pushed a cup toward James when he pushed open the screen door.

"Thank God you're here. I could really use a friend today. Can I think out loud with you for a minute?"

"Coffee smells good," he said, accepting the cup. Claire tugged at her shirt, hoping he wouldn't notice the coffee stain, but it was too late. "How much have you had?"

She gave him a playful, sarcastic sneer and grabbed the list from the counter, shaking it in the air. "I've been up since three. I'm really overwhelmed. I tried to prioritize everything I need to do, but I don't even know where to start on some of this."

James lowered himself into a chair at the table. "What's the first thing on your list?"

"Bookshelves. I need bookshelves."

"That's not the first thing on your list."

"Yes, it is." Claire straightened her back, defiant.

"You prioritized all of the problems in your life and bookshelves are at the top? Doubt it. Let me see."

Claire held the list away when he reached for it. "No way."

"Why not? Let me see the list. I'm objective. Maybe I can help make sense of it."

"Fine. I'll tell you." There was no way she would hand the notebook to James. The last thing she needed was for him to know he was on her list. "I hate the bathroom. I want to paint it blue. I'm sorry. I know you worked really hard on it, and it's a great bathroom, but I don't like that pinky peach color. It makes everything look girly."

"Really? That's the first thing on your list?" James raised his hands. "I'm not offended. Your grandmother picked the color. But peach, good for ice cream, bad for bathrooms. Got it."

"And I want to paint the bedroom a calming color. I have to figure out what's wrong with my car. And I do need bookshelves, so I can get those boxes of books off the floor. I have to decide about work. Am I going to open a small veterinary practice here at the farm or somewhere else? I've never even run my own practice before. There is a vet in town. Maybe they're hiring? I've barely stepped foot off the property."

She fell into a seat at the table and waited for a response from James who stared into his coffee cup. She'd hoped for the James who offered practical advice and a voice of reason. Instead, she got the wall. Wondering what private battles he waged behind his closed doors, she turned her back on James, left the table, and prepared a bowl of cereal.

"The upstairs. I'll help you repaint it, if you want. It could be fun. And I can probably build some bookshelves from all the scrap wood laying around here. Then…"

James was interrupted by John, who made his morning beeline for the fridge. "What's this about bookshelves?" He pushed the contents of the fridge aside, searching for his morning orange juice.

"Grandad, I was telling James that I want to repaint the bathroom and bedroom, and I need bookshelves. He offered to make them from the scrap wood in the back." She turned to James. "You're not being paid to do things for me, and I don't want you to feel like you should do this stuff in your spare time. I really don't want to impose. I was just venting."

James moved his coffee cup, leaving a ring on the sales ads. "I really don't mind helping you paint."

Claire looked out the window at her Wagoneer. It needed new brakes and reeked of gasoline. As if reading her mind, James put down the paper and made his own list. "Your car is a priority. It's a mess. It needs brakes and a fuel pump, and you're missing a side mirror. I'll take a look at it tonight, pick up whatever I need to fix it, and do it in the morning. Then we can go into town for paint. It won't take long. You'll feel better once that stuff is out of the way."

John picked up the newspaper James had laid down and interjected. "Kids, nothing is happening here today. The ground's still wet, and it'll be at least two weeks before we can plant anything. There's nothing to do but wait. You'll make Lily the happiest woman in the world if you two head out of here and take the day to square all this away. Claire's been cooped up in this house with us old people for months. Go out and do what you have to do."

"It's supposed to be hot out tomorrow." James hadn't pried his eyes off the Wagoneer. "It would be good to get the car fixed today."

Claire shrugged. "It's up to you. It's your schedule I'm interrupting."

Sections of the newspaper scattered on the table while James searched for the one he'd put down. Seeing it in John's hands, he settled for the entertainment section. "All right, then. Finish your forty-third cup of coffee and let's hop to it."

"Okay! I'll be right back. I just need my shoes." She gave John a peck on the cheek and dropped her bowl in the sink. "Thanks, Granddad."

Claire scrambled up the stairs and paused in the doorway, scanning the floor for her sneakers. Her eyes fell on her wardrobe, the doors open, skirts and tops on wire hangers hung in a colorful row. The green shirt that brought out her eyes. She brushed aside the urge to change her clothes, to alter her appearance for James. Her energy was better spent suppressing those feelings. The impulses to look nice and glance too long were increasing in number and frequency, but their friendship and working relationship were far too important to jeopardize. The effort not to stand too close or to touch was exhausting, and it was becoming more difficult to spend time with him. Every moment he let his guard down made her want more. Perhaps it was that wall, and the need to know what was on the other side, that made him so attractive.

She tucked a tube of lip gloss in her pocket, tugged her shoes from under the edge of the bed, and bounded down the stairs.

* * *

James listened to Claire's footsteps overhead as she looked for her shoes. "You don't mind if I dig through that wood out behind the shed to make these bookcases she needs?"

"Course not. It's scrap. That's what it's there for." John pulled hot toast onto a plate, then rinsed his hands and dried them on a ragged dish towel covered with dancing geese in blue bonnets.

"You sure you don't mind me spending time helping her square things away?"

"I always said I wasn't getting involved in this. Look, son, I'm not good at these things. Lily has much stronger feelings about this than I do, but I really don't have a problem with it. If you think you're doing something wrong there, you're not. You're both responsible, intelligent people, and you have to take risks sometimes. Lily and I are fine with it if you—"

James took a deep breath and shook his head, forming a protest, but Claire's voice on the stairs saved him the trouble. James pushed away from the table and grabbed his keys from the edge of the counter, eager to escape. "Let's go take a look at your car and figure out what we need."

* * *

Claire hoisted herself into the passenger seat and grabbed the handle on the dash. It was smooth, damp with dew. James started the engine, and she ran her finger along the narrow ledge beneath the windshield and around the thin ring that framed the speedometer, removing the dust. Small rocks kicked up from the tires, their pings and dings and clunks knocking the silence out of the morning air as he backed down the driveway.

Claire watched their silhouette on the grass, traced by the sun. They were fused into one entity, something new with a willfulness of its own. Carefree. She turned toward James. He looked different in his Jeep. Content. Leaning a little in his direction and yelling to be heard over the engine noise and the wind, she said, "This car suits you."

He glanced over at her. "What does that mean?"

Her Wagoneer seemed like an entirely different machine compared to James's CJ-5. Hers had an automatic transmission, and his car had three shifters. Hers had carpeting, chrome, a radio, air conditioning, a tilting steering wheel, and interior lights. His had a flat dashboard and a metal floor. When it came to cars, Claire was intimidated by what she didn't understand, and little was left to the imagination in his Jeep. With nothing to insulate her from the car's mechanics, James's CJ-5 seemed to require special skill and bravery to operate.

"It's not...complicated."

James gave a rare laugh. "Oh, so I'm simple?"

"No! I mean, it doesn't have all those gauges and electronics. It's not trying to be anything more than what it is. Not trying to please anybody. Everything here has a function. It doesn't hide behind...frills. Also, it's a little mysterious. Intimidating."

Claire scolded herself for saying too much. The Jeep came to a stop at the curb in front of the hardware store. James reached down by his left knee and pulled the parking brake without looking. It creaked and clicked in place. He leaned toward Claire and gave her a coy smile as he took the key from the ignition, making accidental eye contact that made her breath catch in her throat. "Thanks for noticing that I don't have frills," he said. "And I hope you don't think I'm intimidating."

She struggled to climb out of the car. Her knees wouldn't hold her. She tucked her hands in the back pockets of her jeans and followed James into the hardware store. The door pushed into a small brass bell.

A raspy voice called from behind a wall of cardboard boxes that surrounded the register. "What brings you by today, James?"

"Hey, Dan. Paint. A towel hook. A little trash can, if you have the right one."

"You must be painting the whole farm." Dan emerged from behind the counter, a small, sprightly man with outstretched hands to grasp Claire's. "Ah, Claire. Finally. We've heard a lot about you around here."

Claire was careful not to crush his hands. Delicate skin hung from his bones. His face was gaunt, but his eyes sparkled. "That must be my grandparents."

"Yes, yes. Your grandfather is in here often. Your grandmother used to come by but not as much since she broke her hip. I hope she's well. Terrible thing, to break a hip."

"She's doing okay, thank you. I'll let them know you asked after them." Claire followed Dan down a narrow aisle, squeezing between boxes of pesticides and varnishes.

"Here are all of the paint choices. You're here to replace that peach paint in your bathroom? I told James that was a bad idea, but he listened to your grandmother. She has the worst taste in wall coverings. Must have been forty years ago she ordered that wallpaper with birds on it. Be glad you didn't have to live with that." Dan patted Claire's arm as he slid past her toward a barricade of paint cans. "I'm sure you'll pick something lovely. Let me know when you're ready. You can just drop everything you want up there by the register, and I'll put it on the farm account."

Claire handed her paint choices to Dan, and James collected paint rollers from a rack at the end of the aisle. "We have errands to run in town. We'll swing back by and pick up the paint later, if that's all right by you?"

"Sure thing, James. I'll just put everything in the back of your Jeep out there."

"You can't tell him no," James whispered to Claire as they walked to the back of the store. She tossed a towel hook into a small white trash can. "I've tried. It hurts his feelings. And he knows everything about every building in this town. In twenty years, he'll remember that you bought this towel hook. And he'll tell you if you're making the wrong choice. Your grandmother is about the only person who never listens to him."

"I'm not surprised."

They left their purchases at the counter and took a slow walk through town, peeking in the laundromat window, the bank, the market, and the salon, stopping at the five-and-dime store. Several residents smiled or stared at the sight of James with an unknown woman, fumbling through surprised introductions.

"This entire town knows you." Claire hoisted her purse strap higher on her shoulder.

"I've lived here my whole life. I don't see why they wouldn't."

"But...Oh, what a cute place." She stopped at the door of Angie's Diner and looked at her watch. "It's almost eleven thirty. Is it too early for lunch? I'm starving."

"I could eat. Definitely." He stepped ahead of her and opened the door.

Another bell announced their arrival. Elk River liked its bells, as if it didn't expect visitors, so it went about its business as if one would never arrive. A woman in a pink apron waved from behind the lunch counter. "Well, look who it is." Angie stood, hands on her hips, with an expression of mock surprise. "Hello, James! Sit where you'd like. I'll come harass you about your lady friend in a minute."

"Like that," Claire whispered, setting into the booth seat across from James. "I thought you were private and kept to yourself. Seems like there's a Farm James and Town James. Everybody here seems to know you."

"They know *about* me. That's what happens in a small town. I went to school with Angie's daughter. My dad and I used to come in here all the time. That's what happens in a small town, I guess."

"Not where I grew up. We have townships and main streets, but there's new construction everywhere. There are more people I don't know than people I do."

Claire looked over the menu. Eggs and sandwiches. It all looked good, but nothing jumped out. She ordered tea and chicken salad on rye under Angie's critical but friendly gaze.

"She seems protective of you." Claire pushed her utensils to the side of her placemat and looked down at the ads. Mechanic. Oil service. Tree trimming.

Two plastic cups and bendy straws landed between them. Angie tucked a pencil behind her ear and turned to Claire. "Welcome to town, hun. Come by here anytime. I do spaghetti dinners on Tuesdays. There's always a line, but it's worth the wait. You'll meet the whole town if you come by early enough." She patted James's shoulder on her way to the kitchen. "She'll fit in just fine here."

Claire felt her face grow warm. She knew she must be a shade of pink brighter than Angie's apron. James unplugged from the diner, lost in an ad for a chimney sweeper. She couldn't let him slip away. "I've been giving a lot of thought to what I want. I can't just wait for something to happen, you know? I just have to do it. Jump in head first." James sat up straight in the booth. She was losing him. "I think I'll set up the practice at the farm first. If I can extend the driveway to the back side of the barn, I could make a separate entrance with parking back there. My dad gave me a personal loan to get started, so I have enough money to get all the equipment I need. If I work from the farm, that money would go further. What do you think?"

She let out a slow breath and thanked Angie out loud for the sandwiches and silently for the interruption and the chance to catch her breath.

"I can't see anything wrong with your plan." James collected his sandwich. He was back but for how long? "Extending the drive would be easy and that end of the barn is just storage. It could all go somewhere else. I guess John would know if there are zoning issues, but they have that lawyer who could probably help."

The trick to keeping James happy and focused was to give him a puzzle to solve. "I don't need a lot. Room for vaccines and equipment and a little exam room. An office. I really just want to treat small pets and focus on the farm." She tucked stray lettuce between the slices of bread. "I haven't completely decided yet, but I think that I will take on the farm when the time comes. I can put my veterinary knowledge to use here. I love Elk River. I just need more exposure to the farm. Being there all the time would give me more experience than if I spent most of my days in town."

"That does make sense."

James hadn't closed the door yet, so she gave it a push. "Have you decided what you're doing with your land? Are you planning to stay here, or do you have a dream of moving to some big city?"

"Me? In a city? Nope. I'm staying put. I like working for John and Lily and being on a farm. For as long as the farm will have me, I would stay."

"Grandma said everybody else has already decided. They've either met with the builder or put their plot up for sale. You're the only one."

"Really? I've been setting money aside to pay the taxes on it, but I haven't decided about living there yet. I like my apartment. I don't know what I would do with a house. Probably end up selling it."

Claire gave the door another nudge. "Apartment? Is it here in town? I guess it's not far from the farm."

"Not far. About two blocks from here. It's not much, but it's quiet, and I've lived there for a long time now. It just feels like mine."

"Sounds nice. I like that about Elk River. How quiet it is here." And just like that, the door was closed again. James's eyes focused on something behind her. One of the old photos of town that lined the walls, perhaps. Or maybe nothing at all. She took the napkin from her lap and lay it on the table. "You know, I'm sorry I keep imposing on you. I feel like I keep tearing you away from work. My grandparents offer your time, and I know you're being paid to chauffeur me around town, but I'm sure there are things you'd probably rather be doing at the farm." She pushed a potato chip around on her plate, summoning the strength to push her way in and ignoring the voice that told her not to. "I just want to say, I do like the company."

James was visibly uncomfortable. She crushed a chip against the roof of her mouth and let the salt sting her tongue. The sounds of the diner disappeared behind the crunching. A wrong move, one poorly chosen word, could ruin their working relationship. She tried to anticipate what he might say, tried to prepare the appropriate apology, but James spoke first.

"You like *the* company. Or my company?"

Claire ran her fingernail along the ridge of a chip, collecting salt that she wiped on her napkin. She swallowed hard and rubbed at a knot in her shoulder, glancing at the kitchen, wishing Angie would make an appearance and hoping she wouldn't. Daring James not to look away, she lifted her chin and locked eyes with him. Her voice was steadier than she felt. "Yours, James. Your company." She bulldozed through the discomfort. "I'm hoping you'll help me paint. And show me how to make bookshelves that won't fall down. And let me help work on the car. And then maybe someday you'll ask me out for drinks, if they do that around here, because if I don't find some whiskey in this town soon, I might cry. And also because..." She came to an abrupt halt to collect her thoughts, and James put his hand up.

"You don't have to say it."

"Yeah, I do. I want to spend more time with you, because lately, your company is the company I like best. And I would like more of it."

Claire lost him. He disconnected and drilled a hole through his plate with his stare. Losing his friendship and breaking her own heart seemed inevitable. She should have waited for signals. She never should have opened the door to her heart so wide while trying to nudge his open inch by inch.

"Say something. Please." She widened her eyes and blinked at the ceiling, drying her tears before they could fall. "Please. Don't punish me for my honesty."

Outside, a woman placed bags into the trunk of her car. When she slammed the trunk lid, James snapped to attention. "Okay. Honesty. What if I told you that...What if I said I felt those things too. Liking your company. Wanting to spend more time with you. But that it might not be a great idea."

"No, you're right. You work for my grandparents, and if I take over the farm someday, I'll need your help. The farm can't risk losing you if things didn't work between us, and it got awkward. Even if I don't take over the farm, I'd still see you all the time. They're family to both of us, really." She sat up straight and put her palms on the table, a failing attempt to harness her posture and gain composure. "I owe you an apology. I'm sorry. I value our friendship, and I don't want to jeopardize that." Claire brushed crumbs from the table. "Someday we can tell a funny story about how I used to have a crush on you."

"Yeah." Something flashed across his face. "Important points, but that's not all of it." Anger? Was he wounded? Did she hurt his feelings?

"Oh, good. There's more rejection that I missed."

"It's not like that," James replied softly. "That's not what I meant."

James tapped his foot on the floor. He didn't look forthcoming.

"Help me out here," Claire asked, just shy of begging. "What did you mean? What other reason is there? Not like I'm excited to hear it, but you wouldn't bring it up unless you wanted to tell me."

"There's a lot you don't know about me."

"You have eight kids?" Claire tilted her head and went through a random mental checklist of major turn-offs. She needed to lighten the mood. "You're a conspiracy theorist, and you totally bought that Roswell stuff? You're a serial killer and your apartment is full of bodies?"

James gave a faint smile, and it faded fast. "No. I wish my life had been that easy. You went to college, but out here there's not a lot of opportunity, you know? After high school, I worked for a while. Then almost all of us, me and my friends, we went to Vietnam. Fourteen of us. We fought together. I'm the only one who came home. While I was gone, my dad died. So, yeah. I'm not boyfriend material."

"That's not true—"

"It is true. How am I supposed to communicate with someone about my feelings when I don't even know what they are or if they're real?"

The sounds of the diner fell away. The knives and forks and the clatter of dishes all faded behind the ringing in Claire's ears. James looked at her, not past her, and as much as she wanted to look away, to lower her eyes, she refused. He didn't just open a door for her, he busted through concrete to get there, and Claire finally understood. He never talked about a future or a past and when he talked about the present, he fought against regret. His independence and isolation weren't a lifestyle choice or a part of his personality, they were layers of rust left behind after his exposure to unspeakable truths.

Claire swallowed hard. She knew that James didn't want pity. He just wanted to be accepted on his own terms. "I'm sorry that I pushed you into that corner. I don't even know what to say. Except thank you for trusting

JENNIFER M. LANE

me. And I hate that you went through that."

"It's okay. No one's ever tried to claw their way in before."

"You're pretty good at putting up walls to keep people out."

"Practice."

"Really? No one? It's been, what, six years since you got home? Seven? You haven't let anyone in?"

"Not a single person. Who would want in on this? If I really care about somebody, why would I invite them into this?" A flash of anger crossed his face.

Was he saying he cared? Claire fought back tears, again. "I'm sorry. I didn't mean to make you mad."

"I'm not mad at you. I'm mad at me." James dug his wallet out of his back pocket and threw a ten-dollar bill on the table. "Let's go." It came out like a bark, and Claire startled at the change in tone. He bolted from the table through the door, and she followed him onto the sidewalk and down the street.

"If you want a drink, let's have a drink."

Claire jogged a few steps to catch up to him and called out, "Wait. James, wait!" She wanted to grab his arm and bring him to a halt, to dig at the root of his anger, to apologize, to take it all back, but she was afraid to make things worse.

The car was running before she was in the passenger seat. She glanced at the paint and supplies in the back of the car. "Where are you going? Are you leaving me here?"

"Of course not. Get in. Hurry."

She hopped into the passenger seat and held onto the grab handle. "Where are we going? We were supposed to paint. And my car. Are you still going to help me fix my car?"

"Of course, I'm gonna fix your car. We have all weekend. This is more important right now."

"*What's* more important?"

James released the parking brake and pulled the car away from the curb. She watched his hand on the shifter and wondered where his hands had been, what they'd held, what he had seen. Two blocks west and one block north, he turned into an alley between two buildings. It opened into a small parking lot. The Jeep rocked to a halt at a reserved sign.

"This is it." James lifted his chin, nodding toward an apartment over the news stand. A flight of stairs led to the second floor where a little patio balcony hinted at the home behind. "That's where I live."

"You brought me to your apartment."

"Yup. Come on. You said you wanted whiskey. Let's have a drink and talk this through."

"It's barely noon." Claire raised an eyebrow.

"It's one drink, Claire. We can wait a few more hours if you want, but if you want to know what it's like to walk through hell, accept the drink."

Her mouth dry, she stepped out of the Jeep and tried not to stumble up the stairs in his wake. A little table and two chairs rested on the balcony, the perfect perch for watching a sunset. She rested her hands on the railing and peered down at the Jeep. It looked small. James held the door open for her, and she stepped into a cozy living room, its walls lined with books on shelves he'd made from timbers and bricks. A sofa and coffee table sat to the right. Behind the sofa, a half wall provided a view of the kitchen with its almond-colored refrigerator and stove. To the left was a hallway that, Claire presumed, led to the bedroom and bathroom. It was bright and cheery, though sparsely decorated.

James went directly to the kitchen. Cabinet doors closed. Glasses touched. The sound of a cork. Claire sat down at one end of the sofa. A binder lay on the coffee table, open to a photo album page with a receipt for oil and ice cream. She pulled the notebook onto her lap and flipped to the beginning.

"This notebook…" Her voice was loud enough to be heard from the kitchen, but James was already standing next to her, handing her a glass that contained an inch of amber liquid. She looked up at him like he was the first person to offer her water after a year in the desert.

James sat next to her, far enough to keep his distance but close enough to see the bill of sale. "This is where I keep car maintenance records."

"You keep maintenance records for your car?"

"Yes, it's the next natural step after actually performing the maintenance." His sarcasm was playful. "Someday, I'll teach you about that."

"Someday? You don't talk much about the future."

James shrugged it off and flipped a page of the notebook. "Anyway, this was the first thing I came across to put everything in after I bought the Jeep. I was looking for a folder or an envelope. It was on sale at the five-and-dime. Seemed like a good enough solution."

Claire flipped through the pages. "It's just receipts and notes about repairs and oil changes?"

"And the sales record. The little sales brochure from the dealership. Pretty much anything about the car I just stick in there in case I need it someday." He watched her thumb through the pages. "There's nothing personal in here. It's just a bunch of car stuff."

"But you could put other things in here, too."

"Like what?"

"Pictures and memories. When you go somewhere, you could put little souvenirs from adventures in here," she said. James wrinkled his nose and shook his head. She pointed at the receipt. "No, look. This one. To you, this is a receipt for oil. To me, it's from the day we ate peach ice cream after that storm. There are so many stories in here. You could add pictures from everyday life. At the barn. Behind your apartment."

"Won't it clutter up the maintenance records and make it harder to find things? Isn't that what photo albums are for?"

"Yes, but you're keeping your car records in a photo album so…" James looked disinterested, but she wouldn't be dismissed. "Come on! Look around you! All of this changes. Buildings and developments and highways are going up everywhere. This place won't look like this forever. Wouldn't it be neat to have something to look at years from now to remember what it was like? Like a scrapbook through the eyes of your car. You love that car."

James shrugged and turned his attention to his drink. "Well, you take the pictures, I'll put them in the notebook."

Claire closed the binder and set it aside, holding a sip of whiskey in her mouth to enjoy the numbness. It made her mouth water. "Does that mean I get to have more of your company?"

"Something tells me you wouldn't go away even if I wanted you to."

Claire took another sip and patted him on the knee. Regret washed into her with the whiskey she swallowed. She had never touched James before. He bristled at her side, and she decided to level the wall before he could raise it. "Thank you for the whiskey. And thank you for letting me in."

He swirled the golden liquid in his glass and looked down into it, silent for so long that Claire's heartbeat echoed in her ears. "Claire, I don't really know how to talk about this stuff. The few things I remembered, I tried hard to forget. The things I forgot, I wish I could remember."

The kitchen clock counted the moments that passed between them. "James, you don't have to. You never have to."

"No, I do. It's time. I don't need to live like this." He reached out and tucked a stray strand of brown hair behind her ear. She froze.

"Claire, I'm not good at this emotional honesty stuff. I'm not even good at emotions. But if we're going to figure out what we are to each other, we have to talk. You have to know everything. And you might have to be patient with me."

* * *

Her hair was soft. James wanted to trail his fingers through it, but she tensed at his side and he pulled his hand away. Clutching his glass, he chose his words carefully and watched as she clung to each one. He hadn't discussed his time at war with anyone. Not with Tom or John or Lily. He ignored Tom's mentions of friends they'd lost until Tom learned not to speak of the past. Now, James accepted that it was time for redemption and deliverance. He'd let go of the guilt. He deserved to let go of the suffering that he'd clung to out of habit. He didn't need Claire's sympathy, and she didn't offer any, only an ear and the friendship that he had denied himself for too long. She was his pardon.

"So, are you saying that you don't let people in because you're afraid you'll lose them?"

He took his time, and she let him. "I saw people die. I saw most of my friends and a bunch of other really good people torn to pieces, and then I came home. Everybody here lost somebody, but I somehow got home. I don't remember everything. Just clips. Snapshots. Quick little movements. Sometimes I'm grateful for that. Fear? I don't know anything about fear. I couldn't feel anything at all for the longest time. Feelings are distant now, because I want them to be. I don't like to lose people. If I don't have people, I can't lose them. But it's more than that. If I can keep some distance, I don't have to answer any questions. I don't have to explain." The more layers he peeled back and the more he revealed of himself, the more vulnerable he felt. He smoothed his pants over his knees, wanting to run, to escape to a smaller, safer place. Being in his home hadn't made the conversation any easier.

Claire placed her drink on the table. "I grew up under the blue skies of suburban Philadelphia, and I've only ever lost a few pets and a grandparent. I can't relate at all to what you feel—or don't feel—but I want to understand. Are you telling me that in all these years, you haven't let one person in? Like, really in? No messy, sloppy love? No raw emotion with anyone? At all?"

"Claire, the only people I talk to are you, your grandparents, and Tom. You know more about what goes on in my head than they do. Everyone else out there is just scenery."

"Thank you for not calling me scenery." Her small smile was encouraging. "So, if you're not surrounded by women and attending keg parties when you're not at the farm, what do you do when you're not there?"

"I read. A lot. I tinker with the car. I go fishing. Watch television. That's about it. I stay busy."

"Can I ask you something personal?"

He offered her a hint of a smile. "Why stop now?"

"Do you ever get lonely?"

James let the glass linger beneath his nose before he took a sip, the smell of wood and sour alcohol filled his senses. He downed a sip. "Are we still doing the honesty thing?"

"Yes. Absolutely."

"In general? Not really. I've never been much of a people person." He looked into his glass, at his last sip of whiskey. "No. That's not the whole truth. I do get lonely. Something funny happens, and I want to tell you. I read a good book and want to give it to you. When I go to sleep, I look forward to our morning coffee. Before you, I never looked forward at all."

* * *

The remains of dinner spread across the little table on the patio, packets of soy sauce and mustard strewn among cartons of rice. The sun burned like fire, and the porch was soaked in orange light. James didn't want to take Claire home. His elbows dug into his knees, and he watched ripples form in the amber liquid of his glass when Claire scooted her chair closer. Instead of shutting down, he faced her instead, their knees touching. He locked eyes with her and waited for her to speak first. This time, he didn't want to turn away from what she might say. He wanted to be there to hear it.

"Thanks for today," she said.

"For what? For talking?"

"Yeah. For trusting me. It's a big deal. I don't take it lightly."

"I know you don't." James reached out and played with the button on the end of her sleeve. "You should know, if you change your mind tomorrow, it's okay. I don't want you to. But if you wake up and feel like…We don't have to have a conversation about it. You can just walk away, and it'll be fine."

"James, you're such a dolt. I'm not going to run. There's no reason to run."

"I'm just letting you know that you can, though. And you won't hurt my feelings. Nothing will be different."

"I promise, I'm not running. And everything is already different. We're different. I hope we are, anyway. Are you afraid of that?"

James put his hands on her knees. "Not of us. Afraid of me. I've put so much effort into staying away from you. I'm afraid you'll show me who I really am."

Claire wound his fingers in hers. "I know who you are. If I like him, you will, too."

His fingers warmed by her touch. "How is this supposed to go?"

"You mean this? Us?"

"Yeah. If you aren't running, then what's tomorrow like?"

"It goes the way it goes. What if we didn't put any labels on it? What if we just did our own thing?"

"And you're not running?"

"I'm not running. I'm giving you space, but I'm right here. Are you running?"

"No." James shook his head. "What if, tomorrow morning, bright and early, I come over and fix your car. I'll teach you how to fix your brakes. Then we can paint the bathroom and build bookshelves."

"I'll be up by dawn."

"Okay. Sunday, we'll finish up anything we didn't get to and then we can stand in the barn and map out what you want to do with it."

"And tonight?"

James leaned in and traced her jaw with his thumb. "I wish I didn't have to take you home."

"Then don't."

* * *

Claire held the railing and watched her feet on porch stairs at the farmhouse, intercepting James. Her head throbbed. She grabbed him by the elbow and pulled him out of earshot from the house, pushing a cup of coffee into his hands. Steam rose from the cup into the unusually brisk morning air. "Prepare yourself. There are questions."

"Questions? Are they mad? Were you out too late? It was only midnight. Do you even have a curfew?"

"No, not mad. It's not like that. They're curious. And I think we're gonna get a lecture."

"What did you tell them?" James asked with mock amusement.

"The truth. That we sat at your place, talking."

71

"You mean, part of the truth."

"I'm not gonna tell them about that."

"I'm teasing you. There's nothing to worry about. This is Lily's biggest dream come true. Let's just go in there and be honest." He took a sip of his coffee. "This is it, then."

Claire stumbled as she turned toward the house, and James caught her arm. "Are you okay?"

"Yeah. Stupid feet. They're just not connected to my brain today." She rubbed an ankle, and James lifted her chin, looking into her eyes. She put her foot down for balance and stumbled all over again.

"Let's put some ice on that."

"Nah, it's fine. But I could use some aspirin for this headache."

James followed her into the kitchen where they joined John and Lily at the little table. She was worried what her grandparents might say, how it might affect James. She worried about the nightmares, if unearthing memories would change him at all. She worried that he'd be so good at hiding it that she might not know until it was too late. Or if she did, that she wouldn't know how to help.

"Look, John." Lily was her usual playful self, but her intentions were clear. "It's the man who kidnapped our granddaughter!"

"Grandma, be nice. James was too nice to kidnap me, so I had to kidnap him myself."

John cleared his throat and lowered his newspaper. "The two of you must have had a lot of talking to do."

"We did. Sir." James exchanged looks with Claire. She wondered how their relationships might change: boyfriend, coworker, grandfather, and boss.

"As long as you are careful and responsible." John returned to his newspaper.

Lily reached out and patted their hands. "James. Claire." They were either in for a stern lecture or a supportive pep talk, but Claire didn't want either.

"Grandma, Grandpa. James and I have decided to start a relationship. We want to thank the two of you for all the effort you put into encouraging it. A lot of thought went into this. We considered all of the consequences, and this is what's been decided."

Lily clasped her hands, the corners of her eyes wrinkled, but John remained stern. "Just be responsible. I don't want to have to send her home to her father and fire the best employee I have. Just you two remember, there's a natural order to things around here. Don't ruin this farm."

"Yes, sir. I mean, we won't."

Claire smiled and rubbed her temple. She was eager to have James to herself again. "If you don't mind, I'm going to take an aspirin and put James back to work. I'd like to get my car fixed before it burns the barn to the ground."

CHAPTER EIGHT

James packed his paperwork into his bag, slung it over his shoulder, and stepped through the kitchen door onto the farmhouse porch. Lily was in the porch swing, where she'd spent the spring of 1971, knitting uneven blankets and tiny sweaters for the great-grandchild she deemed inevitable. John, now retired, was at her side, watching nature have its way with the land while James and Claire shouldered the burdens of the farm.

The sun slid toward the horizon, taking the warmth from the air as it went. Claire emerged from the veterinary office in the barn and waved at the gathering on the porch. Lily waved back before shuffling into the house in search of brighter light, and John followed, leaving James at the top of the stairs. He waved a green folder.

"The plans are here. Do you want to look at these?"

"Are you afraid you'll pick the wrong wall colors?" Claire dropped onto the swing next to James. He moved at lightning speed, once she'd convinced him to build the house. He was excited to move into the future. It was murky around the edges, blurred like an old photograph, but it was clear that it was with Claire.

"I'll probably pick the wrong everything." James opened the folder and handed her the plans. There were four different options with different windows and dormers.

"I like this one. It has a cute front porch. I've loved having a porch."

"Three bedrooms, two bathrooms. That's a lot of house for the two of us."

"It doesn't have to be just the two of us."

"The two of us, three cats, fourteen dogs, and a turtle?" James shot her a sideways glance, and she jabbed an elbow into his ribs.

Claire returned all but one of the plans to the folder. She traced the walls of a second story bedroom. "What about a tiny little James?"

"The world would be better off with a tiny little Claire." James wrapped one arm around her and pulled her close. "You know me better than I do. There may be gaps in my parenting ability."

"You should give yourself more credit. You're not an emotional wasteland."

James snorted. "Thanks."

"Silly. You know what I mean. The nightmares you worried about never happened. You talked about your love of the Jeep for fifteen minutes this morning. You're looking at house plans. There was a time when you didn't plan groceries for a week."

"I do most of this stuff for you."

"A few years ago, you couldn't do them at all. I don't believe it's just for me. Even if that were true, emotional acts of kindness? That wasn't like you." Claire scraped at a patch of rust on his jeans with her thumbnail. Most flaked away but some remained, embedded in the fibers.

The porch swing rocked when James pulled Claire closer. She looked past his Jeep, past the barn, toward the town beyond.

"Come on. You take great care of the Jeep, and it can't even talk. Somehow you just know what it needs, and you're the same way with me. You'd be an amazing dad. But only if you want to."

"I don't have a problem with kids. So they're sticky, and they smell. They're pretty noisy. But I bet ours would be the best kids ever."

She searched his face. "Really?"

"Someday, future Mrs. Wife." he said. "Three bedrooms, two blue bathrooms, and a porch, huh? Nice choice. They said if they start next month, it should be done just before the wedding."

* * *

Claire drove them into town for errands in the Jeep, stopping at the Fotomat booth.

"Hey, it didn't stall." She handed money to the girl inside.

"You're getting the hang of it." James waited in the passenger seat, twisting the ring on his finger, an absent-minded habit that came with its newness. Just two months old. It was cool to the touch and shined in the summer sun. Two envelopes of pictures landed in his lap.

"Trade ya these for that hair tie in the glove box?"

"You got it." James pushed the button, and the glove box door dropped open. "What photos are these?"

The Jeep inched forward into a smooth acceleration. "A little bit of everything, I think. Remember when we went fishing down by the creek, and you changed the tire out in the woods?"

"That was so long ago." James held the photos tight and flipped through them as Claire steered around potholes. "That kayak you made us buy. Here it is, tied to the Jeep."

"I thought you loved that kayak."

"I liked not drowning in that kayak. Here's all that snow piled on the Jeep after that blizzard. Thought the snaps were going to give on the soft top before I could get it all off." James waved a photo in the air. "I like this one."

"Which one is that?"

"The Jeep in front of the barn, under the sign for your office."

"That was the day I opened. Can't believe we waited that long to develop that roll of film. Glad we found it in the move."

"Aw. This one goes in the notebook." They were standing arm in arm on the porch of their new house, Claire in her flowing white dress, him in the suit he borrowed from Tom. John and Lily and Claire's parents stood to the side, and the Jeep was there, peeking from around the porch.

Five miles from home, they picked up speed and drove in silence. The engine roared, and the body panels rattled. James tilted his head back and looked up at the sky, the way Claire often did. She said it was the definition of freedom, to ride in the passenger seat, under a deep blue sky, the earth passing by her feet. She would watch the clouds as if she could see beyond them to something greater. Birds played connect the dots with the clouds, and James wished he could see the heavens through her eyes.

James sat up and collected the photos when Claire pulled into the driveway.

"I'm feeling a little dizzy, James. Do you mind bringing the bags in? I want to sit on the swing for a minute and rest on the porch."

"Of course. Do you want to go in and lay down?"

"Nah, it's probably just allergies or a cold or something. It'll pass. Do you want to sit with me for a bit? We can add the pictures to the notebook and have some tea?"

"You got it." James carried plastic bags full of dish towels, bath mats, toothbrush holders, and curtains in one hand, and supported Claire with the other. He settled her into the unpainted porch swing, kissed the top of her head, and pushed the door open with his hip.

Tan shag carpeting stretched across the living room. The smell of timber and paint mixed with adhesive still swirled in the house. No wonder Claire had a headache. Plastic bags fell from his arms to the sofa, and he opened a window to let in fresh air.

The counters were bare. James searched the pile of appliance manuals, greeting cards, and housewarming gifts on the kitchen table and found the notebook, one corner of its black plastic cover nicked and scratched. He took it and a glass of tea to Claire.

She held up a photo of the two of them, arm in arm on the porch. It had been taken on the last day of construction. The Jeep rested in the driveway. "Look at this lazy guard dog."

"The Jeep?" James laughed. "Lazy guard dog. That sounds about right."

The swing creaked, and Claire's toe grazed the floorboards with a low scraping sound, a calm, rhythmic brushing. She handed him photo after photo, curating a collection of images, reminders of their time with the Jeep. James smoothed the plastic covers over diagonal lines of adhesive.

"Wanna see?" He slid the notebook onto her lap. A drop of condensation fell from her glass to the cover. She wiped it away and flipped through the pages.

"We've done a lot with this Jeep. I almost forgot about that kayak. It's probably still in the barn. We should dig it out sometime. Hey, we could go fishing."

James laughed. "You hate fishing."

"I hate falling in the water."

"I don't recall you liking fish all that much either."

"Ew. You're right. I don't." She wrinkled her nose.

"Maybe not fishing. Besides, we need to keep you out of danger." James closed the notebook and pulled Claire close. "You think the headache could be a sign?"

"I really don't think so. Sorry."

He tangled his fingers in hers and felt the coolness of her ring against his hand. Her expression changed, as if she drove into a tunnel. "Hey, you okay? What's going on?"

"Maybe it's time we talk about it. This has been really hard. Fun. But hard. On both of us. Do you want to stop trying?"

"Claire, no. Not if…do you not want to have a baby anymore? Did you change your mind?"

"No, it's not that. It's…it's heartbreaking. I feel deficient. Like something must be wrong with me."

"It's probably just bad timing. Or maybe it's me. We could always adopt. Even if it never works out, I'm good. I have everything I need right here. Anything else is icing on the cake."

The ringing phone echoed through the house. Claire winced. James leapt to his feet, careful not to rock the swing.

He called to Claire through the open window. "We have to go. It's the farm. It's John."

* * *

People gathered in clusters in the farmhouse and the yard, holding coffee and tea and talking in hushed voices. The screen door slammed a hundred times. Feet shuffled onto the porch and into the kitchen. James listened to the voices of sympathy but absorbed little. Claire covered casserole dishes, and he tucked leftovers into the corners of the Philco refrigerator, pushing aside the nearly empty container of orange juice. It expired two days ago. He wasn't ready to throw it away yet.

A tap on his shoulder. Angie tugged at the sleeve of her black dress.

"You two come down to the diner when you're ready. Anytime you need a meal or to get away. It's on the house." She hugged Claire. "I'm very sorry. Everybody loved John so much."

"Thank you, Angie." Claire took her hands. "I never knew you could die of a broken heart but…he missed her."

"They were a pair. Inseparable. And they loved the two of you so much." Angie smoothed her sleeve over her arm, her lower lip tucked beneath her two front teeth. James wondered what she felt, what any of them felt. What grief was like without the numbing distance that he turned to like an old friend. He applied a fitting smile and nodded.

"James, I never told you this, but I had the biggest crush on your father. He was such a handsome man. So charming. It was the best part of the day, serving him coffee. And I always had a soft spot for you. Seeing you and Claire happy together, I know he'd be just as proud as John was. That Jeep was the best thing that ever happened to you."

"The Jeep? I thought you'd say Claire."

Angie touched Claire's arm. "Claire is a walking miracle, but you wouldn't have any of this if it weren't for that Jeep. What will happen to the farm? Will you two move in here?"

James let Claire give the account they'd shared so often that day, that they planned to rent out the house they built and move into the farmhouse to tend to the farm. Claire would keep her veterinary practice, and James would be closer to work. It's what John and Lily had always wanted. He nodded his agreement and slipped past the people and onto the porch, down the stairs and across the gravel drive. He pushed open the barn door and stepped into the cool, dark corner where his Jeep took shelter. His breath was shallow and shaky. He pushed as much air as he could from his lungs and sank into the driver's seat, his hands on the cool, thin steering wheel.

Angie was right. If it weren't for the Jeep, he never would have stopped at the side of the road. He never would have met John or Lily or their granddaughter. He never would have found his footing in those fields. He'd had every intention of using the Jeep to run from town, to run from himself, and never look back, but the Jeep had other plans.

* * *

Autumn surrendered the last of its leaves to the winter of 1974. James swept away the last of the stray wheat and chaff that had drifted into the barn and closed the door on what remained of Claire's veterinary office. The rooms were empty now. The walls were bare. Claire was gone.

Someone was burning leaves in the distance, past the tree line. Near the house James built just a few years before, when they were first married. It smelled earthy and sweet. Like harvest time. He paused to take in the smell and wished it conjured something, some happy memory. Anything to keep the heartache company.

James climbed the farmhouse stairs, passed the porch swing where they watched their daughter take her first steps, and flinched when the screen door slammed behind him. He felt swallowed by the wave of the memories carried by the sound of the door. Like being consumed by a whale. He lowered his body into his chair at the kitchen table.

At first, he kept the medical bills in a folder by date. He replaced them with updated past due copies, and then with the angry pink invoices as they arrived. Doctors. Surgeons. Cancer treatment. Medicines. Therapies. End of life care. Funeral. Headstone.

One folder became two. He cut back where he could and stopped spending where he couldn't. He sold their little house. He sold her equipment. It took more than a year, but he managed to pay most of the bills. The few that remained were big and persistent. They threatened to put a lien on her farm. Their farm.

He embraced the sharp pain in his chest and cherished the agony he couldn't feel before. Her memory and his heartbreak, indivisible. He would rather chip away his protective rust and carry the anguish forever than to forget one moment with Claire. He had a daughter to raise, and James wasn't sure he could do it without his Claire.

He ran a hand through his hair and went to the counter. Before Claire got sick, before cancer nibbled away at her brain, and she couldn't stand, she loved to look out the window above the sink. Past the porch. Past the barn and the fields. Past the trees. Beyond the sky. James focused on a spot much closer, at his Jeep and the empty space where her Wagoneer once sat, leaking.

He thought he knew the cost of loving Claire. Terrified that she would show him who he really was. Losing control of the facade and meeting the man he buried on the battlefield. But she knew him all along, and she showed him with a bloodletting. Now he had to live with that man alone. Sentimental and wounded. A new kind of empty, collecting every emotion, however painful, to keep himself from caving in. But he was stronger than the man who stepped off that bus ten years ago. He wouldn't have any of this—the farm, Claire, their daughter—if it weren't for that little Jeep. It had carried him so far. It just had to carry him a little further.

CHAPTER NINE

The screen door slammed, and ten years of memories fluttered to the surface. James choked back anger, the kind that arrives on the heels of grief, and waited for the memories to settle like plastic beads in a snow globe. He hadn't noticed Angie's arrival, the sound of her car on the gravel drive obscured by Walter Cronkite on the television, talking about water and a gate. A deep breath held long enough to slow his senses brought him back.

His knees ached from kneeling, pushing a little toy car across the floor. He gave it another push and kissed Catherine's golden hair, receiving nothing in return. His daughter's attention was planted on the car's path toward the hearth. It overturned, its wheels caught in a gap in the old wood planks. He picked it up and put it into her little outstretched hand. Walter Cronkite faded to Captain Kangaroo.

When Angie's keys hit the counter, James loosened his jaw and stood, stretching, adjusting the waist of his jeans. On the way to the kitchen, he glanced at the clock. Beside it, and on every flat surface around it, dozens photographs of Claire smiled into the house. She would never be absent from their daughter's life, and he would do anything to keep the farm, to raise their child in the place where they'd found happiness.

"Thanks for coming," he said. Sliding his wallet from the counter and shoving it into his back pocket, he felt his other pants pockets for the key. "I know it's a lot to ask. There's probably a line at the diner for you already."

"I'm happy to help wherever I can, James. I know things have been rough." Angie's eyes didn't match her smile, and James ignored the sympathy. She dropped her apron onto the back of a chair, her attention turned toward the child in the living room. "I can't believe you let her play with that rusty thing."

"If I judged everything I came across by its rust, I'd—" James patted his shirt pockets. "What am I forgetting?"

Angie stepped past him to lean in the living room doorway, and his eyes followed her. He spotted the black binder on the kitchen table and seized it. "Notebook. Almost forgot. Hour, hour and a half tops, Ang. Thanks again."

He had already turned to leave when she said, "Take your time. Diner can't open 'til I get there, anyway."

James pushed through the screen door and winced when it slammed again. He wanted to rip the door from the hinges and throw it off the porch, but he knew the anger was temporary.

At least you can feel it.

He would worship the memories of that sound one day, if he could manage to hold onto the farm. He leaned against the porch railing and shoved his heels into his sneakers, letting the heat of anger fade. The loss of Claire made him heavy.

The hollow wooden thud of his feet on the stairs ended, and he shuffled through the gravel to his little green Jeep CJ-5. Sliding into the driver's seat, he looked across the dashboard at the gauges for the last time. The paint around the rim of the speedometer was chipped. The white lettering on the fuel gauge was just beginning to yellow after a decade in the sun. He reached across the dashboard and touched the metal bar that served as a grab handle for the passenger seat. The empty seat added more substance to the car than any passenger ever did.

With the turn of the key, the engine rumbled to life and memories boiled within James. Driving it away from the dealership. Breaking down in front of the farm. The drive from his old apartment above the newsstand on a typical morning, the sun just beginning to hint at day. He shut his eyes and swallowed back the hot, bitter taste of recollection. Lifting his chin, he straightened his shoulders against the ache, listening to the idle change. When he and the Jeep settled, he backed down the driveway.

James turned left and headed for town, passing Angie's Diner, the bank, the market. Places he'd once avoided, with their pitying stares and empty condolences. It was a new kind of numb. Not the empty, distant kind he felt after the war, but the cold kind of numb that comes from listening to the same tired expressions.

The CJ-5 shuddered to a stop in front of the bar, and he cut the engine. He leaned to collect the notebook from behind the passenger seat but paused and opened the glove box. Inside the shallow storage compartment, wrapped around an old tire gauge, he found the small leather band that Claire used to tie back her hair in the wind. He wound it around his fingers, pushed the pain aside, and tucked the small coil into his pocket along with the key. Then he threw the tire gauge back in the glove box, grabbed the binder, and walked into the bar, taking in the smell of wood soaked in beer and last night's fried food.

"James. Haven't seen you in here for a while." Tom lifted his chin and a glass from behind the bar. "Beam, neat?"

James shook his head and mustered a sarcastic sneer. "It's eight in the morning. Coffee?"

"The old you wouldn't have said no. You never know around here. One coffee, then."

When James took a napkin from the top of the stack, the light above the bar caught the thin gold band on his finger. He spun it around. It wasn't something he ever wanted. He never sought the ring or the marriage that came with it, but now both were a part of him. Like a scar he turned to for comfort.

Tom set the coffee before him, and the world came back into focus. A thin brown drip made its way down the side of the mug, seeping into the napkin. He saw Tom's eyes bore into the notebook and hoped he wouldn't ask what was inside.

"What brings you by?"

Hot liquid stung James's lip. "Meeting some guy here. Selling the Jeep."

"Really? I can't believe you're selling it. You and that Jeep are inseparable."

James blinked down at his cup on the bar to avoid Tom's raised eyebrows.

Tom stepped back and stuffed his hands in his pockets. "I'm sorry, man. Claire was amazing. Everything about her, she just…she lit up this town, that's for sure. I don't know what to say."

"It's okay. You don't have to say anything."

The cooler hummed a one-note soundtrack. A block of ice clattered into the ice machine. James was thankful for the break in the tension. He cracked his knuckles, trying to think of something to say to let his childhood friend off the hook. He didn't want the sympathy.

"It's been, what, a dozen years since you came home? Just the other day, I was just thinking about when you stepped off the bus and came through that door. You used to come around all the time." Tom shuffled his feet and reached for a toothpick.

"Ten years. It was 1964. That damn war." James gave him half a smile.

"I'm not making this place a habit, if that's what you're getting at. Not for the whiskey, anyway."

"No, I wasn't thinking that. Just…how much you've been through. And that Jeep. That's a shocker."

"Yeah, well. Can't hold onto anything forever. It all has to go sometime. Apparently."

"We should go out. Do something. Catch some fish."

"Yeah, we should." James offered the closest thing to a smile he could muster. He let it fall.

"I gotta finish stocking this cooler. Let me know if you need anything?" Tom turned the dial on a little radio, and Harry Chapin sang into the room.

When the door opened, striking the bell, James spun to face the newcomer. "Hey, you William?"

"Yes, sir." The young man wore a new suit. He looked uncomfortable in it, like it wasn't his style.

James shook his hand and tried not to crush him. "I got a few things to pass on to you here." He patted the black binder. William hopped onto the stool next to him, and Tom stepped into view, drying a glass, ready to take a drink order.

William shook his head, declined the offer. "Nothing for me, thanks."

James took the key from his shirt pocket. One small key on a bent keyring. He laid it on the bar between them. "Take her for a drive?"

"I'm okay without one. I grew up around cars. Gotta get back to Clayburn anyway."

James was relieved. He didn't offer twice. He would rather finish his coffee and catch a ride home than watch someone else with his Jeep.

"It's in excellent shape, like I said. No rust, no major issues. You just have to keep the carb tuned and remember not to downshift into first while you're driving. The choke is sensitive. Take your time. And you have to come to a complete stop before you can shift into first gear."

In his mind, he was reaching for the binder, clutching it to his chest, and screaming *it's mine, you can't have it.* Every receipt, from the day he bought the car to the last can of oil, was in that notebook. There were scraps of paper, hastily written notes about maintenance, like the time he replaced the throttle cable. It had started to snow, and Claire brought him hot chocolate in that old thermos.

James wasn't the kind of man to keep a diary, but it was the closest thing he had to a record of his past. He had copies of every photograph at home. Those wouldn't haunt him. It was the memories stamped into each receipt that tugged at his sentimentality, the remnants of mundane days like buying oil and ice cream after Claire taught him about petrichor. But the book belonged with the car.

He leaned over his drink, his head tilted. Forcing half of his face to smile, he wondered if he'd ever drink coffee again without thinking about his old Jeep. And Claire. His hand was steady when he pushed the binder closer to William.

"This notebook has everything. Every receipt for every dollar I ever spent on her. I did everything myself. It's all in there, plus some odds and ends. I wrote detailed instructions for you for everything I could think of." James risked a breach in his steel exterior, but he opened the notebook anyway, laying the cover down on the bar. The first photo sleeve, yellow with age, gave an off-white border to the original bill of sale. His heart unraveled a bit at the sight of the pen in the front pocket. "I used this at the dealership the day I bought the car. I don't know why I put it in here, but it stayed." James resisted the urge to pocket the pen. "Just...keep good records and pass them on. Take good care of the her. These Jeeps last forever if you treat them right."

James stopped himself before he sounded morose. William shifted forward on his seat and retrieved an envelope from his back pocket. He laid it on the bar between them and lifted the notebook gently.

"I hate to run, but I need to make it back to Clayburn before lunch. The money's all here. You can count it if you want."

James shook his head and gave a small, forced smile. "That's okay. I trust you. I've got your number. Just remember, you can't downshift into first too early. Come to a full stop before you downshift until you get the hang of it. She's a good girl, but she's a little more than ten years old now. It's going to need something eventually. Take care of it."

William slid from the stool and walked toward the door with the notebook cradled in his arm. "I will. I promise."

7 2 9 0 5 8 4

CERTIFICATE OF OWNERSHIP OF A MOTOR VEHICLE

PLATE NO

TJ 2643

VEHICLE IDEN. NO.

8305 165111

NAME

WILLIAM R. NORMAN

DATE OF ISSUE

10 9 74

STREET

11 STICKNEY AVE #721

CITY

CLAYBURN

MAKE	YEAR	MODEL	MILEAGE
JEEP	64	CJ-5	7386

CHAPTER TEN

William was raised in a Volkswagen bus in campgrounds and fields and parking lots by a carefree and loving set of parents who, for all their individuality, were not much different than their carefree friends. Resentful of bureaucratic restraints and fearful of the government, they wandered but were never lost, except in the eyes of the Internal Revenue Service.

Along with other children in their roving caravan, William was homeschooled by whichever studious adult was compelled to captivate them for a day. While most of his friends enjoyed literature and the arts, William was exceptional at math. He devoured numbers. By the age of eleven, on the day the bus broke down in Elmwood, he was managing his family's meager finances, but he was not so exceptional that he could create money from thin air.

"At least we broke down near a town instead of up in the mountains somewhere." William's mother watched through the window of the repair shop as her husband and the shop owner peered at the engine. "This is going to cost an arm and a leg."

"I don't know how we're going to afford this." William chewed at the side of his thumb. He didn't need to look at his ledger or count the cash.

They were in the single digits. He could control the numbers, but he couldn't make his parents be practical.

His mother put her hand on the back of his head, an unnecessary reassuring gesture. William knew how it would play out. They would find the town restrictive, but he would be set free. "Your father and I can get jobs. Make a little money. We can get back on the road in a few weeks, maybe."

"We could always stay here, Mom."

"We'll have to for a little while."

William remembered passing the sign for a school, duplexes with For Rent signs, a deli, a general store. He wished for a bedroom of his own with walls and a kitchen, for a bookbag and a table where he could do homework. But he failed to form his hopes into words before his father and the shop owner entered the lobby, stomping their boots free of dirt and pebbles.

The shop owner was a round and sympathetic man. "I was telling your husband here that this engine, it's just done for. I can put a new one in there, but it won't be cheap. The next best thing is to look around at these junk yards. It'll still cost a good bit of change, though."

William looked at his mother. She tugged at her ear, a gesture that meant she had given up on a difficult circumstance.

"All's not lost. Let me call some of the folks from church. This is a nice little town, and someone will be able to help you for a day or two while you figure something out."

William's father nudged a pebble across the floor mat, pushing it closer to the door. "This town seems nice. On our way here, I saw a little deli with a help sign in the window. And it looks like there are a lot of places for rent. I hate to impose but…"

"It's not imposing at all. I'll call Aida from the church. She owns a few houses along Redfern Road. I bet she'll work with you on the rent until you can get on your feet and get some money saved." He clasped a hand on William's shoulder. "I have a son about your age. His name's Mark. He should be here soon. He'll be happy to meet you. Why don't you folks help yourselves to some coffee."

* * *

Over the years, the bus became a landmark. The tires rotted, and it sank to the ground in front of the garage. Rust took hold and ate through the frame. The shop owner used it for parts until it was sold for scrap. While it was hauled onto a flatbed trailer, patrons of the tavern across the street gathered on the sidewalk and peered out the windows. But William's father had said goodbye years before. The day the bus left town, he was working at the deli while his wife waited tables. William did his homework in the kitchen of their ground-floor apartment, next to the town laundromat, the dryers rumbling through the wall in a comforting cadence that felt like home.

He loved those dryers, that table, and having dinner around it. He loved checking a mailbox, and biking home from school with his best friend, Mark. Elmwood was home, but his heart wasn't there. It was a stop on his way to a big city, full of lights, activity, and opportunity. He yearned to be a part of the world that his parents had tried to avoid. He wanted to work on Wall Street or in Washington, where the numbers were bigger.

The night before graduation, on the eve of their freedom, William and Mark armed themselves with beer, cigarettes, and restless youth and climbed the water tower.

Williams's foot slipped and mud from his shoes landed in Mark's hair. "Watch it up there."

"Geez. I can't climb this thing sober. It's going to be a blast climbing down when I'm drunk."

"You won't get drunk off three Miller High Lifes." Mark shifted the weight of the backpack and stepped onto the bottom rung of the ladder. "I take that back. Maybe you will, ya geek."

William walked around the platform and took a seat on the ledge, kicking his feet and looking out over the town. There was far too much black between it and the horizon for his taste. Not enough city lights. Mark sat next to him and pulled two beers of out his backpack.

"What time you think graduation will end tomorrow?" William opened the can and tucked the tab in his back pocket with the key to his new apartment.

"Before lunch, I hope. I gotta get back to the shop. Garage is full of cars."

"That sucks." William flung mud off his shoes to the ground below. It was a long way to fall. "I gotta run, too. Last bus to Clayburn leaves at twelve thirty."

"You got that apartment?"

"Yeah. I took a bus out there last weekend. I start that mailroom job on Monday. It should pay the bills while I save up for college." He squeezed the empty can, bending it in the middle, and took another from the backpack. Should. He should want to celebrate, to jump to his feet and howl at the moon. But the closer he came to the unknown, the more he settled for *should* over *would* and *could*. For all his boasting about leaving, he didn't want Mark to know that, though. "God, I can't wait to get out of this town."

"Doesn't seem like this town's been that bad to you."

"There's nothing here." It was the truth. "I don't want to work at the beer store or at the post office. Best I can do is hope some bank opens a branch, but I don't wanna sit and deposit checks all day. There's nothing here, man. This place is dead."

96

"What, then? You're too good for this town?"

"I didn't say that." William's cheeks grew warm from the guilt and accusation. He didn't think he was any better than anyone else. Certainly not Mark. He just wanted something Elmwood couldn't offer.

"That's what it sounds like. What's out there is just so much better than what's here?"

"If I stay here, I give up on my future."

"Oh. Since you put it that way. We'd hate for you to have a dismal future. It's probably better if people like you don't live in small towns like this."

"What's that supposed to mean?"

Mark hopped to his feet and brushed flakes of yellow paint and rust from his pants. "My whole life's here. There ain't nothing out there that's any better than what's here. But if it ain't good enough for you and you're just gonna be miserable living here, then go."

"I wasn't saying that…"

Mark turned to climb down the ladder. "Clean up after yourself up here when you're done."

The next afternoon, as black and white mortarboards fell to the ground around William, he looked across the field to where Mark stood. He wanted to apologize, to pat him on the back and invite him to visit, but the ceremony ran late, and he still had to run back to his parents' apartment for his duffle bag. There wasn't time. If he didn't leave, he would miss the last bus out of town. He had dreams to catch.

* * *

Dry hands, paper cuts, and eye strain from fluorescent lights hadn't been among William's dreams, but they were a part of life in the mailroom of Allied Insurance Company, where William worked with three other men, sorting and opening and sealing envelopes.

Every opportunity for advancement was pounced upon and missed, as William was passed over in favor of candidates with more experience, more education, or more knowledge. He never complained, but it was clear that he didn't belong. While his coworkers dreamed of vacations, private islands, and fast cars, William dreamed about college.

"What if you won the lottery? A million dollars? What would you do with it?" Freddy pushed a stack of outgoing mail through a postage machine.

"College. A giant library with all those books to read. You can even sit in on classes that you don't sign up for. I would go to school for business and then roll it right into a master's degree in finance."

"You have strange dreams." Freddy threw junk mail into a giant plastic trash can. "But if that's what you want, I don't know why you won't try."

"Something will happen for me one day. Just like it will for you." William kept telling himself that, but the columns of mail slots were looking more and more like prison bars.

"No, man, stuff doesn't happen for people like me." Martin moved the stack of magazines to a cart, preparing for morning delivery. "You're not like me. You can make stuff happen for yourself. When are you gonna stop hanging around this place? Go to school and get out of here?"

William never said why out loud. He kept secret the fact that his parents had denied him a formal education until he'd enrolled himself in the seventh grade. That he knew about campsite outhouses, the spiders and smells, and the way people looked at you when you went into a store and used the restroom without paying. He knew the questions people asked when they found out how you lived. And he knew that they treated you differently after you told them.

A clock over the postage machine buzzed, saving William and setting them free from work. Pushing through the mailroom doors, he joined the line of agents and filing clerks through hallways and revolving doors and onto the streets of Clayburn. Over crosswalks, through courtyards, and into cars and buses, the streets bustled with businessmen and women heeding the call of the five o'clock commute. William's journey was a four-block walk down dirty sidewalks littered with cigarette butts and beer cans, a twenty-minute bus ride, and three more blocks to his apartment. The idea that he had to grasp the future and make his own change rather than waiting for it to happen to him played over and over in his mind. Two blocks from home, he dug a quarter from the pocket of his corduroys and paid for a newspaper at the corner deli.

No elevator led to the seventh-floor apartment where William lived behind a dented door. He kicked it open and turned on the light. One lamp flickered to life, illuminating mismatched furniture, most of which had been scavenged from thrift shops and moving neighbors. It was dark, dated, dismal. It wasn't much, but it was his. He tossed his key onto a scratched and worn end table by the door and walked straight to the folding card table that served as a dining area. Opening the newspaper to the Help Wanted section, with a red felt-tipped pen, he circled anything that looked promising.

Paper after paper, rejections followed résumés. After weeks of searching and being gracious in defeat, William listened to another rejection, coiling his finger in the phone cord while clinging to his last threads of hope.

"May I ask why?" William asked the woman who called from the financial firm of Parker and Lowell. "It was a filing position. I met the qualifications. I'm curious if there's anything I can improve on. To increase my chances."

"I'm so sorry." She sounded remorseful. William wondered how many people begged for filing positions. After a short pause, she added, "I couldn't say."

"Anything at all? My whole life I've wanted to work in finance. Any feedback you can give me would be great. Even for a filing position, isn't it good for an employee to have passion for the industry?"

"I understand. I do." Her tone dripped with sympathy. "Can you hold for one moment?"

He listened to enough saxophone while on hold to wonder if he was waiting for anyone at all. "William?" The man didn't wait for a response. "Richard here. I am sorry to say we offered the position to another candidate. My secretary said you wanted feedback. We don't usually do that, but I liked you. You were a strong candidate. Smart. Very capable. Too smart for that position."

"Thank you, sir. Then—"

"It's a little more than that. Appearances are important. Yes, it's a filing job, but this position can be seen by clients, and I'm sorry to say that appearance makes an impression."

William ran his fingers through his long hair, looked at his corduroy-clad knee, and thanked the man.

If he were a business, he would have a five-year plan, a ten-year plan, goals and deadlines toward achievements. He would have control of his assets and be using them to his advantage. But all he had was a twenty-year-old lamp, a folding card table, and a checking account.

He spent the night at that table, with a paper and pen, and mapped his strategy.

The next morning, he tossed a coin to the man who operated the news cart and took a newspaper from the top of the stack. With it tucked under his arm, he stepped through the door of the tailor at the end of the block to buy a white shirt and simple suit. Three doors down, he dropped into a seat at the barber shop, waiting his turn while browsing the newspaper. With a tight budget, there was only one car worth circling in the sales section: a green Jeep out in Elk River.

* * *

It was simple math. If time were money, William was wasting it on public transportation. If he was going to go to work and go to college at the same time, he couldn't afford to spend all his time waiting for buses. The Jeep was intended to be an inexpensive solution, an expanded opportunity. But he stood over the engine, high from the scent of leaking fuel, wondering how he was supposed to make it through business school if he couldn't even operate a car. The only way to fix it was to fix his broken friendship with Mark.

William brought the car to a stop in an empty bay of Mark's garage. The engine was still running when Mark lifted a hood latch. "I could smell this thing coming," he said. "Was it like this when you bought it?"

William cut the motor and reached down by his left knee, engaging the parking brake. "No. But it wouldn't start and then it smelled funny and didn't sound right. Then I started messing with it. I saw my dad do this a million times, but I guess I did something wrong."

Mark raised the hood, and with a gentle thud, rested it against the little bumper that protected the windshield. He peered into the engine bay. "To start with, you're running really rich."

"What does that mean? How can you tell?"

Mark's eyes were wide, his eyebrows raised. "You're kidding, right? Smell it."

William accepted his defeat. "Just tell me it isn't expensive. I spent half my savings on this, and I'll never make my money back if I have to sell it this way."

"Well, I can tell you what part of the problem is." Mark stood, motionless, burning a hole through William with his stare. William had always intended to apologize. Weeks had turned to months. Months into a

101

year. Life droned on. He opened his mouth to speak too late, and Mark cut him off. "You've got the fuel mixture screw almost all the way in, so it's dying for air. Did you touch this?" Mark pointed to the small brass screw that protruded from the carburetor.

"Probably?"

"Let's take the whole thing off and look at it. Sometimes the float gets stuck. Gunk gets in there, and it sticks. It happens. It's an easy fix." Mark turned from William and the car, collecting screwdrivers and wrenches.

"Easy for you to say. How long will it take?"

Mark loosened the bolts that secured the carburetor to the engine. "However long it takes to get it right, if you know what I mean. Don't go anywhere. I'm going to walk you through it, so you know how to do it yourself." Mark handed him a small pile of bolts and screws. "Keep track of these."

William inhaled, drawing in the smell of fuel when Mark removed the carburetor from the engine. "This Jeep is terrible." He needed the right time, the right words.

"I beg to differ, Bill. This is a fantastic car. I would say it's the perfect car for you. It just needed maintenance, and you don't know how to listen to it. It's a machine. It's constantly aging and parts are always wearing out. Your job is to keep it from doing that."

"You're saying that something will always be wrong, but it's not a bad car? I guess it's a good car if you're a mechanic." William rolled the little brass and stainless screws in the palm of his hand.

"It's definitely better than that old bus." Mark carried the carburetor to his workbench and disassembled it, lost and rambling in his own world. "This car has been trying to become something else since it rolled off the assembly line. The metal wants to be rust. These hoses are drying out. A brand new car has a long way to go, but this one's starting to show its age.

Your job is to figure out what you can do about it. That doesn't mean it's a bad car. Just like people. Sometimes things just go wrong. Doesn't mean it's a bad person or a bad friendship. It just needs a little maintenance."

William gave Mark a knowing smile. "I may not be good at machines. Or good at fixing much of anything. But I do know when I screw up."

"Do you, though?"

William's shoulders fell, and he looked at the ceiling in surrender. "I do. It's not that I didn't want to apologize. I'm at work all the time, and I still barely make ends meet. I could have called, but I kept thinking I'd get back here sooner than later. One thing led to another."

Mark pulled a dirty rag from the back pocket of his jeans and wiped his hands with it. "I get it. How much longer would it have taken if your Jeep didn't break down?"

"The day after graduation was already too long. Look, man, you're my best friend."

"Were."

"Come on, man. You're the only real friend I ever had. And this town isn't that bad. Honestly, I wasn't as excited to leave as I made it sound. I was terrified. The longer I went without saying I was sorry, the harder it got. I really am sorry, though."

"Problems don't fix themselves. Funny how you end up in this hick town every time a car breaks down." Mark turned back to the workbench, making adjustments to the carburetor.

William couldn't help but smile. As usual, Mark was right. "Just 'cause my life's different than yours, doesn't mean yours isn't worth anything. I never meant it to sound that way."

"But that's how it came out."

"You should know by now that I'm not a words guy like you."

Mark finished his adjustments to the carburetor and carried it back to the car, bolting it to the engine. "It wasn't even that big of a deal."

"Maybe there's hope for me, yet."

"Of course there is. We all come around eventually. Go start the engine." Apology accepted.

William started the engine. Mark waited for it to warm up and made one last adjustment. He listened and watched for leaks before closing the hood and giving it a pat. "There you go. Back on the road."

William turned off the engine and stepped out of the Jeep. "Thanks, Mark. I owe you. A lot."

"Nah, you don't own me anything. Just buy me a beer sometime." Mark took the rag from his pocket and wiped his screwdriver clean. "You still at that insurance place? You should be running your own business or doing brainy things at a desk."

"I'm trying. Not doing very well, but I'm trying. I bought the Jeep so I can get to work and school. I'm just finding my way, I guess."

"Don't lose momentum. You can be just as stuck in Clayburn as you'd have been here. You weren't entirely wrong, up at the water tower. People rely on me here, and I don't want to be anywhere else. I belong here, but you don't. You have potential for something else. Don't get lazy."

"Maybe potential isn't enough. Maybe being smart and good at taking tests and moving money around on paper isn't enough. If I go out there and I fail? That's an expensive mistake."

"We're talking about two different types of expensive. You could make a million dollars in that mailroom and sitting there could still be an expensive mistake. That place will crush your soul. You could use your giant brain to change the world. The world just isn't ready for you yet." Mark patted the hood of the Jeep. "This car's okay for you right now, but you should be in a fancy European thing, taking it to a dealer for service."

Everything came easy to guys like Mark, with looks and personality that almost guaranteed success at anything. It was hard to hear advice from a guy who never had to overcome insecurities. William rubbed one temple. "This garage, everything that happened. Were you afraid you'd fail?"

"I didn't have enough time to think about the big picture. I didn't ask to lose my dad. I didn't ask for everybody to quit and to have to run this place by myself. You just figure it out. Once you get started in business, it's just jumping the hurdles."

"Yeah. My big picture has me homeless, holding onto a giant pile of debt, begging my way back into the mailroom."

"You gotta shake that fear. It's like cars. They can sit in a garage and go nowhere, but they're only doing their job if you drive them. They all go through the same road salt and mud. Some of them coming out looking like that rusty Buick and others come out great, like your little Jeep here. Neither one is a failure. They only fail if they never leave the house."

"Cars, huh? It's always about cars with you."

"Destiny, Bill. Come on, do you really want me to be more successful than you?"

William rolled his eyes at the suggestion. "Yeah, yeah. I get it."

"Just get out of there. Whatever you do, go be happy. It's really unfair to the rest of us if you don't. And stop being a stranger."

* * *

William drove cautiously for a few miles, analyzing every sound and smell. By the time he got to Clayburn, he'd regained enough confidence to celebrate. He stopped at the corner deli for beer. The owner never questioned his age, and he never offered.

At home, he pushed open the door and flicked on the light. He jiggled the keys out of the lock and tossed them onto the old end table. The brown paper bag rustled, and the bottles clanked against one another when he dropped the six pack onto the folding card table. He looked down at the notebook and slumped into a chair, exhausted and pensive. Wondering how he could have gone so long without learning about basic car repair.

Opening a beer, he turned the bottle cap over in his fingers, placed it upside down on the table. He gave it a flick. It ricocheted off of the brown paper bag with a thud and clattered to a stop.

The notebook was open to a diagram of a carburetor and the neighboring pages could have been ripped from a family photo album. The guy who sold him the Jeep with a pretty girl. A child standing on the driver's seat, using the steering wheel to balance. There were pictures taken at places all over the county. Some he recognized. Some he didn't. Looking at the happy couple, he felt like a lonely and inadequate participant. They'd gained so much from the Jeep, and he'd only found a new way to fail. He pulled a few sheets of paper from the briefcase his father gave him as a graduation gift. Pausing only to take sips of his beer, he began to write his story.

He'd spent so much time worried about getting an education, focusing on books and stuffing himself with facts and figures. It took a car, a pile of metal and grease, to show him the difference between knowing and thinking you know. What else did he take for granted? His friendship with Mark. What his parents gave up to fulfill his need for legitimacy. None of them argued or tried to change his mind. They let him harbor resentment until he figured it out for himself. His letter followed the path of that resentment on its way to redemption. It shined light on the pot holes he never paved over because it was easier to sit still than face the unknown at the end of the road. By the time he finished writing, he knew his fear of failure was only eclipsed by his fear of success.

William swirled the dredges of his sixth bottle of beer and watched the last warm sip settle in the amber glass. Two pages of small, precise handwriting revealed more than he intended, but after committing it to paper, he felt obligated to include it. He peeled the plastic covers from two new photo pages and added his narrative. While returning the unused sheets of paper to his briefcase, out of sight and out of mind, William found one blank college application.

The next morning, he ran the application through the postage machine and threw it into an outgoing mail bin. Each day on his way home from work, he stopped at the post office and sat in the Jeep, rifling through stacks of junk mail and coupons, telling himself that he didn't care if he received a rejection letter, and frustrated that he hadn't received anything at all.

Under a January sky that threatened to erupt with snow, the steering wheel pressing into his leg just above his knee, he sorted mail. Envelopes and scraps of paper fluttered to the back of the Jeep. The electric bill. A letter from his mother. An off-white envelope with a navy blue seal and the outline of a clock tower. The engine idle pulsed through him, and the heater shook the letter in his hands. A small drop of blood formed on his thumb, another paper cut. He stuck his finger in his mouth and shook open the letter. Bracing it against the steering wheel, he bit the side of his thumb.

CHAPTER ELEVEN

The Jeep rolled to a stop at William's usual parking spot on campus in the shade of a tall tree. He kept his hand on the shifter, securing the transmission in second gear to keep it from slipping. What he couldn't learn about the Jeep from the notebook, he learned from Mark, and when his questions sounded too silly to ask, he taught himself. He knew from experience that a small adjustment to the clutch cable would keep it from slipping, so he pulled a wrench from the front pocket of his backpack, lay on the tarmac, and made a small adjustment.

"Need any help down there?" A pair of boots appeared at his side. Girl's boots.

"I think I'm good. I'll know for sure when I head home." William finished tightening a nut.

"That's good. I wouldn't know how to help anyway. I really like your Jeep, though. Always have."

"Yeah?" William slid from under the car and sat up, resting his arms on his knees. There weren't many old Jeeps on campus so it would make sense that his stood out.

"I do. My dad has a Commando." She reached out a hand. "I don't think we've ever met. Rebecca."

William showed her his palm. It was black with grease, pocked with rocks and dirt from the parking lot. "William. And grimy. Feel free to pass on the shake."

"I liked your presentation on international mergers. Dr. Jones's class last semester?"

"Dr. Jones's class?" He hopped to his feet, and she stepped back to give him room, shuffling her books from one arm to the other. They hung against her hip at the end of her arm, and William couldn't help but notice the way her jeans fit. He wiped his hands on a rag he kept in the back of the car.

"Anyway, I just wanted to say that I like your Jeep. I did a study of Willys-Overland, Bantam, and Kaiser in that business history class our junior year, and I thought it was interesting."

"Wait." He tossed the rag into the Jeep and slung his backpack over his shoulder. How had he never noticed her before? "We're in the same classes? And we've never met?"

"Seems that way." Rebecca turned toward the building, and William fell into step next to her. "What year is it?"

"What year is what?"

"Your Jeep. What year?"

"Um, it's a sixty-four."

"Is it a Kaiser or a Willys?"

He shook his head to clear the fog and returned her smile, surprised to meet a girl in business school who knew the difference. "It's a Kaiser. An early Kaiser. They still used the Willys tailgates when it was made, but Kaiser owned the company at that point."

"They're pretty bare bones, aren't they? I tend to think of them as more of a rural thing? I don't see many of them around campus."

"Maybe. I dunno. If so, I don't mind that it's a rural thing. I grew up in…not the city." Proud of what he'd overcome, how he grew up was no longer a source of shame, but he still rarely spoke of Elmwood out of habit.

"Me, too! That's why I was surprised to see one out here."

"Yeah? It's been a great car. A little learning curve at first, but it's fun in the summer. And nimble, too. I can park it just about anywhere." Four concrete steps led to the heavy metal door. William held it open for her, and when she passed, he could smell her shampoo. Like flowers and herbs. Like summer. He tightened his grip on the strap of his backpack.

At the threshold, she turned and stopped, blocking his path. "This might sound forward but would you like to get a cup of coffee after class sometime?"

William glanced back at his Jeep and hoisted his backpack higher on his shoulder. Heavy books inside it jumped.

"Yeah. Sure! There's a place a few blocks up. Beans and Leaves? We could walk there after class sometime." He heard himself offer up the idea before he'd thought through the consequence. He was there for an education, not a distraction.

"I love that place. It's so homey. How about today? This weather's perfect."

Distracted by the footsteps and laughter echoing in the stairwell above them, William didn't have much time to deliberate. "Meet you at the fountain after class?"

"That sounds…perfect."

He spent the next hour thinking less about arbitrage pricing theory than about Rebecca's shampoo. He roused at the scraping of chairs against the linoleum, the closing of books, and papers rustling into piles. He stacked his notes carefully, pages he knew he would have to read later, and shoved them into his backpack.

* * *

Campus felt like home to William. He knew every uneven slab of sidewalk, and the distance between every cozy reading tree and the business library. Crossing it next to Rebecca felt natural. Crisp, brittle leaves skipped across the pavement ahead of them, swept up in little funnels of breeze, gathering in piles at curbs and drifting across academic lawns. The frantic pace of warmer days was over. Students and professors bundled in sweaters slowed their strides.

They settled into a little table by the window. Rebecca clutched her tea and peered over it, studying him with her large brown eyes. He took too big a sip of his coffee and burned his lip. "What are you gonna do after school? Have a job lined up?" she asked.

"I do. I'm heading to Washington after graduation. I really like federal economic policy. I accepted a job at an economic development think tank."

"Washington! Me, too." Her cup clattered against the saucer when she set it down, and she twirled the little paper tea tag between her fingers. "It's not one hundred percent yet. I'm in the running for a position at the Campaign Finance Institute. How did you find the think tank thing?"

"One of my...our undergrad professors...Dr. Lee? He has a friend who works in economic development in DC. He shared one of my papers with him, and I got an internship there last summer, which turned into a job. They do all of the typical economic development stuff, jobs and real estate. But they also work with lawmakers on tax policy, and that kind of thing. It'll give me exposure to a lot of different agencies and types of work. The pay isn't fantastic, but it feels like the right place to start." William felt himself rambling and begged himself to stop. He'd always been dumb around girls but being with Rebecca was like an out of body experience.

"I haven't met many people who like tax policy." Her eyes narrowed and the corners of her eyes lifted. William felt the tips of his ears grow hot. "When are you moving to Washington?"

"Assuming that I finish my Masters next semester, probably around the middle of June. What about you?"

"Same. I should be in Washington next summer. With or without a job, that's where I want to be, you know?"

William's backpack slid from the chair, and a wrench tumbled from the front pocket to the hardwood floor. Rebecca picked it up and passed it to him. "Hey, you said you grew up in a rural area? Is it around here?"

"Close, I guess. About forty minutes. Elmwood. We moved there when I was twelve."

"My dad has clients out there. He's an accountant. It's a cute town."

"Yeah." William smiled into his coffee. "Yeah, it is. It's just slower than I want."

"Boy, can I ever relate to that." Rebecca threw her elbows on the table, folded her hands, and leveled with William. "You had no idea who I was when I talked to you this morning, did you?"

Why was she so direct? And why couldn't he keep up? "I'm sorry. I didn't. I have been going through school with blinders on. I'm pretty focused, I guess."

"I know! I have been sitting in rooms with you, next to you, across tables from you for five years and this morning you didn't even recognize me." William winced, and she waved it off. "It's okay. I'm not offended. You *are* really focused. It's part of what makes you so mysterious."

"Mysterious? There's no mystery to me."

"But there is. Right now, I'm trying to figure out if you have room in your world for anything other than school and tax policy."

"Like, room in my world for a date?"

"Yeah. Like, room in your world for a date. I mean, there's a lot of coincidence here. Washington. We're in the same classes, we like the same subjects. It would be stupid if we didn't see each other again. More warm

113

drinks? Maybe a whole meal? What do you say?"

He'd invested so much in school, taking on debt, defying the odds that he'd stacked against himself. He kept raising the standards he had to meet. Losing focus, even wasting one hour, could set him up for failure. He couldn't take his eyes from the goal, but he also couldn't take his eyes from Rebecca. His heart was disconnected from his brain. "I can't argue with that logic. Obviously, you're a very smart woman."

"I've always thought so."

* * *

Rebecca proved to be the biggest distraction when she wasn't around. She moved into William's apartment as their last semester of graduate school began. With the draft of her thesis under review by advisors half a semester early, she took on the task of merging their two households while William clicked and tapped on a Smith-Corona typewriter at his old folding card table in a corner of the bedroom.

Stacks of boxes of duplicate textbooks took over the apartment. With limited shelf space, Rebecca tamed their belongings into one manageable set. When she moved a black binder, a scrap of paper fluttered to the floor. A fifteen-year-old receipt. She sat on the sofa, hunched over the binder, looking for the place it belonged. The first pages held fading receipts for car-related items. Oil. Spark plugs. Battery. Then photographs and personal notes were scattered among the facts. Black and white photos preceded the orange and yellow hues of the last decade. A woman in cut off shorts and a plaid shirt with her hand on the tailgate of William's Jeep. *Claire, 1970* was written along the thin white border in pen.

A couple with a kayak. A house. A baby. Then two pages of the small, even handwriting that she knew to be William's. She pulled the notebook closer and started to read.

"Whatcha got there?" William stood next to her, looking down at his note. "Oh God. That was so long ago."

"I feel horrible. I wasn't trying to snoop. A receipt fell out of it when I moved it, and I sat down to put it back, but then I saw the pictures, and I got sucked in. If I'd known, I wouldn't have read it. You sound so sad and defeated. I'm sorry."

"I don't mind." He sat next to her and tilted the notebook so he could see it. "I was afraid. Everything was falling apart."

"You? Afraid? Of the Jeep?"

"Definitely afraid of the Jeep. And everything else, too. I got in a fight with my best friend just before I moved here."

"Mark? The guy I met at the garage?"

"Yeah. I was stuck in a dead-end job for years, too afraid of failure to apply for school. And I blamed everybody but myself. I bought that Jeep because I thought it would help me and then it broke down. The only way I knew to fix it was to take it to Mark. If it weren't for that car, stupid me probably never would have fixed the friendship."

"So it did help you, then. Just not the way you expected."

"Talk about naive. I mean, you met my parents. You know how I grew up. I thought I knew everything about cars by osmosis. Turns out I knew nothing at all. I had to run home with my tail between my legs after treating Mark like he was an idiot for staying in that little town."

"I can't imagine you saying something like that. You always seem to know what to do and what to say. And not knowing how to work on that car. You just fixed mine. You're like, my superhero."

All he did was change the oil, but he didn't bother to tell her how easy it was. "It was a rough time, finding myself. Learning to listen." William gave her a sidelong look. "Besides, us superheroes aren't born this way, you know. We're formed by adversity."

She closed the notebook and set it aside, sliding onto his lap and running her hands through his hair. "I do feel bad for reading that note, though. I didn't mean to pry."

"Don't feel bad about that. There isn't anything about me that I don't want you to know."

"Yeah? Well, why don't I just follow you back to that room you've been typing in all day and get to know you a little bit better?"

"Why? You want to read the third draft of my thesis?"

"Nope. Not even a little bit."

* * *

William pushed the apartment door with his hip, nudging a bag of shoes into a box of books. He stepped into a river of carpet that flowed through boxes and bags and dropped their groceries into the abyss. Rebecca stood, lost, with an envelope of photographs in her hand, scanning the room.

"What are you looking for?"

She brushed hair away from her face with the back of her hand. "That black notebook with the Jeep records in it. I just unpacked all this stuff and got used to where everything was. Now it's time to move again, and I can't find what was right in front of me yesterday."

"What do you want with the notebook?" He stepped over boxes and a pile of towels.

"I wanted to add the graduation photos that my mom took of us with the Jeep. I swear it was somewhere in this area yesterday." She spread her arms over piles of blankets, towels, and sheets.

"Here ya go. I wondered why you wanted a picture with the Jeep." William retrieved the notebook, toppling a stack of blankets, and they both leaned forward to meet halfway. She took the binder from him, avoiding a fall into a stack of pots and pans. "We should talk about what we're going to do with the car, actually."

"I know. It's not practical for DC, but it's *the Jeep*. You love that car."

She rested the notebook on a trash bag full of winter coats, placed the photo on an empty page, and smoothed the cover back, lining up the corners.

She did everything with such precision, and William still felt like a bumbling fool. "We've been through a lot together, me and that Jeep."

"It's not up to me what you do with it. What do you want to do?"

William put his hands in his pockets and shrugged. "If it goes, it has to go to the right place. It's a decision we should make together, I think."

She moved a box of kitchen utensils from the arm of the sofa and sat. "That's a big conversation. If you really want my opinion, I have a soft spot for the Jeep. I do. But I also think it's drafty. It smells. And there are better cars out there. It's unfortunate, but you are going to be judged by the car you drive. It's two steps away from being rusty."

"It is not rusty. It's the opposite of rusty. It's amazing." He picked at a small tear in the cover of the notebook. He knew everything about that car. Being without it would feel like starting over.

"What's that look? What are you thinking?"

"What if I fail?" William thought there would be a point where he'd stop feeling this way. High school. College. Grad school. When would he stop being so afraid to fail?

"Fail at what?"

"Out there. What if I fail?"

"Well, I think the first thing that happens is they come and take your degree off the wall."

William rolled his eyes. "I can be stupid sometimes. I'm my own worst enemy."

"We all are. What are you afraid of, exactly?"

"This is huge, this change. Doesn't it feel huge to you? Like we're on the edge of something massive, and we can't make it stop?"

"I guess it's a little scary. And exciting. I don't want it to stop. Isn't this what you always wanted?"

"Yeah, but it's still scary. Selling the car, packing all this stuff, leaving my apartment? What if I go out there, and I lose everything?"

"I hate to tell you this, but you *are* going to fail. Spectacularly. We all are. You're gonna make mistakes and apologize for them and then make new ones."

"I know that. I do." He looked at the notebook on Rebecca's lap. Inside was a letter, written by a younger William who'd taken a leap of faith. "It's just cold feet, I guess."

"You seemed fine until we talked about the selling the car. You know you don't have to sell it. Not if you don't want to."

Across the sea of boxes and bags, beyond furniture stacked in tidy piles either to be kept or sold, sat a little table. On that table lay the key to the Jeep. The key that James had carefully passed to him at the bar many years ago. "That car was the first thing I bought that was really mine."

Rebecca adjusted the notebook on her lap and reached for his hand. "Hey, no one's forcing you to sell it."

"I know, but it's time. I've known for a while. Every time I drive it, I feel like I'm saying goodbye."

"I know what you mean. I got choked up in the market the other day. I've been going to that little store for years, and it's hard to believe that we'll move, and I may never step foot in there again."

"Do you ever feel like some dean will walk up to you and tell you that it's all been a mistake? That you're not supposed to graduate?"

A dimple formed in Rebecca's cheek when she smiled. "All the time."

"Like everything out there is a test. I know it's completely irrational, but I feel like I'll have to come back here again, and I'll need the Jeep. Stupid security blanket, I guess. Like, as long as I have that car with me, I can get back to where I came from."

"I didn't know you felt that way about it."

"I didn't either." William had always excelled at the tangible equations of life. Intangible things like impossible dreams and letting go were so much harder to grasp. "I'll talk to Mark. He's done some work on it. He might know someone who'd be interested in it."

"That's a great idea." Rebecca passed the notebook to him. "Then let's not pack this. Set it somewhere so we don't forget to keep it with the Jeep?"

* * *

Mark's garage smelled like metal, oils, and damp concrete. To William, it smelled like his teenage years. He stepped into the garage and found Mark deep in a Chevy Nova.

"Billy. You know, you are welcome to come by here more than once a year." Mark's voice had a metallic ring to it, echoing in the engine bay.

"You're the one who told me to go to school."

"But I also told you not to be a stranger."

William accepted Mark's outstretched hand. When he took it back, it was smeared with grease and oil. Mark tossed a red rag his way and he caught it before it hit the floor. William wiped his hands, and inspected his shoes for garage fodder.

"You should know better than to come in here with your fancy clothes on. How is the old Jeep doing?" Mark asked.

"That's why I'm here. You know anybody who might want it?"

"What kind of shape is it in? Have you destroyed it yet?" Mark tugged another rag from his shoulder and used it to wipe grime from the distributor cap of the Nova.

"It's in great shape. I learned from you, so..."

"It's, what, seventeen years old now? That Jeep's just broken in. Olivia was looking for a car for Ben. She might want it."

"Ben is old enough to drive?"

"Makes you feel old, doesn't it? She promised him that if he saved, she'd help him get a car. He mowed every lawn in town, but Liv's been saving for him to go to school and money doesn't go as far as it used to."

"This might be a good fit, then. Tell her to make an offer, if she wants. I'm motivated to sell it, and I'm happy to negotiate."

"She's off today, but I can catch up with her and get back to you tomorrow. If she doesn't want it, I can ask around."

"Thanks." William walked toward the garage door and patted Mark on the shoulder as he passed him. "I hate to rush you, but we move in a week." Mark looked up from his distributor cap. Answering the unasked question, William said, "Both of us. Washington, DC. I got a job in economic development. Rebecca's in finance."

Mark's head was still buried in the Nova. His voice was muffled, but his point was clear. "I told you, man. I knew you were going to do big things. Stay in touch? Don't forget where you came from."

"How could I?"

CHAPTER TWELVE

"Teenage boys. You know, you have as many moods as there are Alpha Bits in that bowl." Olivia slipped a spoon into Ben's cereal and sat across from him in the kitchen of the little house she rented on Main Street. A truck went by, bumping over a pothole.

Ben refused to look his mother in the eye. "You promised. You said when I turned eighteen, if I saved enough money, that you would match what I saved and help me get a car." He pushed the cereal away.

"What is this? A hunger strike? Honey, I tried. It's hard. The cost of everything keeps going up, and I am doing the best I can. I'll still help you; we're just going to have to get a cheaper car, that's all. A thousand dollars doesn't go as far as it used to. We'll find something. It'll just take some time. I am not going to take away from the money I set aside for college. Go get ready for school, or there won't be any car at all."

He pulled the bowl closer, sandy milk from his Alpha Bits splashing onto the table, taking in mouthfuls of soggy letters. "I mowed a billion yards for nothing."

"And delivered papers and weeded every garden in this town. I know. Would you like to know the kind of humiliation I endure at the grocery store? Or maybe you'd like to know how much I wish I could give you a brand new Camaro every day of the year." She ruffled his hair and kissed the top of his head. "Finish your cereal and get in the shower so I'm not late for work."

"You never come through for me."

"Oh, don't I? You're not dead, are you? I learned how to feed you and keep you alive, unlike every house plant I've ever met. I'd say I did okay. Get dressed."

Olivia won the daily battle to get Ben from the table to the shower, to collect his homework and to deliver him to school, but she was later for work than she'd hoped. She still beat Mark, though. She started the coffee, tidied the garage, and settled into the chair behind her desk in the lobby of the garage, opening envelopes and sorting checks and bills and junk while coffee spat into the pot.

Her desk faced the windows, giving her a view of the only red light in Elmwood. The repair shop sat at the northeast corner of the intersection of Rural Route 62 and Redfern Road. Across one street was an old inn that served greasy lunches on the first floor. Cardboard boxes that hadn't moved in a decade occupied the second-floor windows. Across the other road sat a gas station that supplied the town with a dual-ding soundtrack whenever a car or driver was thirsty. The remaining corner was home to a gravel lot, once the home of a lumber yard that succumbed to a devastating fire, which fueled town chatter for a generation.

Mark's shop occupied a long concrete building that once displayed the latest in affordable furnishings. Olivia kept her desk far from the long, curved window where Ben played with toy cars as a child. It was old and drafty. Plus, she enjoyed a view of the street. Behind her, a narrow hallway led to Mark's garage. A series of doors along the hall opened onto a storage room, a small closet, and a bathroom, all of which were Olivia's domain to keep tidy and Mark's domain to move through like a bull in a china shop.

She poured a cup of coffee and typed, waiting to hear the shop door and Mark's heavy steps in the hall. She didn't look up when he entered the room. "Six soda cans, two empty coffee cups, and a mysterious roll of toilet paper."

"Liv, I like to work messy."

"Every morning I go in there to clean, and it's like a tornado went through. How do you even have time to make that much mess?"

"I try to clean…"

"By hiding the dirt under dirt?"

"Cars are greasy. It's the nature of the job. How long have we worked together? Eighteen years? I'm surprised you haven't figured it out by now. I work better in chaos."

"If that's what you call it. That workbench has so much stuff on it you can't set anything down. The books on that shelf aren't in any order at all. Half of them are for cars that this town hasn't seen since the Eisenhower administration. There are chairs everywhere but never where you need one. And why is there toilet paper on your workbench but none in the bathroom?"

"Geez, if I didn't know any better I'd think you were a little mad about that whole toilet paper thing. It gets cold out there, and my nose gets runny." Mark picked up her empty coffee cup and refilled it. "Here, this will make you feel better."

"Thanks. What brings you up the hallway? Something's up. I can feel it."

"Just wondering if you found a car for Ben yet."

"Not yet. I do *not* have the money to buy him a car. He held up his end of the bargain, but I have to buy food and pay for electricity so, of course, he's furious."

Mark fell into the orange wool loveseat across from her desk. He tossed aside a dark green throw pillow and picked up the only magazine on the small coffee table. Deborah Raffin in a pink crocheted sweater had been smiling at the ceiling for months. Mark skimmed the cover lines. "How Charlie's Angels stay so slim." He threw it at the trash can and missed. "We need better things to read in here. Anyway, I have a car for Ben if you're interested."

"Really? You buried the lede there. What car is it?" Olivia stretched back in her chair, hoping Mark's idea of a good car for Ben wasn't far off from hers. "What's it like?"

"William's moving. Selling his old Jeep."

"Oh, I don't know, Mark…" The car was older and not nearly as safe as she wanted for her son. A thousand objections came to mind.

Mark put up his hand to silence them. "It's a perfectly good first car for Ben. He'll learn more driving this than he will one of these new land yachts. It's not that big, so he can't get too comfortable with the girls. Yes, it's old, but those old Jeeps last forever. And you know that I'll keep it running for you. I would never leave you hanging."

She looked past him out the window at the two cars stopped at the red light. She knew she would lose. Mark was always right. But she wouldn't give in without a fight. "How much?"

"How much can you spend?"

"Really?" Olivia scowled at him. "I'm not going to haggle over a car I haven't seen."

"C'mon, Liv. You remember that Jeep. It was just in here."

"Forever ago. I don't know what's been done to it." Olivia didn't want her son driving a car that was nearly twenty years old.

"Okay, how's this? One thousand. If you agree to that, I'll see what I can do."

The price was right. "He'll either love it or hate it. And he's gonna be mad that he didn't get to choose." She turned her attention back to the invoice. "If he hates it, it's your fault." She gave him a firm look. "One thousand. Tops. And you have to tell him it was your idea. He's already mad at me. He'll be furious if I buy a car, and he doesn't get to pick it out. He'll hate it out of spite."

Mark patted her on the shoulder as he walked past her and toward the shop. She smiled down at the word processor. "And thank you, Mark."

"I always look out for you, Liv."

"I know you do. But you know how you could really look out for me? Leave the toilet paper in the bathroom."

* * *

Rebecca stood at the kitchen sink, dabbing soap on William's jeans and rubbing at a stubborn stain. Probably from changing the oil in the Jeep. There was something domestic about it, caring for William's things, knowing he would do the same for her.

William snuck beside her and turned on the water to rinse his hands. "I'll hang at the shop and wait for you."

"I can't imagine I'll be there any later than three. How long could it take to hand me money, take this sofa down the stairs, and put it in a truck? As long as they're not late getting here."

William kissed her on the cheek and pulled the Jeep key from his pocket. "Love you. Be careful. I'll see you later."

"You too. Love you." Rebecca returned to the sink, watching through the window as he climbed into the Jeep. It shuddered when it started, and a puff of exhaust escaped the tailpipe. Her heart squeezed, knowing it was the last time she would see the CJ-5. It had given her the courage to talk to him in the first place. She remembered the notebook.

It rested on a box of books by the door. She dropped the jeans into the sink and ran to the door, grabbing the binder on the way. She ran down the stairs barefoot, reaching the Jeep just as William lifted his foot from the clutch, and it began to drift backward. The hot pavement stung. "Wait!" She yelled loud enough for him to hear over the sound of the engine and exhaust.

She brushed hot pebbles from her feet while clutching the notebook. "Don't forget this. And make them promise to keep up with it." Rebecca wasn't sentimental, but she had a soft spot for the notebook.

"Thanks. I will." William took the notebook from her and dropped it behind the passenger seat. It landed with a hollow thud.

"I'll see you around three!" She patted the flat spot at the top of the fender and felt a twinge of sadness as she heard the metal clang in response.

* * *

William pulled into the only empty bay of Mark's shop, leaving crisscross patterns of dirt on the floor. He closed his eyes as he shut off the engine, listening as it fell silent, exhaust fading in the concrete room. His last words with an old friend.

They were cut short by Olivia. "Bill! It's been a long time. How long has it been?"

Still seated in the Jeep, William cringed and tugged the key from the ignition. "If Ben is eighteen…Let's not. I feel old. I can't believe he's old enough to drive."

"Me either. It's terrifying. For everyone. And it should be."

William reached into the back, pulled the binder onto his lap, and opened the cover. The pen was still tucked in the front pocket. The ink had probably dried up years before. Receipts. Scribbled notes about oil changes. Two pages in his handwriting. He should have removed them, safeguarded his insecurities from the prying eyes of a casual acquaintance. He picked at the corner of the plastic cover, but it held fast to his letter. As if the Jeep staked its claim on William's words, on its role in his life, owning its accomplishment and the fears they faced. He closed the cover, dropped the notebook in the back of the Jeep, and lowered himself to the ground.

He held out the key, dangling from a rusted keyring. The key that started his education, that jump started his relationship with Rebecca, that restored his friendship with Mark. The key that gave him the confidence he needed to take a first shaky step. Olivia held out her open palm. Without regret, he let it fall.

CERTIFICATE OF TITLE

VEHICLE IDENTIFICATION NUMBER		YEAR	MAKE	MODEL
8305 165111		1964	KAISER	CJ5
TITLE NUMBER	PREVIOUS TITLE NUMBER	PREV TITLE STATE	ISSUE DATE	ODOMETER
0232564809	7290584		06/06/1998	UNKNOWN

MAILING ADDRESS

OLIVIA LAGRANGE
24 MILLER DR
ELMWOOD

REMARKS

ODO NOT ACTUAL. ONLY 4
DIGITS ON DISPLAY.

LEIN INFORMATION

WITNESS SIGNATURE

WITNESS TO THE ABOVE DECLARATIONS IS HEREBY MADE

NAME

TITLE   DATE

The Department of Transporation hereby certifies that the
evidence of purchase of ownership, in compliance with
applicable laws and amendments, of the above vehicle has
been recorded and titled with me, and I do hereby issue this
Certificate of Ownership to the above subject to the agreement
or lein, if any, as stated above.

CHAPTER THIRTEEN

Olivia watched her son circle the car. What looked to her like a death trap enthralled her son. She watched him grasp the cool, smooth metal edge of the tailgate and give it a tug. The sound of metal on metal and rattling chains echoed through the garage.

"This is so cool! Thanks, Mark," Ben said.

"You can thank your mother." Mark winked at Olivia, and she accepted the credit.

Before his excitement got the better of him, she had to lay out the ground rules. She knew he'd break at least half of them, and if she didn't keep an eye on him, Mark would break the other half. "There are a few things that we have to do before you can have it, Benny. Mark has to install seat belts. And you'll have to learn how to do the routine maintenance. And I swear to God if you do something irresponsible with this car, I will sell it. Not one speeding ticket."

Mark whispered. "He's hardly gonna speed in this. It won't go that fast."

"Shh. Don't tell him that."

Olivia missed the knowing glances Mark shared with her son, just as she'd missed all the time Mark spent teaching Ben while she was at her second job. But she was painfully aware of how much she'd miss when he started the car and drove away on his own.

"Hey, Bill," she called out. "Do you have any tips for Ben?"

William abandoned an issue of *People* magazine with Princess Di on the cover. He slid into the passenger seat and pointed to the black and yellow plaque that illustrated the shift pattern. "It's a simple machine. Reverse and three gears. Plus high and low gear in the shifter here. Just remember, it's non-synchronized, so you have to be careful if you downshift into first while the car's in motion."

"What happens if you get it wrong?"

"A lot of noise. Eventually, you'll destroy the gear." William's tapped the speedometer, pointing at the fuel gauge. "It can be hard to tell how much fuel you put into it because you can't see. It only works when the car is on. And those gas pumps that stop when the tank is full can't tell with a tank like this. Eventually you'll know when it's full by the sound. It takes a while to warm up on a cold morning. Take your time adjusting the choke. And this book..." William reached into the back and picked up the binder. "This notebook is really important."

Olivia took the binder from William and opened the cover. "What is this? It's like a scrapbook."

"It's everything. The sales record. The pen the guy signed it with. Maintenance records and receipts. Just...keep it with the car? It's almost twenty years old now."

Olivia patted William's shoulder. He'd always been such a numbers guy. She never thought of him as being sentimental. "Thank you for selling the Jeep to us. It will be a great first car for Ben. I promise we'll take very good care of it."

William's feet hit the ground, and he straightened his pant legs. "It'll give him a chance to learn some things, too. No sense relying on those expensive mechanics. They're such a rip-off."

"Ha ha. Smart ass." Mark pushed past William and slid into the passenger seat. "Start her up, Ben."

Olivia stood helpless, clutching the binder to her chest, watching her son drive away in a car for the first time. The smell of the exhaust caught in her throat as it faded from the garage. It helped a little—but not much—that Mark was in the passenger seat. The CJ-5 might as well have been forged in fear, fear that Ben would be irresponsible, that he would injure himself, that he'd move away and never come home, that he'd make bad decisions while choosing his direction. He was taking another leap toward independence that she wasn't ready for. She still had so much to teach him.

The things she couldn't teach him, she knew Mark had or would one day. Things about caring for cars, about finding answers in the stillness of a garage at night, about caring for metal before rust set in. As the Jeep creeped over the threshold and into the sunlight, Olivia took in a breath of fresh air, knowing that she was about to experience the independence she'd never had a chance to taste.

CHAPTER FOURTEEN

The Jeep bobbed and swayed on the trailer behind Mark's truck. Olivia kept an eye on it through the rearview mirror. She sat in the middle, studying the map of Ben's college campus over her son's shoulder. Ben had the window down. She could hear the squeaks and clangs of the trailer as they went over bumps on the highway.

She stood helpless as Mark released the Jeep into a parking lot, sliding it between an orange Torino and a blue Fairlane that needed shocks. Every suitcase and box they unloaded took Ben a little further from her, and she wondered if she'd given him everything he needed. She looked up at the windows of the fifth floor, at her son's new home, and wrung her hands.

While her heart searched her head for the right words, Mark reached into the back of his truck and pulled out an old ammo can. "Hey, kid. I had this laying in the shop, so I put some tools in it for you. Just the basics. A hammer, screwdrivers and wrenches, sockets, the stuff you need to care for the Jeep and for around the dorm."

Olivia's heart gave a lurch, watching her best friend, the most consistent, reliable, and supportive male influence her son had known, make such a gesture. It should have been a father's job, but that was one of many things she'd never been able to give him.

"Thanks, Mark." Ben opened the container and glanced at the tools. "This is really nice of you. Hopefully I won't need to use them."

"Oh, you will. Someday. Remember, if anything goes wrong with the car, just call the shop phone. But call your mother more than you call me." Mark patted Ben on the shoulder. "I'm proud of you. Stay out of trouble." He turned to Olivia. "Dig in the glove box. The camera's in there."

Olivia pushed aside receipts, napkins, and zip ties. The camera and two plastic tubes of film rested beneath a handful of thin paper napkins. She shoved the napkins in her pocket and checked the camera for film. She turned the camera's wheel with her thumb as she closed the truck door.

Mark stepped back and took the camera. "Plenty of film left. You two. Say cheese."

Olivia forced the corners of her mouth into a grin suitable for framing and wrapped an arm around her son. Mark took the photo and joined them, slapping Ben on the back hard enough to put him off kilter and remind him who was boss. "Learn stuff. Have fun. Don't screw up. See ya at Thanksgiving." He walked back to his truck, advancing the film.

Olivia grabbed her son by the shoulders. "Benny, don't forget..."

"I hate it when you call me that."

She lied when she smiled. Her heart was broken, leaving a piece of herself behind. She shoved her hands into her pockets and squeezed the napkins into a ball. "I know. But you'll always be my little Benny. Remember what I said. If you fail one class, I will sell that Jeep. I promise. Just be good and don't screw up."

"Why does everybody keep saying that to me?"

"Because we know exactly what we would do in your shoes, and we want you to be better than us."

Ben smirked. "You maybe. Not Mark."

"Yeah, keep thinking he's an angel." She glanced back at the truck, at Mark pretending to be occupied by playing with the visors.

"He's good for you, Mom. He's always been good to us."

"He has." Olivia wiped her nose with a wad of napkin.

"Mom, do you remember that kid, Chris, from middle school? The one whose parents got divorced, and he started acting all weird?"

"I'm about to leave you at college. Your first day alone out in the world, and you're asking me about some kid from middle school?"

"It's important. Do you remember him?"

"Yeah. What about him?"

"All that time, all he wanted was for his parents to get back together."

"And this is important because?"

Ben wrapped his arms around his mom, dug a real tissue from his pocket, and put it in her hand. "Because I was the only one in our class who understood him. My whole short life, all I've wanted was for my parents to be together. I know Mark's not my dad, but he's the closest thing I've ever had. Now that I'm in college, I feel like I missed my chance to have that."

"Ben. Mark will always be there for you. I'm sorry I never gave you that white-picket-fence family thing, but Mark and I just aren't like that. We just don't feel that way about each other. You and me did okay, though."

"More than okay."

It was another lie. She hated keeping the truth from her son, but she'd been lying to herself about her feelings for Mark for more than half his life. It might have been a habit, but it was still a lie.

Olivia looked up at the row of fifth floor windows. "The second from the left. That's yours, huh?"

"Yup."

"Call me anytime. You hear? Any time, day or night. And don't do anything stupid. Study. Take care of the car. Brush your teeth."

"Mom, I know. Now, go. I'm walking away before you lose it."

Olivia watched Ben disappear through the side door of his dorm before shuffling back to the truck. Mark put his hand on her shoulder and steered her home while she watched the view of the school building fade in the mirror.

"Dinner's on me, ma'am." Mark patted her knee. "You're gonna be fine."

"It's not me I'm worried about."

* * *

Ben's first taste of college freedom tasted a lot like beer, much of it consumed in the back of the Jeep while watching bonfires. A clearing in the woods behind campus made the perfect gathering spot, and Ben became part of a clique who knew it well. The Jeep, without its top or doors, was the perfect transportation to the wooded nook, where free from parents and campus restraints, he partied into the wee morning hours. His grades suffered.

"I will absolutely go down there, bring you back, take that car away from you, and make you get a job." Olivia took advantage of a quiet morning in the shop to call her son about his mid-semester grades. "Think about that. You can work at a fast food hut until you realize that you could have done better, but by then your free ride will be gone. I am not paying for college twice. And I am not paying for you to party."

Ben's response was razor sharp. "You can't take my car away. I paid for half of it."

"Don't mess with me, Ben. That car is in my name. You know the agreement. I will sell it and give you back your half. And don't think it's some big windfall, because you'd have to use it to get your own apartment. You are not moving back home so you can run around all hours of the night while I cook your meals and clean up your mess. It's time to be responsible. You are supposed to do better in life than me. You're supposed to learn from my mistakes. I'm giving you a chance to get a decent education, so you don't have to work in dirt and filth with no hope for a better future. You decide."

Olivia slammed down the phone. She felt Mark's presence in the doorway behind her and said, half to him and half to herself, "That kid is going to be the death of me."

"He's learning. He's just doing what we all did. Pushing boundaries, being young. Give him a chance. If you really want to make him pay for his mistakes, make him work here next summer in the dirt and filth. I'll show him what hard work is."

Olivia blinked at him. "That might not be a bad idea except that I want him to like you. You're the only father figure he's ever had, and you're barely old enough to be his father."

* * *

The phone rang. When Mark reached for the clock, an empty plastic cup fell to the floor. According to the glow-in-the-dark hands, it was just after three in the morning. His wallet fell behind the nightstand when he put the clock back.

"Whoever you are, you have the wrong number."

"This is Officer Martin from the Montgomery County Sheriff's Office. I'm calling about Ben. Is this Mark?"

"It's three in the morning. From where? For Ben?"

"Yes, sir. About Ben. The young man has gotten himself into trouble and…"

Mark tossed a pillow across the bed, sighed, and rolled his eyes. He knew that his role in Olivia's life might require cleaning up a mistake or two of Ben's, but he didn't expect the police to be involved. And not at three in the morning. "What did he do?"

"At approximately twenty-two hundred hours…"

"What?" Mark rubbed one eye.

"At ten o'clock last night we got a call about a bunch of kids parked in a clearing in the woods. College kids go back there and drink and make a mess. Your young man was one of them."

"What's he charged with?"

"Trespassing. Underage drinking. DUI. Between you and me, we don't have any evidence that he was drunk while operating his vehicle. That charge will be dropped. We use it to scare them a little bit. His license is temporarily suspended until he gets a hearing date and enters a plea."

"What does he need from me?"

"He'll be spending the night here with us. He's an adult. You can let him fend for himself if you want to or you can come down here and give him a good, stern lecture. He seems like a good kid who made a mistake. It's a college town. We see it all the time. A good talking-to from their father usually squares these kids away."

"I'm not his father."

The officer laughed. "The way he worried about calling you himself, we figured you were."

"He's afraid of me, huh?"

"I'd say that's true."

"Good. He can't drive that Jeep on a suspended license, so I gotta go get a trailer to bring it home. Then it's another two hours to get there."

"The impound lot opens at eight. We're happy to keep Ben safe. Any time you want to come and get him."

"Good. Make him sweat." Change fell to the floor when Mark placed the phone on the receiver.

The sky was black when Mark paused in front of Olivia's house, the empty trailer following the truck like a willing accomplice. If he knocked on her door and woke her, she would worry the whole way there. He decided to give her a few more hours of sleep. He already felt responsible for enabling Ben's behavior, and he wasn't ready to face her yet, anyway.

At dawn, Mark collected Ben, who muttered his thanks but received nothing, not even a sideways glance, in return. The sun brought some absolution. It wasn't his fault Ben was in trouble, nor was it the Jeep's. Ben created his own chaos by wasting Olivia's time and money. Anger simmered, and they drove in silence to the impound yard where the Jeep rested behind a chain-link fence. Mark loaded it onto the trailer. He wanted to let out his anger, to slam the chains to the ground, but he cared too much for the car and the kid. Biting his tongue, he started the truck.

Miles passed before Mark's voice smashed through the tension in the car like a sledgehammer. "What did you do?"

"Um. I just. We."

"Don't stammer. You were there. What happened?"

Ben stared at the glove box door.

Mark didn't give him time. He let his sarcasm slice between them and gripped the steering wheel tighter. "Did you black out?"

"No. Nothing like that. We were drinking. Me and some guys. It was a nice night, and the top and doors were off the Jeep. There's this creek, and you can follow it back to a field where people hang out at night. Anyway, the cops showed up. I was drunk. They found the beer in the Jeep, and they busted me for drinking and driving."

"How many people were in the car?"

"Six."

"You have two seats, and you put five other people in that car and drove it while drinking? If you had rolled that thing you would have killed everyone. It's not safe to take risks in that car, any car, especially that car, even if you have a seatbelt on. Do you not understand?"

"I know."

"Clearly, you don't know. Clearly, you don't deserve that car. I thought it would be a great way for you to learn and save your mom some money and give you both some independence. Do you know how much your mother hated the idea of that car? I convinced her that you were responsible enough to handle it, and I'm really pissed that you're proving me wrong."

The color drained from Ben's face. He mumbled. "I'd rather have listened to Mom yell than hear you say you lost faith in me. What do I have to do to fix this?"

Hearing Ben beg for an easy answer made Mark even angrier. "You just don't get it, do you, kid? This isn't about someone else telling you how to fix your problems. This is about doing what you're supposed to do because you figured it out for yourself. At your age, growing up the way you did with a mom who works two jobs and gives up everything she ever wanted for you, you should pick going to class over drinking and acting stupid. Your mom has been paying for your free ride to college for more than half of her life. This is a gift—it's a chance to get out of that town and make any kind of life you want for yourself without a bunch of debt. Instead, you're throwing it away. You made this mess, and you need to fix it." Mark released his grip on the steering wheel and shook the blood back to his fingers.

Ben folded his hands in his lap and turned to the window. The odometer could have been measuring the weight of the silence in the truck, but Mark was grateful for it. Until Ben had a solution or the right words for an apology, his silence was his best chance at salvation.

Ben rested his head against the window. "Can I ask you a question? For advice?"

"Yeah, I guess. I don't know if I have any answers."

"What if I don't want to do anything they teach at college?" Ben picked at dirt under a fingernail. "What if I want to do something else? What do I do? How do I tell Mom?"

William came to mind. Yet again, Mark was yelling at someone who should be in college instead of wasting time, but maybe college wasn't the answer for Ben. "That's a big decision. You need to figure it out, fast. If you want to learn a trade, learn a trade, but be honest with her and don't waste her money. She sacrificed a lot for you. More than you know."

"I know she did. It's not an excuse, but all of those people at college want to be…I don't want to be any of those things. How did you know you wanted to be a mechanic? How did you know that's what you were going to be good at?"

Mark searched the dashboard for an answer. He stumbled into it because his father owned the shop. Enjoying it was convenient. "Divine providence? Nature *and* nurture? I guess I wanted to be a mechanic because I liked watching my dad do it. I like puzzles. Every day I get to put one together. Stuff gets old and wears out, and I fix it. It suits me. School was boring. Writing book reports and doing math never gave me a sense of accomplishment. Not like the shop does."

Mark returned his grip to the steering wheel and tapped his left foot against the dead pedal. He never expected to find himself between Olivia and Ben, counseling her son against her aspirations. The truck accelerated, and Mark was grateful when Ben offered up his silence for a while.

"I put a new brake line in the Jeep."

"You did that? When?"

"At school. Couple of weeks ago. You know how the rear line is kind of flexible? I guess it snapped or cracked 'cause I came out one morning, and there was brake fluid everywhere. I traced the leak back to that little connection with the brake cylinder. I called up the Jeep place near school and bought the part and put it in. It was easy."

"And you added brake fluid and bled the brakes?"

"Yup."

"And is the brake pedal okay? Did you need to adjust it? Sometimes you have to do that."

"Nope, it was good."

"Good." Mark shifted in his seat. Anger made room for a little pride. Knowing how angry Olivia would be, sympathy found its way in, too. Mark had made plenty of his own mistakes, but he managed to avoid being caught. "Good job. I'm proud of you."

"Do you want to check my work?"

"No, I'm sure it's fine." He did want to check, and he would.

Ben pulled a copy of *Popular Mechanics* from the door pocket and stared at the submarine on the cover. He smoothed out the wrinkled cover. "What if I wanted to be a mechanic? Would you teach me? Can I work for you?"

Mark let his silence knock the confidence out of Ben. "First, your mother would kill me. Second, I'm not the right person to teach you. Third, I can't afford to pay another set of hands right now." He also couldn't afford to hear what Olivia had to say when he dropped off Ben and the car he couldn't legally drive, along with the news that her son dropped out of school, got a DUI, and decided to follow in Mark's footsteps to become a mechanic in a poor town.

"No, you're right. It's asking a lot."

"Look, I can show you how to do some things. I'm taking apart a Buick transmission tomorrow. You can help but only if you talk to your mom. I'm not agreeing to anything without her say so. For all you know, you'll be on a train to military school."

"I'm not looking forward to talking to my mom."

"Welcome to adulthood and the consequences of acting like a

dumbass."

Ben rubbed his forehead. "I know. You're right."

They were half an hour from their exit when Mark pulled into a truck stop. "If it makes you feel any better, I'm not looking forward to talking to her, either. I don't see the sense in facing her on an empty stomach. I have one more thing to say to you before we go in there. You've got to fix your own mess. Don't let her do it for you. Figure out what you have to do to get your license back, to settle your legal problems, about school, about all of it. Then tell her what your plan is and ask her if she'll support you. That's the difference between being a dumbass and being a man."

"No argument from me. Can I ask you one more thing?"

Mark looked sideways at him with his hand resting on the door handle. "What's that?"

"Are you in love with my mother?"

Mark's laugh was genuine. "Either way, the answer to that question is none of your business."

* * *

Mark drove below the speed limit down Olivia's street. He was in no hurry. Thirty minutes of rehearsing what he would say when she yelled at him for excluding her had resulted in a few options. He wanted to let her sleep? He didn't want her to worry? He had it under control? All of those things were true, and none of them were good enough. He glanced at the Jeep in the rearview mirror and offered it a silent promise of protection. If left to Olivia, it would end up in the river.

"Oh shit." Ben stared through the windshield at his mother. She was in her housecoat on her porch with a newspaper in her fist and an expression that could set the world on fire.

"Oh shit's right."

"What are you worried about? You didn't do anything wrong?"

"Good point. But I feel like I did. She's going to be mad at me, either way." Mark wound the window up, his eyes fixed on Olivia. "Because I didn't wake her up to bring her with me."

"No. She won't be mad at you, but she's gonna kill me."

"Probably. But I'm still gonna get yelled at."

"Thanks, man. It was nice knowing ya."

"You, too, Ben."

Only four steps led from the sidewalk to the porch, but Olivia loomed over the terrified men like a goddess prepared to issue judgement. A slab of broken concrete wobbled under Mark's feet. He watched her expression change from confusion to fury and relief.

"You are supposed to be in college. Why are you bringing my son home? Why is the Jeep on a trailer? Are you in trouble? Why do you know what's going on, but I don't? Start talking. Both of you. Go. Now. Talk."

They spoke at once, over and in defense of each other.

"Liv, I got a call and—"

"This isn't Mark's fault, Mom."

"Everyone is okay. I didn't want to wake you."

Eyes narrowed and nostrils flared, she put up her hands. "Stop. Why isn't Ben in school? Why is the Jeep on a trailer? Mark, explain this."

"Me? Oh no. I'm not here to explain anything. I'm just here to…" The concrete slab wobbled when he stepped back toward the safety of his truck.

Morning dew still clung to the grass and darkened the toes of Ben's sneakers. He lifted his chin. "Mom, I messed up. But I'm gonna fix it. I have to tell you some stuff, but none of it has anything to do with Mark. He was just helping. Can we go inside?"

Mark let a deep breath escape and bowed his head as he inched away. As quietly as he could, he unhooked the Jeep and left it behind.

* * *

Olivia sat at her kitchen table across from her son, her jaw set, tapping her foot. She listened to the November breeze rattle the blinds and tugged the cord of her housecoat tighter.

Ben poked at the ice cubes in his tea. "I know you don't want me to be a mechanic, but it's what I want to do. There isn't anything at school that interests me. I don't want to be a teacher or a nurse or sit in an office. There's a whole world of options out there. I don't have to work at a little shop like you and Mark. I wouldn't mind it, but I can also take drafting and design stuff. I wanna take classes and see what I'm good at."

She leaned her head back. A cobweb connected the light over the table to the drop ceiling. It swayed in the breeze. "I don't care if you work at a little shop. There's nothing wrong with the life we live. I don't care what you do or how much money you make. I want you to be happy and comfortable. If that's your decision about school, I'm fine with it, but you gotta stop making stupid decisions. That is a totally separate issue to your legal problem, and I told you the consequence. I said I would sell that car, and I wasn't kidding."

Olivia expected her son to beg, but he leaned forward and reasoned with her. "Mom, I'm still gonna go to school; it's just a different school."

"This isn't just about school, Ben. This is about the fact that you put five other people in that Jeep, and you drove around while drinking, trespassing, and God knows what else. You can sit there and tell me that college isn't for you, but college didn't force you to make bad decisions. You need to be accountable for this."

"But if I'm going to go to school, I still need a car. I told you, I'm going to do whatever it takes to get my license back and make this right. I don't want you to help me. This was my stupidity."

"Ben, I'm glad that you've taken control of your future and vowed to clean up after yourself, but that doesn't mean that I've forgiven you for your stupid, reckless behavior." Olivia knew from experience that she was most intimidating when she walked away.

"What are you going to do, Mom?" Ben asked.

"You'll just have to wait and see."

CHAPTER FIFTEEN

Dawn picked up pastel hues in the frost outside the shop. Olivia opened the door, pulled her hands inside her coat sleeves, and hit the light switch. Overhead lights flickered and buzzed. She made fog with her breath and wiped her nose on her sleeve while she squinted at the thermostat. Mark always turned it down before he left, his side of their energy-savings debate. The boiler thundered, and air hissed from the grates.

She tugged the green crocheted afghan from the back of the loveseat, exposing a hole in the orange fabric, and huddled inside of it while she watched coffee drip into the glass carafe. She wiped her nose on her sleeve again and pushed a sweeper across the floor to collect Mark's shoe fodder. The clicking of the sweeper and the dripping of the coffee, hypnotic.

"You look exhausted."

Olivia jumped and dropped the handle of the sweeper. "Jesus, Mark. You scared the crap out of me. Why are you sneaking around? It's not funny."

"I didn't sneak up on you. I've been making noise the whole way down the hallway."

Olivia wiped her nose on her sleeve again. "It's so damn cold in here.

You know we waste more money trying to warm it up again."

"Maybe. But it's temporary. We'll be able to waste money someday. Sit. I'll get the coffee."

The tips of her fingers were cold. She fumbled with papers and legal pads from her desk. Huddled under the blanket, she sat at the little kitchen table where they met every Monday morning for an hour that they both considered sacred. Before her, she spread the week's appointments, inventory, and billing. On any normal Monday, their meeting would last ten minutes and the next fifty would be spent laughing. But not this Monday.

"You look like crap." A Garfield and Odie mug appeared before Olivia. Her favorite one. It had a chip in the handle that she'd forgiven Mark for. She wrapped her fingers around it and begged it to warm her hands.

"Thank you. Thank you for noticing."

"You mad at me?"

She shook her head. "No. Of course not. It was good of you to help him."

"So, it's Ben you're mad at." Mark scraped the chair along the carpet and fell into it.

"Yeah. A little. I'm mostly over it, but I was awake on the wrong side of the sunrise. Want to go over the week? Mrs. Kriebel will be in tomorrow. She needs a thermostat."

"That can wait. What's up with Ben? Did you kill him? But most important, what did you do to the car?"

"You're sweet today." Sarcasm was their shared language. Olivia hoped it would lighten her mood.

"I still have sleep debt from collecting your son from prison. Need more coffee?"

"Haha." She took a sip. "Not yet. Still working on it."

"So, what are you gonna do? Are you taking the car away?"

Warming, Olivia shrugged the afghan to the back of the chair. "I don't know yet. I have to figure it out sooner rather than later, though. The thing is, and it's not a big thing, but registration is due soon. I don't want to let it lapse if I decide to let Ben keep it, but I don't want to pay for it if I'm just going to sell it. What do you think? What would you do?"

Mark hung his head, confessing his sins to his priest. "Liv, I feel bad. I was really hard on him. When he told me there were six people in that car, I overstepped my bounds. I told him he was irresponsible, and I was wrong to convince you to buy that car for him."

Olivia shrugged, unconcerned, drawing snowflakes in the margin of a notepad. She drew circles around them, turning them into wheels.

"Liv, he said he wanted to drop out of college to be a mechanic, and he wanted to work here. And I turned him away. He's like a son to me, and I turned him away. I raised my voice at him. I've never done that before."

Olivia dropped her pen and raised an eyebrow. "Well, good for you. Welcome to what parenting feels like. I've been yelling at him for eighteen years. Look, don't feel bad. I know it feels like you crushed a baby bird, but he's not a kid anymore. He needs adults to tell him when he's stupid. You weren't wrong for wanting him to have that car, and of course he wants to be a mechanic. He grew up around here. Same as you."

"But aren't you mad that he wasted all that money?"

"Furious. But I can forgive that. I still don't know what I want to do when I grow up. It's the rest of the mess he created that he has to atone for." Olivia spun the pad of paper around to face Mark, and he turned her snowflake tires into a trail of cars. "As for the Jeep? No idea. I told him that I'd sell it if he was irresponsible, and here we are. If don't, is that bad parenting?"

"You've got to take a long downward spiral to become a bad parent." Mark gave her the notepad and refilled their coffee cups, splashing coffee onto the table and making Olivia smirk. "If you want my two cents, he's capable of taking care of the car. He changed his own brake line while he was down at school."

"Are you serious? He doesn't know how to do that."

"He does, though. He knows more than you think. I checked his work, and it was good." Mark skipped a packet of sugar across the table to her, like a stone across the water. It landed by her sleeve. "If he's going to school to work on cars, it'll help if he has one. And it'll get real annoying real fast if you have to go back to carting him around all the time. Maybe he's already learned the hard lesson. I don't know, Liv. I don't want to be wrong. I don't want him to do something stupid and then I'll feel like it was my fault for convincing you one way or the other, but my gut says the car should stay."

Olivia slumped in her chair. "I know it sounds selfish, but I did look forward to him having a car. It gave me some independence, too. I never really had any before. Sometimes I wonder what it would be like to…to date or stay out really late at night. Things I never got to do. And then I feel guilty. It's scary out here, on the edge of the unknown. I spent all that time preparing him, and I never prepared myself." She rubbed her eyes with the heels of her hands and blinked up at the flickering light above the table. "He should keep the car. We all deserve a second chance."

"You are a great mom, Liv. And you're the best coworker a guy could hope to have." Mark picked up the pen and doodled more snowflake tires. "Don't forget, I have an appointment on Thursday, and we have to close the shop early."

Olivia stood, stretched, and threw the afghan back on the loveseat, covering the hole in the upholstery. "Sure. More coffee?"

"Yup. What do we have lined up for work this week?"

* * *

Mark shook his sunglasses open and walked from his accountant's office toward his truck, wind rustling the Post-It notes that peeked out from the manila folder tucked under his arm. They marked the places where Olivia needed to sign. He stopped to kick a spot of rust off the fender, and it fell to the ground with a crunch. He loved that truck. He wasn't ready to replace it yet.

Pushing aside a cardboard drink holder, he laid the paperwork on the passenger seat. It was no small decision, one of the biggest moments of his life, to give half of his business to Olivia. She deserved more than full-time hours, benefits, and a substantial raise for putting up with him and standing by him after the death of his father and through the lean years. He turned left out of the parking lot and drove straight to Bette's Market, where Olivia ran a register when she wasn't at the shop.

Apples and milk were just an excuse. Mark danced like a toddler in need of a bathroom, animated by his news, his broad smile captivating the other cashiers. The young woman who bagged groceries next to Olivia couldn't pry her eyes off Mark.

"I can't tell you here. Tonight. Your place. I'll bring dinner for the three of us. Pizza? Chinese? After six?" Mark couldn't stop smiling.

"Chinese. Six is perfect." She keyed in the price of the milk without looking. "What's going on with you? You're never like this."

"You'll just have to wait and see." Mark leaned across the counter and whispered. "Liv, it changes everything."

Her face fell as she counted his change, sliding quarters and pennies from the drawer.

"What? What's that look? This is good change. I promise."

She dropped coins into his hand. "I'll have to take your word for it until dinner, then."

Mark winked at Olivia and thanked the bagger who fumbled with the paper bag. He left an anxious Olivia and a lot of giggling, jealous women in his wake.

* * *

Olivia dried her hair with a Mickey Mouse towel and shuffled down the hall at the sound of the bell, which hung from door knob at the end of a strip of old leather. Mark let himself in and dropped rustling paper bags on the counter, pulling containers from the bags and opening lids. He didn't greet her. He moved in an ominous silence. It may have been anticipation for Mark, who had some great secret to share. But to Olivia, it was that moment of still air before storm winds knocked down the castle walls. She had her own news to share and it would all be different when she was done. She left the towel on the back of a chair and filled three glasses with ice, each cube crashing into the glass. It sounded like heartbreak.

"Tea?" she asked.

Mark nodded. "One egg roll or two?"

"One, please."

The two of them moved through the kitchen in a graceful, unchoreographed ballet, perfected over years of friendship and working together. Being in the kitchen with Mark usually felt warm, like home, as if this was how it was supposed to be. Like a family. Like the one Ben wished he had. The one she always wanted. The one she never had the courage to ask for because the friendship meant too much to risk.

The pitcher shook in her hand on her way from the refrigerator. She hadn't given thought to what he might say, what news could change their lives forever. She was busy figuring out how to quit her job without losing her best friend. She'd rehearsed in the car on her way home from the market and in the shower but nothing she came up with sounded meaningful or believable. The silence became too much to bear.

"The girls at the market talked about you all day. What's the occasion?"

"Not yet." Mark tilted a white plastic tray of beef and broccoli, letting it slide onto three plates. "Wait 'til dinner."

"You really like the delayed gratification, don't you?"

While Ben was young, she swore she wouldn't date. She would not bring temporary men into his life, to allow him to feel insecure or compete for her affection. With Ben on the verge of his own independence, hers loomed on the horizon like a terrifying certainty, and the one thing she wanted was the one thing she could never have.

If she ever hoped to have a meaningful relationship, she had to close the chapter on her unreturned affection. With the time and space afforded to her by her new job, she could heal and move on without damaging their friendship or causing a rift between Mark and Ben. Giving Mark her two weeks' notice was hard enough without his electric euphoria.

Staring into a puddle of pork fried rice, she concealed her tears and counted her breaths, holding the last one while Mark set the table.

"You okay, Liv?"

"Yeah. Just tired. On my feet all day. I took a shower, and now I'm wiped out." She moved the plates to the table. Ben plopped down at the table and picked up a fork.

The sound of knives scraping on plates, ice in glasses, and the tapping of Mark's foot against the linoleum kept Olivia on edge. From the corner of her eye she watched him wield a fork. For eighteen years she had exercised restraint. She didn't hug him when his father died, but she showed up with pizza and beer and the office books and taught him how to balance the budget. She didn't shake his hand when he turned his first profit, but she bought him sparkling wine, and they drank it from Dixie cups before lunch. He was her best friend, and everything was about to change. It didn't matter what his happy news was or when he would deliver it. Hers was probably bigger.

"I met with the accountant today." Mark poked at a piece of broccoli with his fork. Olivia lifted her head, swallowing hard, making room to ask questions, but Mark stopped her. "Don't say anything. Don't ask any questions yet. Let me finish. I paid off all but one of the loans on the equipment. I refinanced what was left, and I've started to restructure the business."

Olivia froze, her jaw tight and her eyes wide. "What do you mean, restructure—" When Mark reached down and grabbed the legs of her chair, she gripped the seat. He spun her around to face him, knocking her off balance. He leaned forward and took both her hands in his and looked her in the eye. Ben's fork hit the plate with clang.

"Liv, you can quit that other job."

Her face flushed, her eyes fixed on her hands in his. She prayed hers wouldn't shake.

"It's not just full-time hours and benefits. It's better than that. Will you be my business partner? You'll have a share of the profits now. With those loans gone, we have real money. We can turn the heat on and buy the fancy pens. You could buy this house instead of renting it if you want to."

Her mouth went dry. She slipped her hands out of his and tried to stand. If her knees would let her. "I don't know what to say. I…"

"I know. It's a surprise. I told you it would change everything. But it's so easy. It's just some paper. It's all out in the truck. You love paper. Everything gets better from here."

Olivia couldn't swallow. All she heard was paper. All she felt were her hands in his. Years of hiding her feelings and putting everyone else first.

"Excuse me for a second." She clasped her hands to stop them from shaking and walked down the hallway to the bathroom.

* * *

Mark didn't move, couldn't move. He sat across from Ben, aware of the parts of his hands that had just touched Olivia's. The air where she had just been was still warm. He rubbed the back of his neck and looked at Ben. "What happened here? What did I do wrong?"

Ben lifted his fork and stabbed a piece of broccoli. "I tried to tell you in the truck, but you said it was none of my business. You two are oblivious. She's in love with you, so she can't work with you anymore. She got another job, and she has to quit the shop."

Mark cursed to himself. He walked down the hallway and tapped on the bathroom door. "Liv, please come out." He rested his forehead against the trim, his eyes fixed on the door knob, pleading with it to turn. "Ben told me you got another job, and I get it. I do. If you want to quit, it's okay. Just tell me. I can hire Ben to help in the office until I find someone else. You know I don't want you to leave. We're still friends. Come on. Open the door. Please. Talk to me."

He only mentioned half of what Ben said. He'd rather hear the rest of it from Olivia. What if it wasn't true? He'd waited for her, hid his feelings from her and from himself, for so long that he couldn't tell fact from fiction between them. After all these years, had he missed his chance?

The door opened, and her feet appeared, her eyes red. She looked small, shaken. One look. Both of them knew that there was no going backward, no way to unknow what had been spilled out between them. The only thing Mark could do was step into the void, assess the damage, salvage the pieces. But that they could never go back to being what they were before.

Mark hunched, his eyes level with hers, but she looked at the floor. "Liv, for eighteen years, I've—"

She threw up a hand. "Stop. If you mean it, and you'll hire Ben to fill in,

I'd like to just start that tomorrow."

Her words knocked the wind out of him. He stepped back and blinked, trying to grasp one emotion from the dozens that flitted through him like fireflies in the dark. He willed his mouth to form the questions. Where was her new job? When would he see her again? Why wouldn't she listen to him? Was Ben right? Did she love him? But the look on her face kept him silent. He shook his head. "Okay."

But it was not okay. In desperation, he reached out to touch her shoulder, to pull her close, but she twisted away. "Liv. Can I come find you tomorrow, so we can talk? Please. You know I'll always be here. This isn't a big deal, we just need to talk about this."

She shook her head and cut him off, again, with a near whisper. "Maybe you should go. I'll pay you back for dinner."

There had to be something he could say to fix it. When it came to his feelings for her, honesty had never been a luxury he could afford—with Olivia or with himself. Anything more between them had always been up to her to create. His two-decade habit of hiding his feelings was hard to break and blurting them out had never been his decision to make. The words wouldn't come. He couldn't find the truth among the lies he'd told himself.

"Whatever. You don't have to pay me back for dinner."

He backed down the hall to the kitchen, where Ben was still eating. "You want to take over your mom's old job?" The words stung. He wanted to storm down the hall, drop to his knees, and beg her to stay.

Ben nodded, his mouth full of food. "I guess."

"Eight o'clock tomorrow morning. I'll work around your school schedule. We'll talk money tomorrow." He left. The bell that hung from the doorknob rang in his wake.

CHAPTER SIXTEEN

Mark rolled new tires across the concrete floor of the shop. He stacked them, the hollow thud echoing off the walls. William watched him work, playing with a tire gauge.

"Everything in here has something to do with her. I hate feeling this way."

"Maybe you need a vacation." William looked at the numbers etched into the white plastic. "I don't even understand what happened. *When* did this happen?"

"A month ago. I don't understand it either. I keep replaying this thing over and over. It's annoying. I never think this much." Mark carried tires two at a time and stacked them next to William along the wall. "First I told her that I was going to make her a partner. Then she hid in the bathroom. Ben said she's in love with me and got another job, which makes no sense at all. She comes out of the bathroom and kicks me out of the house. I ask her if we can talk about it later, and she's like, 'No, get out.'"

William rubbed dirt and dust from one eye. "How did she say it, though? Was she sad or angry?"

"Both? I don't understand why she'd get mad at me for offering to make her a partner. Thanks but no thanks is all she had to say. She never even told me that she had another job. I heard it from Ben. And if Ben's right, if she is in love with me and can't work with me anymore, then why won't she talk to me?"

"You guys have been friends for a long time. If it's true, that's got to be hard for her. Have you talked to Ben?"

"God no. The last thing I want to do is put him in the middle of this. He's going through enough without thinking that the two adults who always looked out for him are never going to talk to each other again."

"That's fair. Look, don't get mad at me for saying this, but everybody knows that you're in love with her. You've liked her since the day she started working here. Have you told her that? Have you even admitted that to yourself?"

"Yes? No." Mark kicked a stack of tires into a neat column. "It happened so fast I didn't have time to process anything. It's not like it's easy to admit that after almost two decades of denying it and keeping it to myself. What was I supposed to say to her? That I've been in love with her since before I could drive? That I've spent most of my life getting really good at not letting her know how I feel because it's her call to make, and if I slip, even a little, it could destroy the shop and our friendship and hurt Ben? That I would rather close the shop and live on the street than having nothing between us at all?"

William snorted and raised an eyebrow. "That might have been a good place to start, yeah."

"Something else to add to the list of things I should have said but didn't." Mark heaved two more tires against the wall.

"What *did* you say? Nothing?"

"She didn't even acknowledge what Ben said. Just the part about the job. It happened so fast. I waited for her to say something and tried to figure out what I was supposed to do, but the ball was in her court, you know? Then she kicked me out of the house. That fast."

"There's only one way you're gonna find out what she's thinking. Know what I'm saying?"

Mark took a small screwdriver from his pocket and picked a rock out of the tread of a tire. He'd played it over so many times he was numb. "I know. I gotta make her talk to me."

"I think you're putting the emphasis on the wrong syllable here."

"What do you mean?"

"Seven, eight years ago, we stood over there, you and me and the Jeep, and you told me that I had to take control of my own situation."

"I said that?"

"In a roundabout way. It sounds a lot like you've been sulking and trying to figure her out instead of figuring out yourself. Instead of making her talk to you, why not ask her to listen?"

The last of the tires inside, Mark leaned against them and shoved his hands in his pockets. "You always were the smart one."

"Except that I suck at communication, and what I didn't learn from Rebecca, I learned from you. Mark, you already know what you have to do. You're just afraid to do it. You've always wanted more with her."

Mark squinted into the bright sunlight beyond the open garage bay door. Breeze brought the last of the autumn leaves into the shop. "I've been waiting for her for years. Two decades. What we had was never enough for me, but she was the one who had to call the shots. After all these years, she chose anything other than me. She left the shop to get away from me and won't even talk to me. Maybe I'm a little bit angry about that."

"Write it down. That's my best advice. It clears the fog. You could sit around here feeling confused and sorry for yourself because you're too afraid of what she'll say, or you could go out there and try to fix it. You don't want me to be more successful than you, do you?"

Mark forced a small laugh. "Yeah, I get it. How are you and Rebecca?"

"Good. We're getting married next year. She's a keeper."

"Congratulations. You should have told me earlier. You two need to come around more. Maybe she could talk some sense into Liv. And I'd better be invited to your fancy DC wedding."

Jealousy sank a small fang into Mark. Eighteen years of practice made him an expert at burying his feelings. Unearthing them from beneath the rubble was an emotional archeology of which he was short on training.

That night, he lay in the darkness, searching the shadows, trying to find the right combination of words to make Olivia understand what she meant to him. He could accept any decision she would make about working at the shop, but he owed it to her, and to himself, to unearth the truth that he'd hidden for so long, to put his heart into words. If after knowing the truth she still didn't want to speak to him, then he would have to accept that outcome.

By the yellow glow of the lamp on his nightstand, Mark wrote the only letter he ever wrote to a girl. The next day, he added a healthy bonus to her last paycheck and placed it in an envelope with the letter. He kept it close to his heart, in his pocket, for two days, promising himself that he would deliver it by hand and watch her read it.

The letter sat on Mark's dashboard, and he sat half a block from Olivia's house. John Mellencamp sang "Jack and Diane" on a radio station that wasn't quite tuned in. Wind rattled past the car, and he shivered, warming his hands in the air that pushed through the vents. The night air smelled like snow. A couple strolled past him on the sidewalk, laughing, arm in arm and he looked away, toward the little green Jeep in her driveway, behind her Gremlin. He knew she was home. The lights went off one by one until only the Christmas tree was left, blinking red, blue, green, and yellow. It fell dark, and he missed his chance, yet again, to fix what was broken. The man who fixed everyone else could never seem to get it right for himself.

* * *

Olivia woke to the sound of thumping on the roof. Squirrels? Raccoons? She rubbed her eyes and looked at the clock. It was bright for five in the morning.

Another thump. Snow.

She slipped her feet into her slippers and twisted into her robe. The thermostat read sixty-seven. She bumped it up two degrees on her way to the coffee maker. With a flip, the toggle switch glowed orange, and the machine began its burble and hiss. Olivia reached behind the Christmas tree, pulled the curtain back from the living room window, and frowned at the foot of snow and her Gremlin. There was no way that car was going to get her to work in this.

"Mom?" Ben stood at the end of the hallway looking like he lost a fight with his pillow. He blinked against the light.

"It snowed, Ben. A lot. You'd better get moving. Mark's going to need you at the shop. The phone will be ringing off the hook, and there'll be dead batteries and cars in ditches all over town. You're about to have a busy day."

"It's too early for snow."

"Exactly. And no one remembers how to drive in it. I imagine Mark'll be—"

She was cut short by the phone. Ben reached around the wall, groping for the receiver. Her stomach wound into a knot at the distant sound of Mark's voice. Instead of ripping the phone from Ben's hand and pouring her heart out, she pulled back the curtain and watched snow fall on the cars.

"He's coming to pick me up on the way into the shop."

"Good. I was going to drop you off on my way into work, anyway. I don't want you driving in this. When is he coming by?"

"He didn't say."

"Get in the shower and make it quick."

Ben shuffled down the hallway. The coffee maker sputtered and spat the last of the coffee into the carafe as she watched the snow fall on her Gremlin. Its tires were bald. She would have to take the Jeep.

* * *

Mark sat in Olivia's driveway, waiting for Ben, knowing it would be a long day. Snow covered the windshield before the wipers made their next pass, but he could make out the glow of the lights from the house and the bumper of her car in front of him. He was warmed by the heater and a sense of relief. The Jeep was already gone. Olivia wasn't home. At least she wasn't out there in the Gremlin with its bald tires. Ice clinked against the roof of the truck. The snow was turning to sleet. Ben's silhouette moved past the windows, and the lights went out. A blast of cold air and frozen mist pushed into the truck when Ben climbed in.

"Looks like it's turning to ice." Mark blinked at the balls of ice bouncing off his windshield. "Did your mom go to work?"

"Yeah."

"Does she have a long drive?"

"Not too long." Ben buckled his seatbelt.

"She knows what she's doing. We better get moving. It's gonna be a long day."

As far as Mark was concerned, Ben's desk still belonged to Olivia. He frowned down at it as he made his way through the shop. The stacks of invoices, scraps of paper, and paper clips bent at odd angles were sacrilege.

"It's gonna be a busy morning. Can you clean up this mess? And keep up with the phones. The afternoon will slow down and then you can finish inventory before we run out of everything."

"Sorry, Mark."

"It's cool. You're good with the phones. Just keep up with that. It's gonna be rough today."

Ben was as bad at paperwork and office tasks as he had been at going to college, but at least he didn't drink or sleep through his job. He was horrible at taking inventory and placing orders with vendors, but the customers liked him, and Mark valued that above cleanliness. He watched Ben slump in his seat, pull the papers into a pile, and place a notepad on the desk, waiting for the phone to ring.

The calls came quickly. A dead battery. A blown thermostat. A car in a ditch. Ben coordinated tow trucks. The sixth call came from their parts delivery driver, with a report that he had seen the Jeep in a ditch from the other side of the highway.

Mark paused at the door, took a few deep breaths, and steadied himself. The buttons of his jacket wouldn't line up, and his hands shook. He abandoned the effort and tugged down on the hem at his waist. "Watch the shop," he barked at Ben. "Answer the phones, but don't tie them up. And don't go anywhere."

"Are you bringing her back here?" Ben tapped his pen against the desk.

"Haven't thought that far yet." Marks squeezed the door handle, his knuckles white. "I'm sure she's fine. Stay put. And keep the phone line open."

The roads were cleared of cars but covered with ice. He could barely make out the Jeep on the shoulder. Mark stopped his truck in front of it, fastened his coat, and slipped on patches of ice toward Olivia, who stood by the fender, hands in her coat pockets. The snow blew sideways, and wind whipped through his hair. He kept his eyes on his feet, unprepared for the range of emotions he felt. Anger was a protective choice.

Sleet and snow collected on Olivia's coat and in her hair. He wanted to brush it away from her face, but touching her wasn't an option. It had never

163

been an option. "Where is your hat? Why are you even out in this? You shouldn't be out here." He yelled over the deafening sound of ice pounding the pavement and enjoyed the catharsis.

"Yeah, then why are you out here? And don't yell at me. I didn't ask you to come out here and shout at me. How did you even know I was here?"

"The Napa guy saw the Jeep and called the shop. You think I'm going to get a call like that and leave you out here to die?"

Mark shoved his freezing hands in his pockets and skidded on the ice as he inspected the Jeep, ice and slush splashing away from the edges of his boots. The car rested in the ditch, tilted toward the passenger's side, as if it leaned on the snow-covered berm to take a nap. He opened the door, overcome by the smell of it, recalling how much he enjoyed working on it with William and Ben, but his anger boiled to the surface when he saw the shifters. He spun to face her. "You didn't have it in low gear?"

"No?" Olivia winced and shrugged. "It was only snow."

"Until it was ice."

"It changed over so fast. I didn't think about it until—"

He slammed the door and loomed over her. His anger tried to fall away but he held onto it. "Until you were sliding off the road? Of all people, Liv. You know better, and you shouldn't be out in this anyway. When it's not sleet, it's a white out. You can't see three inches in front of you in this."

"I'm not a damsel in distress. Why can't I go out in this? You're out in this. You even drove my son to work in this. Where the hell do you get off—"

"And I would have driven you, too."

"I don't need you to drive me to work. I can take care of myself." Puffs of fog escaped through her flared nostrils. She looked every bit the dragon he knew she could be.

"I never said you couldn't. I know you don't need me. You've made that really clear, thanks." He wanted to grab her by the shoulders, to draw her close and keep her warm and safe. He put his hands in his pockets instead. "Why is it a crime to want to take care of—"

A plow passed, scraping chunks of ice from the road and spraying sleet against the highway barrier. Pebbles of salt showered from behind the truck. Balls of ice and perfectly formed snowflakes intermingled on the sleeve of his coat. He watched them slowly melt while the sound of the truck faded away, taking the anger with it.

"If you hadn't left the shop, none of this would have happened." Mark threw his hands up. "You know what? I'm done standing out here in this mess. We're not getting anywhere. Do you want me to take you home or would you rather stay out here than spend twenty minutes in the truck with me?"

"Whatever, Mark." A tear fell, and she brushed it away. Maybe she felt something after all, even if it was an angry tear.

"Can we pick up Ben at the shop? I'd like to get him home before this gets worse."

"Yup. It's on the way."

"I gotta get my stuff from the Jeep."

He nodded and held out his arm, offering support, but she waved him off and inched past him toward the Jeep. Mark made his way to the truck and started it, adjusting the air vents to warm his hands. In the rearview mirror, he watched her give the Jeep an apologetic pat on the fender.

With no one to tease him about his clutter, he'd allowed scraps of paper, pens, and gloves to take over Olivia's seat in his truck. Scooping them up and shoving them behind the seat, he made room for her again.

* * *

Olivia sat as close to the door of Mark's truck as she could. She tucked her hands between her knees so he couldn't see them shaking. Warming them was a secondary benefit. Her heart raced, her chest tight. The air between them thickened with the unknown. The truck's wet brakes squealed when he stopped in front of the shop. Through the window, she could see the light on at her old desk, her son on the phone. She paused with her hand on the door handle and broke the silence. "I said I didn't need it, but thanks for coming to my rescue. Even if I'd called, I wouldn't have expected you to." The way she'd treated him, she didn't think she'd deserve it.

"I wasn't the one who walked away. You're the one who shut me out, not the other way around."

Water dripped from Olivia's hair onto the sleeve of her coat. With the engine off, the heat in the truck began to dissipate, and the windows started to fog. "I'm sorry that I wouldn't let you talk. I'm sorry that I ran away." She shivered and pulled her elbows in for warmth, her eyes fixed on the glove box door. "I'm sorry that I never told you the really important things."

"It's not too late to tell me the important things, Liv. I've got all day. I've got things to tell you, too, if you'll listen." Mark inched the door open.

"Can we go inside and talk about this over coffee like we used to?"

"Yes. Finally. But you have to make it because Ben's coffee sucks."

Olivia led the way into the shop. While the coffee maker spit out ten cups of coffee, she peered behind the machine, the sharp edge of the counter cutting into the palms of her hands. Crumbs and dust covered the counter. Dirty cups were piled in the sink. She shook the dish soap container. Empty.

"Ben, do you have a list of supplies you need to order? Add sponges. And dish soap. You'd better add coffee to it, too. God, don't run out of coffee. Mark will die."

Ben scratched the list onto a scrap of paper by the phone. "Are you guys okay now?"

"I don't know, Ben. I'm gonna try to fix it." Olivia turned her back on the dirty cups, folding her arms across her stomach for warmth and protection.

"I don't think you'll have to work very hard," Ben muttered.

"I hope you're right."

"Heater's on back there. Is the coffee ready?" Mark appeared in the doorway, picking dirt from his fingernail with a pocket knife. Olivia knew his displacement activities well. "And don't look at that sink. It'll only disappoint you."

The last of the coffee sputtered from the machine, and Mark pulled two cups from the shelf, pushing her Garfield and Odie mug into her hands. "Hasn't been used since the last time you were here. So you know it's clean."

Olivia followed Mark down the hallway on autopilot. The ghosts of things she thought she'd never experience again moved through her. The smell of coffee mixed with rust and cold concrete. The sound of shop stools scraping across the floor. The smell of the kerosene heater. She settled onto a stool and watched Mark pace. It hurt to see him uncomfortable, but at least she wasn't the only one.

Weeks of playing out the conversation they should have had, sleepless nights and long commutes thinking through what she would say if given the chance, and she was still unprepared. Warmed by liquid courage, she opened the floodgate. The words came to her one at a time.

"I don't want it to be like this anymore. How do we fix it?"

"You're the one who left me, Liv. You hid in the bathroom and then never talked to me again."

"I'm sorry for that. You're right. It was horrible of me to treat you that way. It's no excuse, but I had a million thoughts in my head, buzzing like bees, and I couldn't get a grip. I found out that morning that I got the other job. I was terrified to tell you, and my stomach was in knots all day. Then you showed up at the market, so excited, and you make that amazing gesture. Imagine how I felt. I thought, maybe I'll just splash some water on my face and figure out what to say. Then Ben told you that I...and everything just fell apart. We fell apart."

Mark leaned next to her, against his workbench. The wood creaked. "I don't blame you for getting another job. Honestly, to think about it, I'm surprised you hung in here for so long. I get it. I would have missed you, yeah, but I understand that. What I didn't understand was how running away from me and kicking me out of your life made things any better."

"That wasn't what I was trying to do. I never intended to damage our friendship, and it wasn't about the money. I took that job to put space between us." Olivia couldn't skirt her feelings for Mark anymore. She couldn't avoid that Ben blurted out her love for Mark, that her son was right. That she couldn't spend the rest of her life loving someone who didn't love her back. The only way forward was to face it head on, even if it meant hearing Mark voice his rejection. Whether they could laugh about it and be friends, or part ways without anger, the sooner it came, the sooner she could move on. "Ben's an adult now. I'm terrified, but I'm ready to live the rest of my life. I don't want to spend it alone. If I can't spend it with you, don't I deserve a chance to get over you, so I can spend it with somebody else?"

"You never gave me a chance. You never even let me say anything."

"I really don't think I could have taken the rejection. I didn't want to hear you tell me that you don't..." She didn't need to say it. She tugged her sleeves down over her hands. Looking up at the ceiling, she willed her eyes to absorb the tears, demanding that they wouldn't fall. "What would you have said? What could you possibly have said that wouldn't hurt or make things harder than they already were?"

Mark placed his coffee on his workbench next to hers and put his hands in his pockets. The workbench creaked when he leaned against it. "I've replayed that scene a thousand times. Standing in the hallway outside your bathroom door. I've come up with a thousand great things to say and not one of them was good enough, because I don't know how to show you how vulnerable I am with you."

Olivia reached for her cup, her mouth dry. She hunched over it, trying to seal the hole in her chest. She'd raised a human. Kept Ben alive for eighteen years. But she wasn't sure she'd be able to survive this conversation. Vulnerable?

"Liv, the day we met, you shook my hand, and I spent the next three years trying to find excuses to be in the same room with you. When I was twenty-two years old and Dad died changing a tire, right over there, I had no idea how to run this shop. Everybody quit. But you showed up at my apartment and said we'd figure it out together. The only thing I cared about was you, and you stayed, so I tried. You and Ben are my family. I knew you wouldn't let me love you because of Ben, so I had to protect myself and hide my feelings from you. I had to hide them from myself just to survive. It wasn't easy, standing in your hallway trying to figure out what to say, because I've spent two decades waiting for you. You had your chance to tell me, to confirm what Ben said, to say it in your own words, but you didn't. Because you'd already decided that you wanted any of a billion other guys out there who aren't me. And then you left. Now I have to pick up the pieces and figure out who I am without you."

Gusts of wind pushed against the garage doors and ice pinged against the drafty windows. It collected on the screen as Mark's words formed a hard ball in her chest. A sip of coffee did nothing to open her dry throat. Everything seemed to be caving in. "You did a great job of hiding your feelings. Maybe I was so wrapped up in my own that I couldn't put the pieces together. Maybe I was too afraid to see it. Either way, telling you how I felt was never an option." She couldn't say it. She couldn't say she loved him. He was already moving on and she'd missed her chance. "Telling you how I really felt could have destroyed us and made things hard for Ben." Her eyes fixed on the window, her mind focused on what she had lost. "I'm sorry I made such a mess of things."

"It's okay. You've been forgiving me for years. Let's call it even."

"You think it'll ever be the same between us again?"

"I don't know. All we can do is try. Just don't bring some guy over here and expect me to be happy for you." Mark let out a deep sigh. He emptied his mug. "You know, I think I do know what I would have said. Not that it matters now, but I would have told you I loved you. That I always have. All those years of waiting for each other? We could have been great together."

Olivia let his words sink in, their past tense landing on her chest like a lead weight. The air still hadn't cleared between them yet, and she wasn't refilling her cup until it had. "Could have been? Or will be?"

Mark shifted his weight against the counter. He played with a rusty adjustable wrench, trying to unstick the worm screw. He laid it on the clean workbench and turned to face her. "Let me put it to you this way. The ball has been in your court for a really long time. You tell me."

* * *

The thawing began at sunrise. Water dripped from gutters and tree branches, off the corners of tables and porch railings, and bounced off pavement and rocks. Mark gathered Olivia in his truck and drove to the spot where the Jeep rested against the berm along the highway. The body panels creaked and squealed as he winched the car out of the ditch and onto the shoulder of the road.

"Liv, look in the glove box and see if that camera is still in there."

Beneath the napkins and zip ties that were permanent fixtures in Mark's glove box, Olivia found the camera. Just beneath, she saw her name on a dog-eared, folded sheet of paper in Mark's angular, slanted handwriting.

"What's that?" Mark appeared over her shoulder.

"I don't know. You tell me." She put the paper in his hand.

"Looks like the only love letter I ever wrote to a girl." Turning the letter over in his hand, he remembered how hard it was to tell her how he felt. He pulled her close and shoved it deep into the back pocket of her jeans. "Guess it's time to give it to her."

"What took you so long?"

"She's a little intimidating when she's angry. She always gets what she wants anyway."

"It's a good thing you know that." She held up the camera. "Looks like there's still film left in here. You wanna take a picture with the Jeep for the notebook? I guess I need to record its first dent."

"Yup. Then we gotta get this thing back to the shop and hose all the road salt off of it. If you don't take care of these things, they rust right through."

* * *

Robins pecked the buds off the trees in Olivia's yard. Their feet scratched and clicked along the gutters outside the kitchen window. Ben reached across the table for the cereal box. "You're always here," he teased.

"Yeah? So are you. You want the milk, too?" Mark pushed the carton in Ben's direction.

"Speaking of always being around, I want to be around less."

"Where do you think you're gonna go?" Olivia tugged her robe closed and sat in front of an empty bowl.

"Closer to school. I got a job at the campus bookstore. Jake's roommate moved in with his girlfriend, so I'm going to move in with him. I'll have to quit the shop, which means you'll have to go back to working there. Or Mark will have to start making his own coffee and answering the phone. Either one."

"It sounds like you have this all figured out. You're going to make enough money at the campus bookstore to pay for all that? Also, you're going to work at a bookstore?" Olivia shook the last of the cereal into her bowl. "You do know it's a bookstore, right?"

"I suspect that it might be, based on the name of it. And if I don't make enough money, I'll figure it out. And I'm going to trade you cars. You keep the Jeep, and I'll take the Gremlin. The Jeep runs great, but the Gremmie keeps breaking down. I can fix it with the guys at school. Maybe we can turn it into a race car."

"Please don't." Rice Krispies popped and snapped in her bowl when she added milk. She cast a sideways glance at Ben. "I accept this plan. And I'll take the Jeep, even though I don't really need it. Maybe we can paint it and put the shop logo on it. Park it out at the corner. I do hope you plan to give your current employer formal notice, though."

"Sure. I'll type something up this morning."

Mark drank the milk from his cereal and leveled with Olivia. "Excuse me for interrupting here. But it seems to me that if you came back to the shop, it would run a little better. No offense, Ben."

"None taken."

Mark dropped his bowl in the sink and kissed the top of Olivia's head. "I'm going to take a shower. Tell you what, if you come back to the shop, I promise never to take the toilet paper out of the bathroom again. When can you start?"

CHAPTER SEVENTEEN

For years, Mark cared for the Jeep, checking its fluids and keeping air in the tires, although Olivia drove it less and less. By the time 1994 rolled around, it was too small for their growing family, and it was in the way, shuffled from the parking lot to the shop floor and back as space was needed. Olivia placed ads in the local paper and Mark answered questions, but it was twenty-seven years old and not what most people wanted in a car.

Mark put the finishing touches on Mrs. Kriebel's Buick and sang along with Tori Amos to "Cornflake Girl" on the only station that would come into tune. He waved a wrench at Olivia when she emerged from the hallway, followed by a man in his seventies, but his expectations were low.

"It's not much," he heard Olivia tell the man. "It's just a little four cylinder. It has a dent from a few years ago when it slid off the road in an ice storm, but it's solid as a rock."

"It looks great for its age. I like the green."

"Thanks. I almost painted it a few years ago. Glad I didn't. This is the original paint, and it's held up pretty good."

Mark wiped his hands on his pants and held one out. "You must be Vince."

"Ayup. Nice little Jeep ya got here."

"Third owner. My stepson and wife shared it for a while, and then she used it for a few years. We don't drive it like we should. With a little one, we need a car with more room, you know? No sense keeping it around if we're not using it. Before us it belonged to a buddy of mine and before that it belonged to a guy who had a farm out by Elk River."

Vince walked around the car. He bent to look at the exhaust and ran his hand along the ding in the fender. He was stocky, strong for his age. A man who worked for a living. But he was old enough to see the car for what it was. "It runs okay?"

"Yup. I just replaced the belt and the hoses, and all the fluids are new. New battery. New tires. It's a good little Jeep, but it helps if you know what you're getting yourself into with a car like this. I don't mean this to come off the wrong way, because I've had a few people come by to look at it who think that it's an inexpensive ride, but it's not a good car for a kid or someone who expects modern convenience. I won't sell it to just anybody. It has to go to the right person, you know?"

"I can see how a young driver would make that mistake. Jeeps have a reputation for being durable, and a kid might think it's like the stuff they build today."

"Right. Not at all. I don't want to sell it to somebody who doesn't have the right expectations. I want to make sure that the buyer knows what they're getting."

"That's respectable." Vince continued his inspection. He struggled to lower himself to the ground.

"I have a creeper you can use if you want." Mark pointed to the cushion on wheels that rested nearby, but Vince declined.

Olivia nudged Mark's arm and gave him an approving nod. Mark agreed. Vince did look like the right man for the car.

From beneath it, Vince asked, "There's a drop of oil down here. Does it leak?"

"It sat for a good few months, but I've been running it the last few days, and it does leak a little. Especially after a long drive. Not enough to warrant cracking it open, though. I would say in the next five years, you'll need a new rear main seal and new gaskets around the transmission and transfer case, depending on how hard and how often you run it."

Vince used the front bumper for leverage and raised himself off the ground. "I'm definitely interested. This is kind of a silly question, but do you know anything about maintenance before you got it?"

Mark waved for Vince to follow him to the workbench. "Come on back. I'll show you." He collected the notebook from its resting place between two old oil cans.

"The first owner started this and passed it to my friend Bill. We've kept up with it. Everything is in here. The original bill of sale, and the pen he signed it with." Mark turned the pages, passing receipts, handwritten notes, carburetor diagrams, photographs. He paused at a picture of James and Claire. "I guess this was his wife. They added pictures to it from all over the place." Mark continued to flip through the pages. "Bill and his girl added a bunch of pictures. They look so young. And this is my stepson, Ben. This was the first time he took the car out on his own. His first day at college. I stuck receipts in here and wrote up our maintenance notes. My card is in there, too. If you ever need help, give me a ring. If you buy it, that is."

"I'll take it. I thought the price was reasonable. Can I come back tomorrow to get it? Is cash okay?"

"Cash is fine. I'll be here at seven, and we wrap up at six on Thursdays."

"First thing in the morning then." A handshake sealed the deal, and Vince showed himself out through the garage bay door. Mark ran his hand along the curve of the hood and secured the latches. The pat that he left on the fender echoed through the shop.

* * *

Olivia listened to the gas fill the tank as the bottoms of the clouds turned pink, announcing the arrival of day. She released her seatbelt, which fell with a clunk, and slid over the shifters into the driver's seat. "I wanna drive back."

Mark tapped the last drop of gas into the tank. "I figured you would."

The streets were empty for their last drive at dawn. It had been weeks since she last drove it, taking it into Buck Mountain to a car show behind the fire hall where they left it with a For Sale sign while they ate chicken from a Styrofoam container. It was a breath of fresh air. A simple machine that you could connect to. Driving it was like playing an instrument compared to the stuff that filled the garage with its insulation and check engine lights. Everything new seemed designed to fail. It was easier to say goodbye to new cars, because you barely got to know them at all. Halfway back to the garage, Mark squeezed her thigh, interrupting her thoughts. "You wanna go make out by the water tower?"

"Always." She tapped her watch. "But it's almost seven. Gonna have to take a rain check."

The Jeep left wet tire prints on the garage floor, and the sound of the engine and exhaust thundered through the concrete room. Olivia cut the engine and lowered herself to the floor. She collected the notebook, dropping it in front of the passenger seat while Mark opened the rest of the bay doors. Sunlight and cool air flooded the shop. She gave the Jeep one last pat on the fender, a bittersweet goodbye, before trudging down the hall to make coffee and unlock the front door.

Mark checked the fluids one last time. He was going to miss the little Jeep, but there was no sense letting it waste away if they weren't using it.

Vince's voice rang out in the garage. "Good morning! Hope I didn't get you up too early."

"Not at all. We're early risers." Mark greeted him with a handshake and accepted an envelope of cash. "I forgot to ask you what you were doing with it? Is it just a fun, second car?"

"Oh, it'll get some use. My wife and I own a general store out on the state road to Buck Mountain. Our house is just up the hill from it. Our old car died, and we just need something to get up and down the hill. To get us into town every once in a while. I used to have an old Jeep, not as old as this one, though. They're good little machines."

"Yeah, they're fun to drive around in, and they last forever. Glad it will get some use. Like I said, if you have trouble just give me a ring. The notebook is on the floor there. Keep up with that? There's more than thirty years of history in there."

Mark dropped the key into Vince's open hand and stepped back. He took a broom and swept dirt from a shadowy corner. Vince started the Jeep and backed out of the garage.

"I almost missed seeing it drive off." Olivia appeared next to Mark with two cups of coffee. "I'm gonna miss that Jeep. Of all the cars I've ever owned, I like that one best."

"Why's that?"

"It brought us back together by throwing me into a pile of snow, so…"

Mark wrapped his arms around Olivia, and they stood in the garage bay, in the spot the Jeep vacated. They watched the sky light up as Vince sat at the red light.

"Yeah, you keep saying that, but it didn't throw you into a pile of snow. You drove around in an ice storm."

"It sounds much more romantic my way."

The light turned green and Vince pulled away, grinding a gear as he aimed for Buck Mountain.

CERTIFICATE OF TITLE

	TITLE NUMBER
	53724952470

PREV TITLE NO	DATE OF APPLICATION	MODEL YEAR	MAKE	MODEL	TYPE
0292564809	04/14/1994	1964	JEEP	CJ-5	WAGON

VEHICLE IDENTIFICATION NUMBER	EQUIPMENT NUMBER	CAPACITY	MILEAGE	ODOMETER CODE
83050 185111			000000	EXEMPT

TITLE CHANGES

BUYER INFORMATION

VINCENT BENORE
238 HILL STREET
BUCK MOUNTAIN

BY *V. BENORE* DATE 4/14/94
TITLE

SELLER INFORMATION

OLIVIA LAGRANGE
24 MILLER DR
ELMWOOD

BY *Liv LaGrange* DATE *April 14, 1994*
TITLE

I hereby certify that an application for certificate of title has been made for the vehicle described hereon, pursuant to the provisions of the Motor Vehicle Laws of this State, and the applicant named on the face hereon has been duly recorded as the lawful owner of said vehicle. I further certify that the vehicle is subject to the security interests shown hereon, if any.

CHAPTER EIGHTEEN

The rolling hills of Elk River and Elmwood swelled into mountains. Route 62 wound through them, past abandoned wood-framed houses and barns that tilted behind haphazard rows of pine and birch, hickory and evergreen. It crossed streams that bubbled over rocks, full of clay, fish, and tadpoles. Nestled in a wooded valley was the town of Buck Mountain, where deer outnumbered people, and in the outskirts, the distance between houses created distance between people that was only bridged on Sundays.

When coal was found in the mountains, men with clipboards arrived to exploit it. Armed with a blueprint provided by the company, they built a self-sufficient coal town. When the veins of coal were bled dry, little but pride remained to support the people. To the eye of the average traveler, Buck Mountain was depressed, but to Vince and his wife Pauline, it was the center of the universe.

Downtown, rows of tall, narrow, two-and-a-half-story houses lined the streets, their dormer windows peering down like ever-watchful eyes. The cheap, plastic playthings of childhood—Big Wheels and play sets—gathered mildew on porches. Paint peeled from doors and windows and walls. Flat-fronted stores dumped their customers onto sidewalks that sank and cracked with age. Pebbles, soil, and weeds filled the voids. Cars leaned on weakened struts, sat raised on blocks, and bore the hallmarks of patched repairs, with duct-taped panels and plastic covered windows. People kept to themselves, although friends and enemies chatted and argued, smoking cigarettes as they met on the street. The church and the beer store were popular meeting places, but none could compete with the fire house, which maintained a hall where people gathered to drink. All but the church were foreign to Vince and Pauline.

Like most rural areas, Buck Mountain's zip code extended farther than its visible boundaries. Vince and Pauline owned the last property claimed by the town's western border, where their general store rested at the base of a steep hill, owned by Vince and his wife Pauline. Its weathered slats and beams once gleamed bright white, but time and weather wore away the paint. It was a cornerstone for residents and a landmark for travelers who scattered their cars in the unlined gravel lot, dodging weeds that defied nature, growing in the dust and pebbles. But Pauline refused to tame them. She preferred that God and nature have their way.

Inside the store, the wide wooden floorboards wrestled with the joists, clunking and squeaking under the feet of visitors. Shelves and tables held stacks of food, travel conveniences, equipment for hunting and fishing, and general household goods. They were Vince's territory to keep stocked and tidy, while Pauline tended the register. Next to it, she kept neatly stacks jars of their honey, each displaying a label with her favorite Bible verse, Psalms 40:2. Where the walls were not bare, they were covered with copies of Warner Sallman's *Head of Christ*. Each frame was different, but all had small, yellowed price tags. No visitor had ever been moved to purchase one.

A narrow driveway, no more than two wheel grooves in the hillside, led to the top of the hill. It was bordered by wild grasses and ended at a patch of dirt in a small yard, where the land leveled, and the grasses gave way. The remnants of a garden created a moat of detritus around their cozy trailer, the first luxury to be forsaken when age settled into their knees and hips. Inside, however, was immaculate. Pink and peach, pale green and sky blue, the living room was a sea of floral patterns and hues. And every flat surface held a childhood photograph of their son.

Just outside the front door, the Jeep rested on a patch of hard-packed earth beneath the trees. Pauline photographed it from every angle with a disposable camera from the store. A photo at the store, by the sign at the corner. Another at the house. Next to her beehives. And another when a storm rolled through and a branch from an elm tree pierced a window in the soft top.

The top was aging and faded. Pollen and dirt from their hillside jaunts accumulated in a yellow-brown layer. The door hinges were rusting, and the zippers were stiff. The windows yellowed and brittle. Vince removed the top and draped it over a picnic table, intending to scrub it clean and patch the hole with tape, but as day rolled into night and into day again, the demands of the store took precedence. He put the top in a box, tucked it under the trailer, and never put it on the Jeep again.

Pine needles, sap, leaves and twigs, pebbles and acorns, and all types of weather accumulated inside the Jeep and took their toll as they passed through the interior. The seat cushions cracked and exposed the foam filler. Rubber parts, like the shifter cover and the horn button, hardened in the sun, became brittle, and began their descent into dust. The steering wheel cracked in two places. But the little Jeep continued its daily hill climbs, escorting Vince and Pauline up and down the hill each day in slightly less comfort but with no less competency.

In very bad weather, Vince would cover the Jeep with tarps to prevent snow and rain from entering, but water and weather found a way. He would dry the interior to Pauline's satisfaction with towels and old blankets, but his efforts only slowed the onset of rust. Pauline considered it uncomfortable, utilitarian at best, and she made sounds of disapproval at Vince, who lost the motivation to care for the little green Jeep.

* * *

Vince sat on a floral sofa and tucked the coiled phone cord under his arm. He listened while his son, Peter, typed as he talked. A year had passed since their last call. Maybe more. And he didn't even warrant his son's undivided attention.

"What kind of car did you get, Dad?"

"Are you at work?"

"I'm at home, but I'm working."

"It's nine o'clock at night."

"Deadlines. Gotta love 'em. What kind of car?"

"It's an old Jeep. I got it from that service station down in Elmwood. A year ago?" Vince waved a hand at Pauline, who offered him tea from across the room. Every time he tried to talk to his son, his wife found a way to interject. "At least a year ago."

"The one across from that old tavern?"

"Yeah. Nice shop. Pauline stayed at the store here, and I got a ride from one of the Chess Men."

"The Chess Men?"

"Yeah, the guys who sit on the side of the building here and play chess and checkers all day."

"That's still a thing, huh? Funny. Those guys have been there forever."

"Your mother put in a little coffee station a few months ago. They sit out there all day drinking Sanka, complaining about taxes and their knees."

"Some things never change. That old Jeep? You think it'll hold up? It's in good enough shape?"

"It's been good. It's built to climb over things, so that hill won't be a problem. And since it's old, we don't have to worry about dings from rocks and sticks. It leaks a little, but I can keep up with it."

"That's great, Dad. Sounds like you found the right thing."

"It came with a notebook, too. The old owners put all kinds of stuff in there. Receipts. Pictures."

"Hmm." Peter was distracted.

"I'll let you go. You sound like you have a lot going on."

"Okay. Wait! I was thinking. I have a week of vacation time that I need to use. Why don't I come visit?"

Vince held the phone away from his face. "Paul-eeen! Pick up the other phone. Peter wants to visit."

"I would love to see the store. It's been a long time. What's it been? Five years? Six? And then it was just for a day. We really shouldn't let so much time go by."

Vince heard a click on the line when Pauline picked up the cordless phone that sat on the kitchen counter and moved to the matching recliner. He knew there was no use trying to get a word in once she was involved in the conversation, so he listened.

"The whole family?" Pauline asked. "Even the kids?"

"Unfortunately, just me. The kids have school, then summer camps and scouting. Nick doesn't have as much vacation time as I do."

"Oh, it would be such a joy. It has been so long."

Vince let his wife handle the arrangements. He set down the phone and picked up the TV Guide, flipping the pages without seeing them. A visit from Peter without the rest of the family could mean that his home life were in trouble. Or it could mean that he was ready to put the past aside, to find common ground despite all their differences.

* * *

Peter put his rental car in low gear and climbed the dusty trail to his parents' trailer at the top of the steep incline. Just after sunset, he tumbled into the house with a suitcase, flowers for his mother, and his father's favorite candy—just in time to watch his mother lick frosting from her thumb and place the cake on the kitchen table.

Immersed in nostalgia, he unpacked his suitcase into the dresser he used as a child, and felt seventeen again. Homeschooled. Isolated. Chained to the church and a dogma that taught its followers to love thy neighbor but included him in its list of exceptions. His mother threw away his comics, and his father was silent. The last time he opened the drawers to that dresser, he was packing its contents into trash bags while his parents prayed for his soul.

"Peter. Come wash your hands for dinner." His mother's voice resounded down the hall.

The kitchen was disorienting, with familiar items in unfamiliar places. Opening and closing drawers in search of utensils, Peter found what he needed to set the table for dinner.

Vince attacked his dinner with a fork and knife. "How are the computers treating you, son?"

"The Tower of Babel." Pauline shook her head. It was the same tone she'd use to express sadness about a drought in a land she'd never visit. Peter wouldn't make apologies for being a part of the world.

"It's what I do for a living. I do very well, and I support my family."

"It's artificial. You don't know what's inside those machines. We just pray…"

"I know, Mom." His mother held a staunch belief that the unknown must be corrupt. He inhaled and congratulated himself for not rolling his eyes. "I know exactly what's inside those machines, because I put it there."

"And all that debt."

"I paid off my student loans, and I support my family very well. The kids can go to any summer camp they want. We have a nice house and nice cars." Cars. The Jeep. Peter latched onto the easy transition. "Speaking of, what's the story with the Jeep out front?"

"The old car died, and your father found this to replace it."

He wanted to ask why they didn't start a prayer chain and perform a laying on of the hands to bring the old car back to life, but he doubted they would see the humor in it. "Do you know anything about it? It has a Willys tailgate."

"What kind of tail?" his mother asked.

"Willys. That's what's stamped in the tailgate that they put on the back of the Jeep." Peter pushed peas onto his fork with his finger. "The company changed a lot over the years, and that's what the older Jeeps said on the back. I was curious if the tailgate was original or not. Do you know anything about it?"

His father put his fork down to answer Peter's question. "That notebook I told you about, with the maintenance records, it's back in your room. The original sale paper's in there too. You can look at it after dinner if you want."

Pauline wrinkled her nose, scowling at Vince's mention of the notebook. Peter couldn't resist. "You don't like the notebook, Mom?"

"Floozies."

"She doesn't like the pictures in it. Some of the girls are a little too liberal for your mother's taste. It's just a car, Pauline. You don't have to wear their clothes, you just have to get down the hill and back in it."

"I put plenty of pictures in there that didn't have girls in short shorts." She picked at her peas.

Peter knew enough about Jeeps to know it was probably an early CJ-5, judging by what he could see in the dark. It had curved fenders, not flat like the really early Jeeps. And it was in better shape than most he had seen.

185

"Do you mind if I take a look at it?"

"What do you mean, take a look at it? You're not going to take it apart, are you?" Vince paused, his fork hovering over his chicken.

"No, Dad. I'm not going to take your car apart." Peter smiled, remembering many of the machines his father had lost to his youthful curiosity. "I just want to see how old it is. I think old Jeeps are interesting. I almost bought one when I was just out of school."

His mother scowled again. "Really? It's like a tractor."

"There's something graceful about how simple they are. You can do the work yourself. The parts are easy to find, even for Jeeps that are older than that. And they're this iconic thing, you know? A solid, American Jeep."

That night, propped against the wooden headboard of his twin-size childhood bed, he read through the binder under the yellow glow of a Tigger lamp and wondered what became of James and Claire.

* * *

Peter woke before dawn to the smell of coffee and bacon. He ran his hand along the panelled hallway and stopped in the kitchen where his mother stood in her floor-length floral nightgown with its ruffled collar and sleeves, a spatula in one hand and a plate of pancakes in the other.

"Sit down, sit down." She waved a spatula at the table. "I'll have breakfast done in a minute. Your father is in the shower. After breakfast, we have to head down to the store, but you can run off to whatever you want. We eat our lunch in the back room, and we close up at six. Do you have plans for the day?"

"No plans. I want to see how the town has changed. Might run down to the car wash, pick up a newspaper. See what's new down there."

"It's a shame you didn't give me more notice, or I could have told everybody at church. They ask about you all the time. There would have been a line to see you. I know how you hate to be lonely."

"It's okay, Mom. You don't have to make plans for me. I'll come by the store later and maybe you can put me to work. If anything needs fixed or cleaned, I'm happy to help."

After breakfast, Peter watched as his father adjust the choke, and the car warmed. The sound of metal on metal, the body panels and leaf springs squeaked as they started down the narrow path. A cardboard box full of clanking honey jars bounced in the back, and the Jeep disappeared down the hill.

Downtown hadn't changed. The bookstore. The newsstand on the corner where kids tried to bum cigarettes. The car wash took change now, instead of tokens. The nostalgia kept the Jeep in the back of his mind. Had it traveled these streets? Brought its owner to these stores in search of shoes and fancy clothes? The car needed as much work as the town, paint wearing thin and age showing through. He returned to the store and parked next to the Jeep in the unkempt lot. He raised the hood and rested it against the windshield with a thud, gazing into the engine bay. Clean, but showing its age. It still had its serial number plate. The labels on the oil filter had turned brittle and flaked away. All of the wear-and-tear items were in good shape: the hoses, spark plug wires, and belt. The wiring was aging, possibly original, but seemed to work properly. Inside the Jeep, however, things looked much worse.

Clumps of dried mud were scattered on the floor and in the rear of the tub. Everything rubber was rotting or missing, cracked, and broken apart. The beautiful, thin, Bakelite steering wheel was cracked. The dashboard was no longer glossy, the clear coat worn away. The paint had worn off the hinges of the glove box door. The floors were scuffed. Metal and rust were visible where the paint chipped away. The seat covers were ripped and torn with dark yellow foam peeking through the gaps.

Peter found a receipt in his pocket and searched his car for a pen. He inspected the Jeep, making notes of parts to replace, starting his list with a new soft top. From his place in the driver's seat, he sensed a presence to his left.

"This your Jeep?" The man was about his age. He held the hand of a toddler who clutched a Buzz Lightyear toy.

"Nah, it belongs to my parents. They own the store here. I'm just looking it over. It could use a few things, I think." Peter glanced at his list and wondered if *few* was the right word.

The man let out a chuckle. "You can say that again. It's all cosmetic, though. Sorry to bother you. Just thought I'd ask about it. I used to have an old Jeep, and we see this one here all the time. My daughter thinks it looks like a praying mantis."

"I can see that, the big bug eyes. That's cute."

The visitor thanked him and started to walk away. "Hey," Peter called after him. "Do you know if there's anywhere around here to get parts for this thing?"

"There's a place about an hour from here. It's a small shop that sells old Jeep parts. There's a junkyard about forty minutes that way, too." He pointed to the east. "I'll write it down for you."

With a destination and directions, Peter thanked him and walked toward the store. He found his mother behind the counter. The clicks of the cash register's keys and the ringing of the bell announced the completion of a sale. He watched her hand a bag to a customer.

"Janice! Look, it's my son." She waved him forward to join them at the register. "Janice, I don't know if you remember my son, Peter. You remember him from church? Peter, remember Janice?"

Peter felt stiff around the contrived niceties of his hometown. He had no idea who Janice was, but church held no fond memories. He took the easy way out. "I do remember. It's nice to see you again." He asked about his father, eager to crawl from under the critical stares, real or imagined.

"He's in the back, hon. Just head right on back through the door, and you'll find him."

Peter made his way past rows of canned food and jarred liquids and pushed open the swinging wooden door to find his father breaking open a case of bars of soap. He must have cut through one with his knife. It smelled clean.

"Dad, I took a look at your Jeep. I know you said that you didn't want to work on it, but there are a few easy things I can do to make it more comfortable and last a little longer. I'm happy to do it. It'll give me something to do." Peter pushed past his father's look of protest. "There are a few places around here that have parts. I'm going to check them out."

Vince adjusted his hat and waved his hand in surrender. "It needs a new top. I still have the one that came with it. A big branch came out of that tree, and it got a hole in it. There's no sense doing anything with it until it has a top."

"Don't worry. I'll take care of it, Dad." Peter started toward the door but turned back to face his father. "Are you sure you don't want to come with me?"

"Nah." Vince had already resumed unpacking bars of soap in little blue boxes. "You go on ahead. I'm not interested in all that."

"You know, I could always stay here and help you with all of this..." Peter's voice trailed off as he looked around the room. Boxes and cartons stacked five and six high. Nothing had changed since he was a kid. He never understood how his father could feel fulfilled emptying cardboard boxes every day.

"That's okay, son. Have fun working on the car."

Peter drove in the direction of the junkyard, wondering what it would take to find common ground with his father.

CHAPTER NINETEEN

Peter surrounded his childhood bed with car parts. A steering wheel. The new soft top. Spray cans of paint and tubes of grease. He rummaged through his father's tools in the workshop at the back of the store. The collection was suited to building and repairing shelves and healing the wounds that time inflicted on the century-old store, but among them, Peter found much of what he needed. He amended the pile with wrenches, sockets, and extensions that he purchased from the hardware store, from the junkyard, and the car parts store. He spent his third night at his parents' house reading a repair manual.

In the morning, he carved into a pancake with the side of his fork and asked his father, again, if he wanted to help. He received the expected response.

"I'm not interested in this stuff, Peter." Asking more than once had clearly agitated Vince. "I just want to get up and down the hill in the thing. I'm starting to wish you'd knock it off before you break something you can't fix."

"But you're destroying it. It has value, Dad. It may not be expensive or have meaning to you, but there are a lot of people who would love to have a Jeep like this in good condition and you're just letting it sit out there and rot. Not to mention the fact that it will get you up and down the hill much longer if you actually take care of it."

His father heaved when he sighed. "I'm not going to argue with you about that car. I'm glad that people want cars like this, but this is my car, and I have a store to run and a home to keep up with, and I'm just not interested in another project." Vince let his fork fall to his plate and leered at his son. "Why are you being pushy about this?"

Pauline dabbed at the corners of her mouth with a napkin. "Can't you just relax, Peter? Why don't you go down to the church and see if anyone could use some help. You could deliver meals to shut ins or volunteer at the pantry for a few hours. They're always looking for someone to clean in the chapel. I can call the church office this morning to see if they have any tasks for you."

"Thank you, but no. I'll finish what I started. That car won't last if you keep treating it the way you have and then you'll just have to buy something else."

Breakfast continued in silence, which Peter preferred to the bickering. He might be a square peg in their house, but he was still their son, and he was allowed to care, even if they didn't like the way he went about it.

Peter watched the little Jeep carry his parents down the hill, and he followed an hour later. Winning the tug of war, he traded his rental car for his father's Jeep and went to work.

The broken slab of concrete behind the store was home to two rotting picnic tables, protected by a rusted metal canopy. Peter dragged the tables with their warped, moss-covered benches off to the side. He parked the Jeep on the concrete slab and removed the steering wheel, the dashboard, the seats, and the gas tank. He took out the shifters and taped off openings. Wiring dangled. He tied it out of the way. Standing to stretch, he noticed his mother, watching him through a window at the back of the store. Peter waved at her and hoped the weather would hold.

* * *

Tomatoes and slices of cucumbers fell from Pauline's cutting board onto beds of lettuce that lined her wooden salad bowls. The usual silence was broken by the sound of Peter singing in the shower. She'd hoped for a peaceful evening, but behind her, Vince waited at the table and fumed.

"I resent him coming down here, implying that we're inept. We can manage our own affairs. I don't need him studying me to see if I'm still capable. I'm not a frail old man who needs his keys taken away." Vince set his glass down hard enough for tea to splash onto the table. "And if he doesn't put that Jeep back together the right way, we won't have a car, because I don't have time for more projects."

"I really don't think it's that sinister, hon." Pauline placed the bowls on the table with a pile of silverware. "I don't think he's trying to take anything away from anybody. I know you don't want to go out there and help him, but you could at least try to appreciate that he's doing something nice for you. Getting him all riled up will just end in an argument."

"Getting him riled up. Wouldn't you know?" He waved a hand. "I won't say anything. But don't you say anything either. Every time the two of you are in a room, you have to tell him that he's going to Hell. Stop forcing your beliefs onto him. You know he doesn't want to hear it."

The bathroom door opened, and steam followed Peter into the hallway. Pauline leaned toward her husband and whispered. "There isn't any compromise in the path to heaven, Vinny. What kind of follower am I if I can't raise my son right?"

Vince's stare could cut concrete. "One who lets her family eat in peace."

"Piece of what?" Peter slid into a seat next to his father and drew his salad closer. He made a utensil set from the pile on the table and sliced into a cucumber.

Pauline knew that if Vince had a chance to answer, dinner would be ruined. "I just think it's wonderful what you're doing with the Jeep." Vince's knife scraped against the plate. She straightened her back and gave him a stare that silenced him.

"Did you see it before we left? I got a lot done."

"I saw you took a lot of things apart."

"Yup. The floor is scratched and bare metal is showing through. There's some surface rust. I'm repainting it so that it won't rust through on you. There's a lot of prep work, and it'll take a few days, but it will be good for the car in the long run."

Pauline clicked her tongue in disapproval. "It was going to rust?"

"It's already rusty in a few places. It happens fast, but I can fix it. It's just stuff on the surface."

Vince bowed his head over his pork chop, and Pauline plowed forward. If she left Vince an opening, she was afraid he would take it. He would fill the room with anger and she'd never be understood. "How did you learn to do all of this? You always liked taking things apart, but you never showed interest in cars when you were young."

"For a long time, I didn't have a lot of money. I had to be resourceful, you know? I fixed my own car when it broke. It's not that hard to do. You just work backward and think your way through it. And I bought a book."

"It's a shame we couldn't have helped you financially when you needed it." Her son rejected any help she offered, as if he were afraid of a catch. Like father, like son.

"I'm independent, Mom. I didn't need any help. It's not like I was starving. And I enjoyed getting through school on my own."

"But you shut us out. You ran away, and you wouldn't come back." Pauline ignored her husband's audible groan.

"The whole point in growing up is to go away."

"But we gave you everything. You never went hungry. We gave you a great education at home because we wanted you to do great things with your life."

"I did do great things with my life. I'm smart and educated, and I have a great job and a wonderful family. There is absolutely nothing wrong with my life."

Pauline laid her knife on her plate, careful not to make a sound. She smoothed the napkin on her lap. A million times she had told her son that every road led somewhere and not every destination was pleasant. "It is not a belief. It's a truth of life that if you do not follow the right path, you are going to hell. It is my job as your mother to let you know when you falter, and my job as a believer to spread the word. How am I supposed to stand back when I see nothing but damnation on the horizon for my son?"

"Damnation?" Peter spit the word. "What about all that judging stuff? Huh? Isn't all that evangelism just a way to convince yourself that it's okay to pass judgement on other people and get them to tow your line so you don't feel insecure about your choices?"

Vince slammed a fist on the table, and Peter put up a hand. "No, I'm not done. There are plenty of good people in the world who do amazing things who don't believe what you believe. You run a store and criticize your only son. There are people out there who protect orphans and fight injustice against minorities, and yes, they prosecute hate crimes. You can't possibly tell me that they are going to hell because they missed an opportunity to tell their son that he's not a good person."

"But that doesn't mean they're going to heaven." How could she have failed at teaching her son that the rules aren't that pliable? That man doesn't get to make them up as he goes along?

"This is exasperating. What does heaven even mean to you?"

"That if we live our lives right and we follow the rules, then we all get to be together and have everything we ever wanted on Earth when we die. But you're so concerned with the here and now that you'd rather spend eternity suffering than be in heaven with your family."

Peter laughed. "All of this is about a magical mansion in the sky? Everything you ever wanted, huh? What are you missing right now? What don't you have? What do you need so badly that you'd cling to ancient dogma that makes you alienate your family? It looks to me like you have a lot. And you're giving up what you could have for something you might never get."

"The word of God says so. And it gives us hope…"

"Hope? That kind of hope was great for people who were being buried alive and crucified by Romans. This is just the latest pendulum swing in a never-ending struggle for power and oppression. We don't need that kind of delusional thinking anymore. There's enough of everything to go around. Except maybe love. We withhold *that*, don't we? If a *real* relationship with your family in this life is worth less than an imaginary land where everything goes your way, then I would like an apology for being the one person you can't afford to love."

Pauline tried to bury the tears with a spoon full of peas. She looked to her husband but he'd heard her message and kept his opinion to himself. This wasn't the reunion she hoped for. It was the same circle of judgement and misunderstanding, and she had to keep going until he could accept her view. Some combination of words had to show him how wrong his path had gone. She lowered her fork to her plate and tangled her hands in her napkin. "That's not what I mean. You can be a good person and not be a good believer."

"Well, I am a terrible believer. You know, it's like that Jeep out there. We all have some surface rust, but you have to fix it before it takes over. Eventually, hate, just like that rust, will eat right through your entire frame, and there's nothing you can do but cut it out and start over." Peter stood and collected his plate and glass. "If you don't mind, I was outside all day, and I wanna go to bed so I can get an early start tomorrow. I am actually enjoying working on this Jeep for you, not because I expect anything in return. Not to prove a point. Just because it makes me happy to do it for you."

Vince dropped his fork to his plate. "We are not inept. You come down here with your fancy life and your computers and things that we don't understand, and you think that you're better than us because we're old and because she's set in her ways, but you're not."

"It doesn't have anything to do with age, Dad. I'm not trying to convert you, either. I don't mean for the life I live to be an insult to you, but if you feel that way, there's not much I can do to change it. I never said any of those things, and if I ever came across like that, then I'm sorry."

Pauline watched her son wash years of hurt and anger down the drain with the remains of his dinner. What if she could never make him understand? What if she went her whole life unable to guide her only son down the right path? Peter dried his dishes and put them away. He walked down the hall to bed, leaving Pauline alone to face her husband.

"Really. What were you trying to accomplish there, Pauline?"

"I was trying to get him to understand where I'm coming from. To understand that the path he chose isn't the path that we want for him. That the church wants for him."

"Maybe it's not a choice, Pauline. We didn't even get to see our son get married because you won't stop."

"It's not a marriage, though. Not in the eyes of God or the church or its laws."

"Ceremony, then. It's a marriage to them. It's all they can have. And those are your grandchildren. They're old enough to understand that their grandmother doesn't like their parents. Why do you think he's here? He's trying to put his family back together, and you're just giving him reasons to leave. Wrap your morality around that, Pauline."

"He called me judgmental. Am I judgmental?"

"Sometimes, yeah. Why can't you keep it to yourself? You've already told him that he's going to hell for living his life. You're done. Obligation fulfilled." Vince took their plates to the sink. "No invisible force is gonna tell me how to treat my family. A lot of families have been destroyed by stuff like this. The only reason we still have him is because he's been the forgiving one."

Pauline slipped away from the table, giving her husband a sad smile and a nod, and retired to the bedroom. From beneath the bed, she pulled the old hat box that once held her mother's Sunday best. Inside were drawings, tin soldiers, the stuffed rabbit that comforted Peter as a baby. She tucked it under the corner of her pillow and laid down to sleep. Religion was so full of contradictory rules. An eye for an eye, but turn the other cheek. Be a good disciple and raise your children on the right path, but ours is not to judge. It was nearly impossible to follow them all. She would err on the side of love.

* * *

Pauline stood on the milk crate in the stockroom. She watched her son wipe sweat from his brow. He pushed a rubber floor mat into the corners of the Jeep, reconnected the battery, and installed a new steering wheel. She jumped when he pressed the horn button into place, and it beeped its approval. Clutching her disposable camera, she stepped down from the crate and searched for Vince among the rows of shelves and at the register, but the store was empty. The screen door creaked when she pushed it open.

"Come on, Vince. We have to go back to the Jeep."

Vince paid the ice delivery driver, who let the door to the freezer slam.

"Is he done?"

"I think so. He put a new top on it. It looks nice." Pauline peered around the corner to where the Chess Men sat on the side porch. She needed someone to take their picture. "Walter! Walter, can you take our picture back there by the car?"

Pauline and her husband stood as bookends to their son. She wrapped her arm around Peter and smiled for the picture. She hadn't framed a new photo of him in nearly a decade. She thanked Walter and took the camera, looking down at the window to see how many more pictures she could take. She stopped when Peter tugged on her sleeve.

"Mom. About last night?"

"You don't have to say anything. You're right. Your father, too. I need to do a little soul searching, paint over some of that rust you were talking about. Things evolve, and times change. We eat pork." She tried to smile but making light of the distance between her and her son wasn't making her feel better.

"That's a pretty big step, Mom."

"Well, I've been more accepting of the weeds in the parking lot than I've been of my own family. Maybe it's time for me to accept that we're all God's creatures, and it's not my job to pick and choose." She tucked the camera into the pocket of her apron. "I hope the next time you come, you'll bring the whole family. I will prove to you that I can be better."

* * *

The mattress on his childhood bed sagged, its springs old and tired. Peter sat on the edge with the notebook in his lap. He added receipts to the first empty pages. A list of work, and a personal note that he'd written on a small piece of novelty note paper followed. His suitcase was already packed, sitting by the door. This time, he left regret behind.

He slammed the trunk of his rental car and turned to face his parents.

"Next year. Next summer. We'll all come."

Pauline hugged her son. "Do you mean it?"

"It's not a threat, Mom." He meant it as a joke, but perhaps it was too soon. "I'm kidding. It's a joke."

She swatted him with the tissue she clutched in her hand. "I know."

"And develop those photos for the notebook?"

"We will. I promise."

"Son?" Vince's hands were deep in his pockets, his eyes cast down at his shoes. Peter hadn't mended things with his father. Not the way he wanted to. "You did good work on the Jeep. I appreciate it."

Peter studied his father. It didn't matter whether he meant it or not. "No problem, Dad. I like doing stuff like that. It was fun."

As he drove down the driveway, Peter looked in his rearview mirror. He saw his father pat the Jeep on the hood as he turned to go into the house. At the bottom of the hill, Peter turned left and headed toward the highway. It was a long way home.

* * *

Cicadas sang their summer hymns and left their shells around the general store. Peter's youngest son collected them in an empty candy jar, showing off his collection to the Chess Men on the porch. His daughter ran the antique register. Peter stood on the porch and watched his father teach his oldest son how to drive the old Jeep in the dusty parking lot. They made circles and figure eights, and came to a stop by the front steps.

"There you go. Just pull the parking brake. By your knee. It's that simple." Vince patted the shifter.

"How old is this Jeep, Grandpa?"

"Gosh. It's going on forty years old, I reckon." Vince took the key from the ignition and lowered himself to the ground. Peter offered his son a hand as the young man maneuvered his legs from beneath the steering wheel, but the offer wasn't accepted. He scampered into the store. Peter and his father stood on opposite sides of the hood.

"It's probably time to get rid of this old thing," Vince said. "It's leaking like crazy. I can't keep fluids in it. It's got a noise that I think is the transmission."

Peter patted the fender. "Can't say I'm surprised. Do you want me to find somebody who could help you fix it? How about that guy you bought it from? He was a mechanic, right?"

Vince shook his head. "It's bad, but I'd rather not put the money into it. I think I'm going to sell it. It's done its job here. Time for someone else to make something of it if they want. Somebody out there will want it."

"Have you looked into what it's worth?"

"Nope. It can't be worth that much. It looks good, it just has normal age issues."

"I'll be sad to see it go. It's a shame I can't buy it from you and take it home with us, but we don't have room for it, and there's never any time with all the stuff the kids are into. And Nick wouldn't enjoy it like I would. He hates spots in the driveway. Are you going to put an ad in the paper?"

"I was thinking I might just make a For Sale sign. Put it in front of the shop and see what happens."

"Don't forget that notebook."

"Oh, we won't. Your mother keeps up with it." Vince looked back toward the store at the screen door that needed repair and the aging porch. "Pauline still in there with Nick?"

"I think so. Funny to see the two of them working together at a computer. We'll show you how to use it before we head home."

"I still don't see how it keeps track of inventory."

"It's easy. It'll help you keep track of the money, too. It's a lot easier come tax time."

Vince tugged at his belt. "It's nice of Nick to set it up for us. Make sure he knows how much we appreciate it. I mean, we'll tell him, of course."

"It's okay, Dad. I know what you mean. So does Nick."

* * *

The Jeep faced the street. A sign in the window said *For Sale -Enquire w/in*. People stopped, peered in the windows, asked questions. The first was a man who wanted it for parts. Next, a young father with low funds and high hopes. Then Walter, one of the Chess Men.

Walter tracked Vince to the center of the store where he slapped orange price tags on jugs of wiper fluid. "You're selling that old Jeep, huh?"

"Ayup. It's making noise, and it's leaking bad from a few places. It needs more work than I care to give it. I'm just too old to be climbing under cars."

"How much do you want for it, if you don't mind my asking?"

Vince pushed his hat up to scratch his head then pulled it back down into place. "You don't want that old thing. It won't get you around these roads."

"I was thinking about it for my land. I've been cleaning all that up."

"You still have all that stuff? From the old flea market?"

"Out of sight, out of mind. I'm never going to open another store, and it's just an eyesore. My son doesn't want all that stuff." Walter raised his sagging pants by lifting his hands in his pockets. "I've been using a hand cart, but it's really slow. That little Jeep would make fast work of it."

Vince pushed a bottle of wiper fluid farther back on the shelf. "You know, the Jeep might hold up for a job like that. It's got a solid engine, and the body is in great shape. If you keep adding fluids to it, it would probably see you through. I don't know if you would make your money back or not, but you could probably sell it as a project to somebody when you're done, or you could fix it up."

"Could do, either way," Walter replied. "What are you asking for it?"

"Twelve hundred or best offer. Why don't I go get the key, and you can take it for a drive? Just remember not to downshift into first in it. You can only go into first when you're at a complete stop. I made that mistake a few times."

Walter exchanged a check for the key, and thanked Vince for the Jeep. For the drive, he purchased several quarts of oil, some tea, and a package of licorice from Pauline. As he turned to leave, she handed him a black notebook.

"I know how much you like antiques. I think you'll enjoy this. The first owner started this book. It has the whole history of the car in there. There are pictures and notes and the full maintenance history. Make sure it stays with the car?"

Walter cradled it in one arm and flipped through the first few pages. "My goodness. I can't believe we ever dressed like that."

From across the counter, Pauline peered over his shoulder. A woman in her short shorts resting against the Jeep, grinning for the camera. The name Claire was written in pencil in the white margin. "Times sure have changed."

"It's like a time capsule."

"That it is. I hope we did it justice."

Walter started the car and adjusted the choke, allowing the engine time to get up to temperature at its own speed. It reminded him of the cars of his youth. Raw. Unsafe. He watched the first dried leaves of autumn scrape across the street and gripped the steering, hoping the Jeep would make it home. And get the town off his back.

CERTIFICATE OF TITLE

VEHICLE IDENTIFICATION NO.	YEAR	MAKE	MODEL	BODY	TITLE SEQ. NO.
8305 165111	1964	JEEP	CJ-5		

WEIGHT	CYL.	IF NEW DATE FIRST SOLD	DATE ISUED	ODOMETER	T.I.M.
			3 JULY 2003	EXEMPT	

VEHICLE OWNERS

WALTER GILMAN
2018 HANSON WAY
BUCK MOUNTAIN 21646

FIRST LIENHOLDER

RELEASE OF LIEN
(FIRST LIEN) Interest in the above
described vehicle is hereby released.

First Lienholder   Date Released

DATE OF LIEN

Signature   Title (if any)

SECOND LIENHOLDER

RELEASE OF LIEN
(SECOND LIEN) Interest in the above
described vehicle is hereby released.

First Lienholder   Date Released

DATE OF LIEN

Signature   Title (if any)

HOWARD STAUB
ADMINISTRATOR

This document is proof of your ownership of this vehicle. Keep it in a safe place, not with your license or registration or in your car. To dispose of your vehicle, complete the transfer section on the reverse and give the title to the new owner.

DIVISION OF MOTOR VEHICLES

CHAPTER TWENTY

Walter inched the Jeep up the driveway, feeling every bump in the cracked asphalt. Dried leaves snapped when he drove over them. Decades of ice, of freeze and thaw, had caused the drive to break down—ant hills, weeds, and moss making islands of the pavement.

At a clearing in the trees, the drive forked, and he stayed to the right, backing the Jeep into a barn. Its large wood doors faced the house. He left them open and walked to his front door, pausing to stretch his knees. In the kitchen, he thumbed through a stack of mail.

"I caught up with the guys. Had breakfast down at Jimmy's in town, then Frank took me out to the general store so I could get that old Jeep I told you about. I just came in for some water. Heading out in a bit to clear out that green shed. Little by little, we're gonna get that cleaned up."

Donna couldn't hear him but after a decade alone, Walter's unbearable loneliness was lightened by keeping her memory informed.

He stood at the sink, looking through the window at the rows of arborvitae. They obscured his view of the forty-two acres beyond. Overgrown with thorny shrubs and creeping vines, it was the final resting place of two dozen residential storage sheds, models that once sat in the parking lot of his flea market. Ivy, moss, and grasses surrounded the structures. Mildew crept up walls and doors. The wood swelled with water. And what remained of his life's work was packed within.

A cardinal landed on an abandoned bird feeder at the edge of the porch and left, disappointed, when the phone rang. The little caller ID box displayed the name of Jack's university. Walter pictured his son at a desk in a room lined with walnut bookcases, advising students on their life path. He grabbed a chair at his kitchen table and watched leaves skip across the patio, pushed by the wind.

"Dad, they can take your house away. You know that, right?" Walter could hear the familiar lilt of judgement slide into Jack's voice. He held the phone away from his ear, keeping his sigh to himself, while his son continued. "The town doesn't care. We have to find a way to move faster."

"What's this we? I am moving as fast as I can. I'm almost eighty years old. Trying to clear out all that crap is hard on a body. The grass grows faster than I can work around it, and it's not easy to lug stuff across that field. All I need is a little patience. It's my property, anyway. I pay my taxes. What do they care what I do with it? You should see the shacks people live in downtown. Windows half falling out of the house. I'm way out here in the woods, and my house is spotless." Walter's voice grew loud and high. "They had to be trespassing to see anything back there. Code enforcement officers. What are my taxes paying these people for, anyway? Running around on people's property and writing angry letters." Walter felt his face flush red with anger. He put the phone on speaker and carried it into the kitchen.

"Don't get mad at me, Dad. I'm not the enemy here. I'm trying to help, and you're trying to leave me with fifty acres of disaster area to clean up when you're gone."

"Of course, this is all about what you'll be burdened with when I'm dead."

"That's not what I meant, and you know it." Jack's sigh was audible. "Look, I'll call the town and see if I can buy you some time. Maybe if we just let them know you're working on it, that'll be enough."

Walter looked out the window over the sink, past the row of trees, toward what remained of his livelihood. They couldn't leave the sheds behind, those model sheds from the flea market parking lot. And they couldn't bring themselves to throw away the contents of the market when they closed it. They always thought that Donna would beat cancer. They'd pay the bills. Repair their credit and start again. "It was the best I could do."

"I know, Dad. It was a tough time. We're on the same team here. I'll call the town, and you just keep chipping away at it."

Walter swore under his breath and closed his eyes, regaining traction. Like hell they were on the same team. But he didn't mean that. His son was just trying to help. Walter carried the phone back to the table and picked at a loose thread in the tablecloth. "I bought that Jeep I told you about."

"That's good news, Dad. You should have led with that. Does it run okay?"

"Yup. It belonged to a mechanic for a few years before Vince got it. It's old, but it's been cared for. It slips a gear sometimes, and it's leaking a lot of fluids, but as long as I keep up with it, it should be all right."

"Is it rusty?"

Walter tried not to read anything disagreeable into Jack's words. "Not anymore. There was some on the inside, but Vince's son did some work to it." Keeping Jack informed was better than being questioned. "You probably want to know what it looks like back there, since the authorities have determined that it's...what did they say? Uninhabitable?"

"I don't wanna..."

"Everything is organized in those sheds. The bins and boxes are labeled."

"There must have been two dozen sheds. That's a lot of stuff, Dad. They're all back there in the field?"

"All of them. We didn't have a lot of time to prepare when we moved them. They aren't on foundations."

"They're rotting? Termites?"

"There are no termites, but it's not pretty. Some of them are starting to fall down. Out of sight, out of mind, I guess."

"What all's in there? That store was huge."

Walter mentally walked through the warehouse, through rows of tables and shelves packed with items discarded by generations. It wasn't an easy trip. It brought back painful memories of packing up the life they loved and the shame taxes they couldn't pay. "There were dolls, toys, records, tools, kitchen stuff, pottery. Home decor. Garden planters. My plan is to unload one building at a time. I'll bring it all up here to the barn and take pictures. Put ads in newspapers and trade journals. That little Jeep will make fast work of it."

A heartbeat of silence. The awkward kind that falls between members of a family when they've exhausted the present. Walter heard clicking on the other end of the line, like the button on a ballpoint pen being pressed again and again. "Alex will be glad to hear you got a Jeep," Jack said.

"Oh yeah?" He barely knew his grandson, a city dweller who moved a lot and designed fancy, new things like bridges and industrial equipment. He'd never seemed like someone interested in Jeeps.

"He talked about getting a Jeep before he moved last time. Maybe we should come down there this summer for a long weekend, and you can show it to him."

"That would be nice. To see all of you." Walter suppressed unwelcome thoughts. Maybe his son just wanted to visit and wasn't checking up on him. He offered his goodbye and stood at the back door, watching bees and birds dance among the arborvitae.

"I always feel anxious and negative, talking to him on the phone. Maybe a visit would be a good thing. It'll break up the monotony around here. And Jack can lend a hand cleaning up back there, if he's so concerned about it being done right." He waved the negative thought away. "I don't mean that."

Deep down Walter knew they wouldn't come. Six years had passed since he last saw Jack, and Alex hadn't visited since he was a child. There would be apologies and a vague offer to plan for another time. Walter hoped that Jack had a better relationship with his son than he did with his father.

He glanced at the phone and considered calling Alex to tell him about the Jeep but decided against it, given the hour. He would call another day.

* * *

A heavy Halloween rain pounded the roof. With a clap of thunder, branches cracked, falling to the ground. The storm left at dawn, and the air hung hot and humid over the morning. Walter sat at his desk, waiting for the sun to dry the earth, skimming the notebook. According to the yellowing papers, it was the Jeep's thirty-eighth birthday.

At midday, Walter and the Jeep crawled through small lakes and over twigs and branches to reach a tan shed with white trim. Inside, teddy bears of all shapes and sizes were packed like sardines in blue plastic bins. One wore a colorful birthday hat and a tiny red T-shirt that said "Happy Birthday" in crumbling iron-on letters. Walter propped it on the hood and dug the digital camera from his shirt pocket. He squinted at the display, tilting the camera to take a photo for the Jeep History Book.

"You're going to a new home tonight," he told the bear, placing it back into the tub and hoisting the bin into the back of the Jeep. "At least I hope you are."

That evening, while Walter waited in his brown recliner, listening to *Wheel of Fortune*, headlights bounced on the living room wall, and a minivan approached the house.

"I'll be right back," he called down the hall. "Just going to meet the lady who's here about the bears." He closed the door behind himself without waiting for a response, and stood on the front porch, ready to greet the visitors.

A young boy dressed like Superman scrambled out of his car seat, through the open van door, and bounced straight to the barn. "Mom! It's an old Jeep!"

"It is, honey. Don't touch," his mother called after him.

"You can sit in the seat if you want," Walter offered. "If it's okay with your mom."

"Be careful. You'll rip your costume before you even go trick or treating." She looked over the teddy bears, examining seams and eyes and ears.

Walter lifted the boy into the seat and thought about Alex again. About things he'd missed.

The woman extended her hand, offering a folded stack of bills. "They're exactly what you described. I'll take them." She thanked him, loaded them into her car along with her son, and they were gone.

The metal screen door wheezed and slammed behind Walter as he slipped off his shoes. "That's it for the bears. We're almost done out there. Gonna have a lot of free time on my hands when this is over."

* * *

The field was wet from the morning dew. Chaff adhered to Walter's work boots and the sides of the Jeep. He passed clusters of empty sheds which sat like abandoned homes in a forgotten cul-de-sac and unlocked the last one, tugging open the rain-swelled door and stepping inside. The air smelled of cedar, pine, and rust. Inside were two old car engines. A few transmissions. Boxes and bins of smaller parts. Maintenance manuals and books about cars.

What he couldn't lift, he pushed aside, uncovering oil-stained cardboard boxes. *Early Jeep Parts* was written on the side of one box in red marker. He placed it on the top of the stack and opened the flaps. Plastic packages of cylinders, gaskets, and seals were neatly labeled. Whether they would fit the CJ-5, he would have to determine.

"What do you think, buddy?" Walter held up a packet of rubber grommets and brass colored seals. "Does this look familiar to you?"

The little green Jeep carried boxes of parts and books to the barn, where Walter lined them against the back wall until he could find the time to sort them. There were different styles of carburetors, boxes of transmission gears, gauges and shifters, and plastic bags of cork gaskets. There were tailgate chains, bags of footman loops that looked like little drawer handles, and even a front grill. Among the boxes of books, he found a service manual—the kind used by dealers and service stations.

The pages were cool to the touch, and the book smelled like an old garage. He turned to a diagram of the transmission and left the book open on the hood of the Jeep, making a mental note to check the fluids. Larger and more frequent spots had appeared beneath it in the barn. Perhaps the gaskets he needed were already here. Maybe he would fix it or sell it. He patted the Jeep on its front fender on his way to the house, thanking it for the hard work and with that, the clearing of his property was complete. Just in time for winter.

Walter wiped sweat from his face and left his shoes by the door. "That's the last of it, love. We did it. There's still some stuff back there, but it's too heavy to carry. I'll just have a scrap guy take it away when they rip down those buildings in the spring. I found some Jeep parts too. Might be enough there to fix up the Jeep if my old bones are strong enough."

* * *

Winter hardened Walter's bones, making his joints thick and slow, but spring came early, its warm breezes pushing the cold aside. He welcomed the changing of the seasons, shoving open the barn doors and sorting through car parts. If he could fix the leaks and restore the Jeep, he could take it to car shows and the vintage car meets behind the fire hall on Sunday afternoons. He knew he had the time and tools, and after much research, he knew he had the parts. But he lacked agility and strength.

In the sweatshirt Jack sent him for Christmas with its ridiculous dancing reindeer, he stood next to the Jeep, his jaw set. Shaking his hands like a boxer before a fight, he crawled into the car and beneath it, unbolting and unhooking the parts that held the transmission in place. He strapped a transmission jack to the crossmember, but he was unable to slide it back to free it from the engine.

He struggled from beneath the car and rested on an old bar stool where he caught his breath and made a list of things that needed replacing. The solenoid. The distributor cap. The wiring. The brake lights wouldn't work. The fuel gauge wouldn't read. The fuel pump was failing. Walter tucked the list in his pocket and tried, one more time, to remove the transmission. He failed.

He inched his way from under the Jeep, closing his eyes hard against the head rush. He would consult the notebook. Perhaps call the mechanic whose card was in the binder, if he was even still in business.

Walter entered the house through the kitchen. "I'm just coming in to take a shower. Calling it quits for tonight. There's a lot to do, and I don't know that I have it in me."

Getting into and out of the shower was not the simple task that Walter took for granted in his youth. He steadied himself with the shower rail and inspected his bruises. Warm water eased his aching muscles, but it could not ease the pain within. Snapshots of the past fluttered like moths before a flame. Sliding into home plate during a baseball game. Playing on the floor as a kid. Swinging from a tire swing beneath an old maple tree. Swimming in the creek. The searing heat of a summer sliding board against the backs of his legs. Teaching Jack to ride a bike and dancing at his wedding. He would trade all the wisdom gained with age to live any one of those days again.

Comforted by his flannel pajamas, Walter stationed himself at his desk. Cool air rattled the blinds through the open window, and he pulled the notebook close. He started at the beginning. James and Claire and their adorable daughter. William's fear of failure. Ben's misadventure at college. Mark and Olivia. Peter's accomplishments. The mended past and hope for the future harbored by Vince and Pauline. All of the stories before his were youthful, full of promise and potential, stories of beginnings. Walter and the Jeep were no longer young.

He wondered what a future owner would make of the things he added, the photos of the Jeep by the sheds, with the teddy bears, and by the barn after a snowstorm. His chest tightened. What if he never got the transmission back into the car? How long would it take for rust to eat its way through, turning the metal to amber dust? Would the Jeep return to the earth? Would his son throw it away as if it were trash?

He tugged a small stack of paper from his printer. Hands shaking, his fingers slipped on pencils and pens in the desk drawer until one caught in his grasp. Blue ink scratched along the paper, fighting the shapes of the letters of his personal note—detailed instructions for his son. Not about the house, his affairs or his finances. Those were in his will. His letter was brief, expressing all of his love and none of his regrets. In his final act as a father, he urged Jack to restore the CJ-5 with his son.

Walter added his letter to the binder, along with the list of things the Jeep needed, and left the notebook on his desk, open to the first page. Gripping the back of his chair, he caught his breath and shut his eyes tight. He moved slowly, pausing in the hallway to kiss the painting of Donna in her wedding dress before settling into the bed they had shared. Through the open window, Walter could see the Jeep resting in the barn. The light from the moon brought life to the headlights, like a night watchman standing guard. Even if his son and grandson never put the Jeep back together, Walter was grateful for its company that night, as he let go of the past and drifted off, at peace, into his last deep sleep.

CHAPTER TWENTY-ONE

Alex scanned his grandfather's driveway. The edges were eaten away by clumps of crabgrass, their lanky, green arms reaching out to consume. Weeds grew between the broken blocks of asphalt. Jack pried his white knuckles from the steering wheel. "I really wish I got down here one last time before...this."

Two barn doors were open, just as Walter had left them. Alex turned in his seat to look inside. "There's the old Jeep he bought." It had to be thirty-five years old. At least as old as Alex.

"Yeah, it helped him clear out that mess, but it's in bad shape." Jack parked next to a Lexus and turned off the ignition. He scowled. "Lawyer's already here."

With a parting glance over his shoulder toward the barn, Alex followed his father into the house. A laptop was open on the kitchen table, and a small stack of manila folders and envelopes rested next to it, each displaying the blue and white logo of Tyler and Rowan, Attorneys at Law. Walter's seat at the table was occupied by a soft-spoken man who stood when they entered and introduced himself as the Tyler half of the firm. "People around here call me Barney." He extended his arm to the empty seats at the table.

"How was the funeral?" he asked with a look that Alex interpreted as business sympathy.

"It was nice. Small, like he wanted." Jack lowered himself into the seat across from the lawyer.

"Walter and Donna were married at that church, weren't they?" The lawyer looked to Alex for confirmation. He felt a tug of regret for not knowing and shrugged, turning to his father.

"In 1948," Jack replied.

"Do either of you need a moment to get a drink or take care of anything personal before we proceed?" Alex stifled a snort. What could be more personal than a death in the family? He brushed aside his disdain for lawyers, a trait he'd shared with his father, and picked at a tear in the table cloth. He was merely a bystander to the proceedings.

"Walter had very few debts. He had enough cash in his accounts to pay the last of his bills. A moderate amount was left over which goes to you, Jack. As for the property, according to the will, he wanted to divide it." Barney placed one folder before Jack and one before Alex.

"Divide it?" Alex pulled the folder close and opened it. A copy of the will was tucked in the right pocket.

"That's correct. He wanted everything behind the tree line sold and the profit given to Jack. Alex, he wanted the front acre, which includes the house and the barn and all of their contents, to go to you. His will included a second option, that the two of you could opt to sell all of the property in one parcel and deal with the proceeds as you see fit, if that's what you prefer. But his first preference was for Jack to have the profits from the sale of the rear of the property and for Alex to take ownership of the front."

Alex looked down at the will in front of him, waiting for the letters to form words. "He gave me the house? I haven't seen him since I was a kid."

Jack shrugged, his eyes following the lines of the will. "He asked about you all the time."

"I had no idea." Alex looked at the furniture, at the kitchen's mismatched modern appliances and old countertops, at pictures on the walls and knickknacks that meant nothing to him. His mind kept wandering to the Jeep in the barn. He ran a knuckle along his lower lip. "It's generous, but I'm not sure I want to settle down yet. I've moved six times in eight years. On purpose."

"And you've never lived outside of a city. You have a lot of debt from grad school, and I can't picture—"

Alex braced himself from tumbling into his father's spiral of negativity. He had a habit of wanting to do the opposite of whatever his father wanted and then seeking his validation. "I don't know what the debt has to do with it. It would actually save money to live here. I wouldn't have to pay rent."

"But you have to work."

"I work from home. All of my work is by email and online. I'm completely portable."

"How are you going to live out here in the woods? And look at this stuff. It's not your style."

The questions and financial implications of keeping or selling the property mounted. Alex scanned the table, looking for a pen to start a list, but his father seemed to have made up his mind.

"Maybe you could give us some guidance. I assume that the property will be kept together, which will make it easier to sell. We'll need a real estate agent. I'll have to hire someone to clear that junk out of the back. Maybe a property manager to oversee all of this? Can you recommend someone?"

It was impulsive. One of the most impulsive things Alex had ever done. But living in his grandfather's house, even for a short time, could solve a lot of problems. He could save a lot of money and put some distance between himself and the noise of the city. It could put space between him and Sarah, too, and the endless bickering that had already torn them apart. "I can work from here for a while. My lease is almost up, and there's no reason I can't stay here while I figure out what to do with the house."

"You're not going to want to deal with all this. Are you seriously considering living here?"

"I don't know what I'm going to do yet. There are taxes to consider. I don't know what all this is worth. My stuff is in New York. There's that Jeep." His words trailed off with his thoughts.

Barney placed his hands on the table and cleared his throat. Alex had almost forgotten they had company. "There are plenty of people who can help you, and nothing needs to be decided today. There's no mortgage on the property, which buys you plenty of time. There are tax implications, like you said. That's laid out in the paperwork here. Alex, you may want to talk to a financial planner. We can help you get started, if you'd like. But there is one more thing that Walter left for both of you."

Barney opened a manila folder and removed a plain, unlined piece of paper covered in shaky blue ink. Jack took it by the edges and laid it on the table. Alex read it while the lawyer explained. "This was found on his desk, on top of a notebook." Barney trailed off. "Essentially, he cared a lot for the Jeep that's in the barn, and he hoped that the two of you might be able to finish what he started."

Alex pulled the letter close, the last remnant of his grandfather's voice. From a vast vocabulary, from the billions of sentiments of love and hurt and loss, the man had pushed his shaking hands and dug these words, this request, from the rubble. Alex thought about his father's tense relationship with his grandfather, all the times his father sighed or let the call go to voicemail, and his own absence in the man's life. Beside him, his father thanked the lawyer. The man stood and collected his things, waking Alex from his scrutiny of the letter.

Jack followed him to the door, and Alex moved down the hall, opening doors and closets just enough to make out the form of the contents within. No one was there to feel violated or to judge him for his transgression, but he felt like an intruder, scanning ephemera and clutter, judging its value. A coffee can of screws and nails. A book of matches. Practical things accumulated during the course of life. The further he moved into the house, the more meaningful its contents became. A shelf of old oil cans. A half-burned candle. Shaving cream. His razor. The objects started to fit together, like puzzle pieces, forming the picture of the man that Alex had only known as his grandfather by name. All of these things were his responsibility now, but it was a legacy he didn't deserve.

On the concrete patio sat a round picnic table with a glass top, surrounded by chairs that were grayed with mildew. Empty terracotta pots still held the soil that fed the last plants to make their home there. Unintentional green stalks jutted from the pots, staking their claim in nature's eternal territorial dispute.

His father appeared at his side, his hands in his pockets. "I expected to be...I don't know...more sad about the place."

"You can be numb and sad at the same time."

"Yeah. Both of my parents are gone now. That's a strange feeling. I don't feel connected to this place at all. I never lived here, and I don't recognize most of what's inside. He thought I was nagging at him about all that mess, but I just wanted him to be free of it. I'm not complaining, but it's funny that's all he left me, and he gave the rest to you."

Father and son stepped off the patio and onto the damp earth, their footprints leaving similar-size depressions in the grass. They stopped at the arborvitae and looked across the field.

"He planted these trees since the last time I was here. He was trying to hide that clutter back there. It's just...blight. I understand what happened. The bills were out of hand, and they just couldn't afford to keep the store open. But still. All that rotting wood. What a mess."

Alex stepped into the overgrown grasses, and his father followed.

"There was a fence here, wasn't there? It was red? Tall. It was probably a normal fence, but it looked huge to me." The wooden fence had bordered the most vast, open field he'd ever seen. It was green and hilly with trees—different types and different sizes—all different shades of green. He remembered wanting to run, climb, and lie in the grass, his father telling him no, but his grandfather releasing him into the wild. He had completely forgotten that first taste of untamed nature beyond a suburban backyard.

"It was a normal-size fence, but you were little. It probably looked massive."

"Why didn't we come here more when I was a kid?" Alex looked down at the ground, thinking about ticks and snakes.

Jack frowned and rubbed the back of his head. "We were two different people. I wanted to live in a city, be a college professor. I moved away and went to school. They sold their old furniture store and bought this place. That junk store they called a flea market was their dream come true. We came here a few times when you were a kid. They visited us. Then life took over. They didn't take vacations, and we were always taking you to robot camp and to see space shuttles. And I was closer to my mom. After she passed away it all just became phone calls and cards."

Alex almost pointed out that calling his grandfather's career a junk store might have hindered their relationship. He was glad that his relationship with his father was better by comparison. No, they didn't see eye to eye. They had different worldviews and aspirations but at least his father never called his work *junk*. That he knew of. They walked across the field in silence, looking at the crumble and decay, remembering the vibrant landscape that once thrived here. Overgrown trees and vines created dark corners where the sun couldn't reach to dry the earth. Mold and moss took hold.

"This place must be full of mosquitoes in the summer," Jack said. "I can't wait to have all of this mess ripped out of here."

Alex couldn't bear any more negativity and his mind kept wandering back to the barn. "Did you read that letter?"

"I skimmed it. I'll read it later."

"That old Jeep. He wanted us to work on it together. He said that most of what we need is probably already there."

Jack grinded his teeth, a habit Alex knew was meant to hide his exasperation. It didn't work. "That's not my kind of thing…"

"Consider it? He thinks…he said it's mostly transmission work, and it's almost out of the car already. We might be able to fix it in a day or two while we're here." Alex hoped that if his father harbored any penitence for what he missed with his father, he might be willing to make up for it with his son. But he also knew that no amount of trying to work on a car in a damp barn would make up for two generations of stubbornness.

"What are you going to do with that thing anyway?" Jack asked. "Keep it? In a city? Where are you going to park it? If it breaks down, where are you going to work on it? Sitting at the curb? It takes a lot of tools to work on a car like that. You can't fit tools like that in your shoebox apartment."

Alex wanted to remind his father that he was perfectly capable of figuring out where to store tools, even if architects weren't the ones to use them. Instead, he picked up a stick and poked at a hole in the ground. "Voles."

He tossed the stick into the weeds, scattering crickets into the yard. "You know, I am capable of thinking through things on my own. I was only

221

suggesting that we consider what was in the letter."

Jack threw his hands up and stomped further into the terrain. "Maybe we can come up with something else instead of working on an old car. Go on a trip. I have a conference in Vegas in July. That could be fun."

"Vegas?"

"Just a thought." His father patted him on the back. "Let's head back to the hotel and see about dinner."

Alex planted his feet, unyielding. "Okay. But I'm coming back here after dinner."

"Why?"

"I haven't decided what I want to do yet. I'd kinda like to take a look around. Make a list of things I'd need to do if I want to move in."

His father blinked at him and shook his head. "Whatever you want. I'm telling you, you're making a mistake, but you gotta learn some lessons the hard way. Let's go get your stuff and have dinner, and I'll bring you back here."

There was a Denny's next to their hotel. Alex spent the twenty-minute drive wishing for a pen and paper. He opened a blank email to himself in his Blackberry and began a list of things to consider. He found himself staring at a Denny's menu without seeing it, grateful they never changed. After a Moons over My Hammy melt, Alex collected his bags from the hotel, and his father dropped him off at the front door of his grandfather's house. Only one lock stood between him, the past, and his future.

He dropped his bags in the bedroom and forced open the window. Tags fluttered from the end of a new mattress, still covered in plastic. Alex came to the slow realization of his grandfather's death. In his sleep. Replacing it must have been an act of kindness on the lawyer's part. He tore the plastic and tags from the mattress and found sheets in the hall closet.

Alex dropped to his knees at the kitchen sink and pulled spray bottles and cans of cleaners onto the floor. He memorized the dents on the baseboards and the grain of the hardwood floors. He removed soapy rings in cabinets and closets and traces of where creams and lotions once rested. What his grandfather smelled like, what he touched, what he consumed. He wasn't erasing his grandfather's memory as much as he rubbed himself into the fibers of the house, making it his own, blending the present into the past.

He found a flashlight and climbed the stairs to the attic. An old mirror. Christmas decorations. He inspected the electrical wiring and the plumbing. In a cupboard, he found a feather duster, and he moved through the house, removing the fine layer of dust that had settled since his grandfather's last cleaning. A trail of photographs led from the living room to the office and his grandfather's bedroom. He examined similarities in noses, jaws, and eyes in an early family photo on his grandfather's dresser. He saw his likeness there. Dusting beneath it, the reflection of the moon in the Jeep's headlights caught his eye.

Alex followed the beam of the flashlight across the driveway and into the barn, where he found a switch. After a click, an overhead tube light buzzed and crackled to life, then settled into a hum.

The barn was deep and long with a high roof and a concrete floor. Two folding tables stood end to end by the wall to his left. One held cans of paint and tubes of cleaners, grease, and lubricant. A crumpled receipt from two weeks ago. On the other table sat the Jeep's top and doors, with a twisted, snaking pile of straps and tie-downs. The Jeep stood alone in the far left bay, propped up on jack stands. A transmission jack was raised beneath it. Parts were scattered on the floor. A cable. An odd metal tube. Ratchets and sockets. A little magnetic parts tray with bolts. It looked as if his grandfather had stood up and gone into the house a moment before. And yet it had only been days. He could feel his grandfather's presence there, through the unfinished project. He picked up the pieces and turned them over in his hands. They were cool and smelled faintly of oils and oxidizing metal.

Alex stuck his head inside the Jeep and took a deep breath. It smelled like rust and soil, oil and leaves, the iron smell of rock, and rubber. It was a comforting smell, replaced by a whiff of gasoline when he leaned on the driver's seat and vapor rose from the gas tank beneath it. He tapped the thin metal tank. A hollow thud and the gentle slosh of fluid within.

The beam from his flashlight fell on the back of the Jeep, on the WILLYS lettering embossed in the tailgate. He traced it with his finger. It was pitted with age. The only rust to be found was on the exhaust pipe, which needed to be replaced. One tail light cover was cracked. When Alex stepped back, he caught his heel on a cardboard box, one of a dozen that lined the back wall. He followed the line of boxes, full of parts. Metal. Rubber. Plastic.

Three books rested on the hood of the Jeep, one of them open to a diagram. He could picture his grandfather standing there, as he would have done, contemplating the engineering of a timeless machine. Alex marked the place with a wrinkled receipt and carried the book into the house.

* * *

A car horn cut through the silence. Alex locked the front door. His shoes collected the morning dew, and he climbed into his father's rental car, adjusting his seat belt. "I think I'm going to keep the house and live here for a while."

The car lurched. "That was a pretty fast decision. I'm not sure you've thought this through."

"I did think it through. I made a list." Alex shifted his weight and pulled a folded piece of paper from his back pocket.

"Of course you made a list." Jack took his foot off the brake and let the car roll down the patchwork driveway. "You have to work. What are you going to do around here all day?"

"I'm gonna work. I work from home. I can work from any home. All I need is the internet."

"You can't live in the country. You'll go crazy out here."

"The cost of living is much lower here than it is in New York. I'll save a lot of money on everyday things. The income taxes are lower here, too. I'll have to pay property taxes, but they're a lot cheaper than rent. Even if I don't like living outside of a city, I can always sell it or rent it out." Alex folded the list and returned it to his pocket. "Plus, I can be here to oversee whatever you do with the land in the back. I really want to do this." The barn faded from view in the side mirror. "Why are you always telling me what to do? Like I'm five?"

"I don't know. Maybe because you tell me everything in the tone of a question, so it sounds like you're asking for my opinion. Maybe I don't want to watch you learn things the hard way." Jack lowered the visor, squinting as he drove through bursts of sun between the trees. "So what's your next move, then?"

"Call the lawyer. Tell him I'll keep the property. Paperwork. I'll figure it out. The rest is easy. Utilities. Move my stuff down here. Sublet or break my lease." Alex peered into the woods, wondering what wildlife he would encounter. "I wanna see where this takes me."

Jack turned the car toward breakfast. "As long as you've thought about it. What about Sarah?"

Alex could never make Sarah love him, and he'd long ago stopped trying. She wanted a suit and tie man who towed her perfectly polished line. Alex just wanted to live a simple life. "That was never going anywhere anyway. She won't be surprised. I'll call her tonight. It'll give her one last thing to yell at me about."

CERTIFICATE OF TITLE

VEHICLE IDENTIFICATION NO.	YEAR	MAKE	MODEL	BODY	TITLE SEQ. NO.
8305 165111	1964	JEEP	CJ-5		

WEIGHT	CYL.	IF NEW DATE FIRST SOLD	DATE ISSUED	ODOMETER	T.I.M.
			13 APRIL 2004		EXEMPT

VEHICLE OWNERS

ALEX GILMAN
2018 HANSON WAY
BUCK MOUNTAIN 21646

FIRST LIENHOLDER

RELEASE OF LIEN
(FIRST LIEN) Interest in the above
described vehicle is hereby released.

First Lienholder   Date Released

DATE OF LIEN

Signature   Title (if any)

SECOND LIENHOLDER

RELEASE OF LIEN
(SECOND LIEN) Interest in the above
described vehicle is hereby released.

First Lienholder   Date Released

DATE OF LIEN

Signature   Title (if any)

HOWARD STAUB
ADMINISTRATOR

This document is proof of your ownership of this vehicle. Keep it in a safe place, not with your license or registration or in your car. To dispose of your vehicle, complete the transfer section on the reverse and give the title to the new owner.

DIVISION OF MOTOR VEHICLES

CHAPTER TWENTY-TWO

Alex stood on one side of the Jeep, his father on the other, magnetic poles tugging at their fate.

"What time are you leaving tomorrow?" Alex tossed two beer caps across the barn and into the trash can.

One missed, and his father picked it up. "As early as I can. Have to be at the airport two hours before the flight leaves, and it's a two-hour drive."

Alex ran his finger over a chip in the paint of the Jeep's hood. "What do you think about coming back down here in a few weeks? Finish this Jeep?"

"I don't want to hurt your feelings but working on cars isn't my thing." Jack swung the Jeep's side view mirror on its hinge. "Another thing you inherited from your grandfather. Taking stuff apart and putting it back together again."

Alex lifted his chin and watched a spider build a web between a clock on the wall and an old gas station sign. "It does look like a lot of work, and it's not hurting anything where it is. Maybe I'll just leave it here until summer when it's warmer out and things calm down. Maybe you'll change your mind by then."

"Doubtful. I have no interest in lying on the floor of a barn, covered in rust and grease. If I were you, I'd get the scrap metal guy to take it away with the rest of the junk. Why don't you let me ask him to take it when he comes for the last of that stuff out back?"

Alex shook his head. "No. No way. It was the last thing he asked. I'll do something with it." He rested his forearms on the fender, holding his beer in one hand and picking at the corner of the label with the other. "What do you have against working on cars, anyway?"

"It's dirty. And it's frustrating. And boring. I don't even like to put batteries in the remote. Hooking up the satellite dish was the most stressful part of the last decade for me. Your grandfather was just trying to teach me a lesson. Again."

"By wanting us to do something together?"

"By forcing me to do things that he knew I didn't enjoy." Jack sighed and sipped his beer. "I don't really mean that. Did I ever tell you the story of our old Hudson Hornet? Something was wrong with it. I was twelve? Thirteen? Sitting on the floor listening to a radio show. Your grandfather came in the house, covered in grime. He asked me to help him, but I didn't want to. You couldn't record things like you can now. Anyway, I was rude, and I got in trouble for talking back. I deserved it, but I was sick of standing around fetching screwdrivers and wrenches. I wanted to read books. He never asked me to do anything like that with him again. For the longest time, I thought I'd won. Now that I think about it, I guess we both lost."

"That's why he wanted us to work on this Jeep?"

"Maybe he was hoping this car would make my relationship with you better than the one he and I had."

Regret sizzled off his father like heat from a newly paved summer street. Alex didn't see a need to let him roast in it. "I don't think we're that far off." The fact that they spoke like this at all was reason enough to believe it.

"We're not. We're not like that."

Alex wiped rust from the side of his thumb with a rag. "We have our differences. You want me to do things your way, and I want to make my own choices. But that's universal stuff. Being stubborn."

Jack sniffed and smiled. "Yeah. And some of this stuff gets easier when you get older. Parents stop trying to keep their kids from making mistakes, and kids stop looking for approval. Even at thirty-four. Relationships change." Jack took a sip of beer and held it in his mouth before swallowing hard.

Alex peeled the rest of the label from his bottle. His father had a point. If he didn't need the validation when he made big life decisions, he shouldn't seek the approval. The days of looking for permission were over.

Jack swirled the last sip of beer and held the bottle up to the light. He tossed it into the trash can. "I think there's an assumption that parents have it figured out. We don't. We're all just learning as we go. And by the time we're old enough to realize that our parents were just winging it, sometimes the relationship is just too strained to make up for the mistakes. Do what you want with the Jeep, Alex. We're good."

Alex's bottle followed his father's into the can. He smiled. "I won't torture you with the Jeep then."

* * *

A warm breeze pushed the cooler days of spring into the past, making room for early summer. Alex spent his Sunday mornings at the picnic table, listening to a regional radio show on his grandfather's old alarm clock. He pushed the clock to the right, then farther away. In just the right spot, the station would come in loud and clear, despite the trees and mountains. Callers advertised yard sales and services. A woman from a place called Elk River offered cakes for children's birthday parties. A man had a boat for sale.

He watched a squirrel bury a walnut in the yard, its butt bouncing in the air as it used all its strength to dig into the hard, dry earth. It was the only life he'd seen for days. The radio station went out of tune, and he pushed the alarm clock on the table again, seeking human connection.

Before him sat a yellow legal pad scavenged from his grandfather's office supplies. On it, he made a list of things to learn. Things his grandfather had always known. Weeds versus flowers. Wasp nests. He needed to go through his grandfather's tools. Lawnmower maintenance. He wondered where he kept the gas can. Everything old or broken had to be replaced. The Jeep.

As the dust settled on his new life, the Jeep was buried under the sediment. It was too old to get him to the store, too slow for the highways, too much work to fit in around his job. A voice cut through the fog. "If you have something to sell, you can call us at eight eight eight…"

In the barn, the Jeep waited.

CHAPTER TWENTY-THREE

Kate glanced down at the scrap of paper where she'd written Alex's instructions. Stay left at the fork in the driveway. She silenced her radio. The Jeep sat on jack stands in a barn to her right, the house to her left, long and low. Weeds grew in the gutters. The roof was shaded by trees. Mossy. A man stepped through the front door of the house and onto the porch, not at all the older man she expected. He was her age, maybe a little older. T-shirt and jeans. Clean shaven. He looked like the kind of guy who went running for fun. She scanned the yard. There were no toys, no flowers, no decorations. She didn't want to stereotype, but this was not the home of a man who had a family. She'd had enough of men. Even the ones with families. This Jeep, if it really was the one, was perfect timing.

She climbed from her car and painted a smile. "Nice to meet you." She looked past him as she shook his outstretched hand. No need to be too friendly.

The barn was humid and warm but cooler than the air outside. Sunlight streamed through the open doors and flecks of dust floated in ribbons of light. Alex leaned in the doorway. She felt his eyes follow her as she crawled in and under and around the Jeep, inspecting places that showed their age, finding the usual wear and tear along with a few surprises. She wiped a bit of engine grease and road grime from the data plate and ran her finger over the serial number. It was the one. When she lowered the hood with a metallic thud, she found Alex on the other side of it. Folding her hands and leaning on the front fender, she had no interest in meeting his eyes or letting him know how badly she wanted the car.

"It's what you described. Just like the pictures." The dust in the barn made her want to sneeze. She transferred grease onto her nose when she rubbed it and stepped back, conscious of her body language and wanting as much distance as she could create. "A few surprises but not much."

"What did you find?"

"There's no way of knowing why he dropped the transmission and transfer case," she said. "It could be gaskets, or it might need a rebuild. Exhaust needs to go. The steering knuckle is bad. The tires are shot, but the wheels look good. The wiring is probably done for. If I'm gonna go through the trouble of rewiring it, might as well switch it over to an electronic distributor and give it new spark plug wires. These engines last forever, though. The body is in good shape. There's a tiny ding on the right fender here, and there are little cosmetic things like that cracked tail light, but that's all negligible." She patted the fender and stood back. "It's showing its age, but it's all normal stuff, except for that transmission question." It was perfect. It was even the same color as in her father's pictures. But she didn't want Alex to know that.

"You know a lot about Jeeps. It's been sitting here for a year, and I didn't notice half of that."

"I've been looking for the right one for a long time. I wish it didn't need so much work, but it is what it is." She accepted a shop rag when he offered it to her.

"I'm a little surprised. People either want a complete Jeep or more of a project. Obviously you know what you're getting yourself into."

"Almost like it was sitting here, waiting for me." She latched her side of the hood. "Do you know anything about it? Any history?"

"I wish I did. I know that my grandfather used it around the property here. Other than that, I have no idea."

The notebook hadn't survived, then. She tilted her head and inspected her thumbnail. She'd detected an accent in Alex. He said in the ad that the Jeep came with the house when he inherited it. This guy wasn't from here, and he'd lost his grandfather. She started to feel bad for him. "I'm sorry about your loss."

"Thanks. It's okay. I didn't know him well." He stepped toward the sunlight. "Well, I'm an architect, not a salesman. I know nothing about Jeeps, and I haven't even looked at it that closely. You're the only person to show any real interest in it, so if you want to think about it and give me a call…"

Kate wrinkled her nose. She wanted the Jeep. Bad. She was disappointed at the condition, but she didn't want him to know that. And she would need to save more money if she had to pay what he asked for it. "I'm not much of a negotiator, but I'd love to try. Can I talk you down a bit?"

"Probably. The important thing is that it ends up in a good home."

"Can I talk you down a grand?" Kate didn't wait for an answer. She put up a hand to stop his protest. She could not lose this Jeep. "I obviously can't take it today anyway, but I thought I'd throw it out there. I live in an apartment over in Lennox, and I don't have a place to work on it. My friend Michelle is trying to convince her husband to let me use their garage. If it's okay with you, think about it and give me a call with a counter offer? Just, please don't sell it to someone else without giving me a chance?" She gave him her most charming smile and admonished herself for pleading with him but gave herself a pass. She needed this Jeep. No other Jeep would do.

Alex raised an eyebrow and a shoulder. "Honestly, it could sit here for a while. I don't need the space. Let me know when you've found somewhere, and we can go from there. I promise you get first dibs."

The voice in her head told her not to slip her hand in his and shake on it, but she did anyway.

* * *

The office still felt like his grandfather's. Alex worked at the old metal tanker desk, with its squeaky drawers and cold metal top. All around him, on built-in shelves, sat books about history and applying value to collectibles. Among them were photo albums and old newspapers. He would get to it all, one day. Donate or throw away what didn't suit him, and hold onto anything personal. Maybe tear down the shelves and line the walls with modern art. Through the window next to his desk, Alex watched a robin turn its ear toward the ground, listening for worms in the soil.

When his Blackberry rang, he looked at the caller ID. It was his best friend and boss. "Eric. What's new?"

"I've got your dream job here."

"Lottery winner?"

"No. How do you feel about two years in Philly?"

Philadelphia. Alex had been trying to get there for years. The closest he came was in the months before he moved to Buck Mountain. "You've got to be kidding me."

"Nope. Huge new development at the Navy Yard. I know you're not usually a site guy, and you love to work from home, but I can put you on as team lead if you want."

"That's a hell of a promotion."

"Promotion? You want a raise, too?"

"Funny. When does it start?"

"We're six months out of design phase. I don't need an answer for a while. If you don't want it, I'll give it to Kelsey."

He could pick up and move. Taxes on the house were cheap. He could shutter it, lock the doors, and still afford an apartment for a few years while he explored a new city. "Pencil me in and send me the details. I really want it, but I have to work out some other stuff first."

"That house at Walden Pond, I assume. How is life down there?"

"Good, I—"

"Wait. I almost forgot to tell you. I saw Sarah. She was all snuggled up with some suit guy. Banker or something. She wanted me to say hi."

Hi? Sarah barely said hi to him while they were dating. Of course she'd moved on first. She probably wanted to make sure he knew it. Anything to drive home the point that he was unlovable. "Meh. Hope she's happy."

"What are the girls like down there, anyway?"

"I wouldn't know. I don't think there's a big singles scene around here. I'm not interest in finding anyone right now, anyway. I did meet one girl. She came to look at that old Jeep."

"You're selling it? It looked cool in the pictures. I figured you'd fix it up."

"And do what with it? I don't have any use for an old car like that. I bought a new Cherokee."

"How much did you get for it?"

"Haven't sold it to her yet. She lives in an apartment, so she has to find a place to work on it, then we'll negotiate."

"You should let her rent out your place. She can work on it there, and you can get to Philly. Finally."

"Eric, that's the most sensible thing you've said to me in really long time."

CHAPTER TWENTY-FOUR

Sleepless nights took their toll. Alex tossed and turned and lay awake at night, and fought to stay focused during the day. The shiny newness had worn off months before. He was surrounded by things that were his but not his own. His identity seemed to fade behind mid-century furniture. In quiet moments, he felt pressed upon by solitude.

He folded the last of his laundry and thought of his father. How he had to prove him wrong. He thought of Sarah, how his idea of freedom led to isolation. Of his friends in New York. Again, he thought about Kate and that spot of grease on her nose.

Sitting at the foot of his bed next to a pile of unmatched socks, he looked out the window of his bedroom at the silhouette of the Jeep in the barn. He hated half-finished projects and abstract problems he couldn't solve. It was time to clean up loose ends.

Alex was not impetuous. Deliberate, cautious, and risk averse, but no one would call him impulsive. Until lately. Ordinarily, he would map out a phone call before he placed it, yet he scrolled through his recent calls and placed one before plotting his proposal.

"Kate! It's Alex!" He cringed. He hadn't thought this through.

"Alex! How are you?"

"Good! I was just thinking…I know you were hoping the Jeep would be in better shape. I'm never gonna do anything with it. It's just gonna sit there and go to waste, so I'll sell it to you for what you offered. How does that sound?"

"That sounds…that sounds great. But I haven't been able to find a place to keep it yet, and I—"

"Don't worry about it. I have tools and a barn and lots of parts, and the Jeep is already here. It would cost you a ton of money to have it towed somewhere. And we'd still have to deal with the transmission and getting it off the jack stands. You could work on it here, if you want."

The offer was met with silence. Alex sat on the edge of the bed and picked up a sock. He shoved his free hand inside it and turned it right side out. Maybe he gave the wrong impression. Maybe he should have given her an easy way out.

"This might work," she said. "You're not a serial killer are you? Do you have a pit in the yard where you'll keep me and feed me moisturizer?"

Alex was terrible at movie references, but this one he got. He relaxed at the joke. "I promise that I'm not. I'm not any other kind of serial killer either. You can even bring friends with you, if you want. Just promise not to sue me if you hurt yourself."

"Okay. The drive to your place is only an hour, and it's a really nice drive."

Alex looked out the window at the Jeep and ran a hand over the stubble on his jaw. This was either a solution to his focus problem or a very bad idea. The image of Kate with the spot of grease on her nose came to mind, and he pushed it away. "I'm glad this worked out. I don't know why I didn't think of it sooner."

"It's a generous offer. I promise not to be in the way. First thing tomorrow?"

"Tomorrow is perfect. There's no such thing as too early. I'm up with the sun these days. Whenever you want to get started is fine by me."

He hung up the phone and scattered loose socks on his bed, looking for more pairs, trying to remember where he'd seen the spare key to the barn. His grandfather's desk. He pushed aside old pencils with brittle erasers and pens without caps, looking forward to crossing the Jeep off of his list of things to do, pleased that he'd found a way to restore something without having to do it himself.

On his way down the hall, he paused at the door to the bathroom. She would need access to the house, to the kitchen. She would be closer than he'd considered. He would have to set boundaries to keep them apart, to keep from giving her the wrong impression, because the last thing he needed was another high-maintenance relationship that ended in anger.

* * *

Six scoops of coffee. Seven? Eight? Alex rubbed the spot in his chest where anxiety pooled and looked out the kitchen window while he waited for Kate to arrive. It seemed like a bad idea, a woman he didn't know in the barn. In his house. He rehearsed his greeting, trying to be hospitable and approachable without being forward or too welcoming.

The sky turned the faintest shade of blue as the sun came up behind the barn. He added two more scoops of grounds to the coffeemaker, set two of his grandfather's diner-style mugs on the counter, and pushed the start button.

Keys. He almost forgot the keys.

The junk drawer in the kitchen held tiny notepads and too many pens. The wood was stained with black, blue, and red ink. He sorted through wooden rulers, paper clips, and dried rubber bands that disintegrated in his hands until he found the keys. One to a padlock and one for the Jeep on a rusty keyring. He heard Kate's car and shut the drawer, poured her a cup of coffee, and stepped onto the porch.

"I hope it's okay. There's more half-and-half and sugar in the kitchen if you want it." Alex kept his distance. The coffee seemed a bad idea. Too welcoming.

"It's perfect. Thanks." She took a sip and stepped back.

Alex was grateful for the extra space. He intended to keep his distance.

"C'mon." He nodded toward the house. "I'll give you the tour."

Alex held the door open, and Kate followed him into the eclectic mix of old furniture and modern architectural prints. Where brown shag carpet ended and 1970s diamond and floral-patterned linoleum began, a small, round dining table sat, illuminated by sunlight that streamed through the sliding glass door.

"Someday, I'll redo this kitchen," he said, more aware of the contrast than he'd been before. Old wood cabinets and bronze hardware, aged by decades of hands, alongside stainless-steel appliances. "Down that hall, the bathroom's on the left. My office is on the right. That's where I am most of the time, if you need anything."

The sliding glass door skipped in its track. "This sticks. I keep meaning to fix it. You just have to lift up on the door a little."

Kate hadn't spoken. She clutched her coffee and nodded while he led her onto the patio. A mulch path led to the right, to the barn. "Use anything you want out there. You can move stuff around. Reorganize it. Make it comfortable. I never go out there except to get the lawnmower. And feel free to come in for anything you want. You can keep stuff in the fridge, too. I won't bother it."

Alex reached into the front pocket of his jeans and retrieved the small, rusted key ring with two keys. "One is for your Jeep, and the other is for the barn door. I usually leave it wide open because nothing ever happens out here, but I figured since it's your Jeep, you should be able to lock it up if you want. I have a spare to the padlock if you ever forget it, but I figured you should have your own set."

He dropped them into her open hand. She smelled like flowers. Some fancy shampoo, maybe. Her hair looked soft. Alex made a rule. No touching.

* * *

Kate held the coffee cup with both hands, clutching it under her chin and letting it warm her, though the air wasn't cool enough to warrant it. She heard the sliding glass door close when Alex returned to the house, leaving her alone with the Jeep. Her father's Jeep. The Jeep that got a flat and left him stranded at the curb of the farm where she grew up. The Jeep he taught his mom to drive. It was a daunting task, bringing it back to life, but she was suited for it. Mostly. Straightening her shoulders and cracking her neck, she began to relax. She opened toolbox drawers, inspecting the contents and closing them gently so the tools didn't slide. She found a small Zenith radio with a tuning dial and corroded batteries. She made a note to buy more. On a little chalkboard, she began a list of repairs, mostly from memory. With the last sip of cold coffee swirling in the bottom of the mug, she stood back and looked at the list. That's when she noticed the silence.

There were no neighbors, no machines, no children. No car doors or apartment doors. Cleansed by the incense of old wood, oil, and metal, Kate moved around the Jeep, running her hand along the fenders, the hood, the raised rear wheel wells that made perfect seats and shelves for tools. She ran her fingers along the curved metal edge of the tailgate and the snaps that secured the soft top. She traced the crack in the broken tail light and opened the fuel cap, taking in the sweet and sour smell of gas.

The Jeep spoke to her, taking her on a tour of its flaws and its wounds. She collected pliers and wrenches and screwdrivers, sockets and ratchets, and began to work, grease and oil and rust etching into her hands. Purified.

CERTIFICATE OF TITLE

9435B4821C6

VEHICLE HISTORY

VEHICLE ID NUMBER
8305 165111

YR MODEL	MAKE	PLATE NUMBER
1964	JEEP	XPN520

BODY TYPE MODEL	AX	WEIGHT	FUEL	TRANSFER DATE	FEES PAID	REGISTRATION EXPIRATION DATE
WAGON			G		$25	06/30/2007

	YR 1ST SOLD	CLASS	EQUIPMENT NUMBER	ISSUE DATE
	1964			06/25/2006

MOTORCYCLE ENGINE NUMBER

ODOMETER DATE	ODOMETER READING
06/25/2006	5248

REGISTERED OWNERS
ALEX GILMAN
2018 HANSON WAY
BUCK MOUNTAIN 21646

I certify under penalty of perjury that THE SIGNATURE(S) BELOW RELEASES INTEREST IN THE VEHICLE.

1a. _6/25/06_   X _Alexander Gilman_
DATE   SIGNATURE OF REGISTERED OWNER

1b. _____   X _____
DATE   SIGNATURE OF REGISTERED OWNER

Federal and State law requires that you state the mileage upon transfer of ownership. Failure to complete or providing a false statement may result in fines and/or imprisonment.

The odometer now reads _____ (no tenths), miles and to the best of my knowledge, reflects the actual mileage unless one of the following statements is checked.

WARNING ☒ Odometer reading is not the actual mileage ☒ Mileage exceeds the odometer mechanical limits.

I certify under penalty of perjury that the foregoing is true and correct.

DATE	TRANSFERER / SELLER SIGNATURE	DATE	TRANSFEREE / BUYER SIGNATURE
_1/25/06_	_Alexander Gilman_	_6/25/06_	_Catherine Colvin_

IMPORTANT READ CAREFULLY
Any change of Lienholder (holder of security interest) must be reported to the Department of Motor Vehicles within 10 days.

LIENHOLDER(S)

X _____
Signature releases interest invehicle. (Company names must be countersigned).

Release Date _____

KEEP IN A SAFE PLACE - VOID IF ALTERED

CHAPTER TWENTY-FIVE

Kate walked up the stairs to her apartment, sore and exhausted. She put Michelle on speaker phone and slid her key into the lock.

"How was Buck Mountain?" Her best friend's voice contained a lilt of sarcasm. "That place is such an armpit."

"It's not an armpit. It's just old. I wasn't *in* Buck Mountain, anyway. I was outside it."

"Fine. What's he like?"

"Pretty good. I can't tell what's wrong with him yet. I know something's up with the transmission."

"Not the car. Alan."

"Alex."

"Sorry, Alex. What's he like?"

"I don't know. I'm not there to make friends." Kate filled her Teacher of the Year mug with water. She set it in the microwave and slammed the door.

"You're going to be on this guy's property. He may try to talk to you. What if he does something completely uncalled for and says good morning. Are you prepared for that?" Michelle laughed at her, but Kate saw nothing funny about it.

"I don't have to make friends with everybody who talks to me." The microwave hummed, and the mug spun around like the wind-up ballerina in her childhood jewelry box.

"I get it. I do. But not every guy out there is Brad. Or what's his name. They don't all cheat, and they're not all out to get you. You have to trust somebody someday."

"I don't have trust issues. I have liking-people issues." Michelle made a sound on the other end of the phone. Whether it was a laugh or a sigh was irrelevant to Kate. Either way, she wanted to change the subject. "What are you doing this weekend?"

Michelle wasn't finished. "Don't change the subject. Tell me what he looks like. Alex, not the car."

At that, Kate laughed. Too impatient to wait, she stopped the microwave with three seconds left, put the mug on the counter, and threw a tea bag into it. "By your standards, he's a God. By my standards, he's still a guy and he's still scenery."

"At least the scenery is nice. What's he do?"

"He's some kind of architect or something. City guy. Likes new things. Looks like he's replacing all his grandfather's stuff. The kind of guy who used to have a gym membership. New Cherokee parked in the driveway."

"Doesn't sound like your type anyway."

"Good news for him, huh?"

"It's not your fault, Kate. You didn't make those relationships fail."

"Hell of a coincidence, then, isn't it? Being cheated on twice in a row. Being cheated on and lied to by someone who asked me to marry him? Like a professional hit. If he didn't want to be with me, why did he bother?"

"The universe is really weird. It puts us through strange crap so we can be where we need to be to do what it needs us to do."

"The universe wants me to fix my dad's Jeep. That's all I'm there to do."

* * *

Alex shivered. The proximity of his desk to the window air conditioning unit sent him searching for a sweatshirt. The late day sun threw light into the barn, and through his bedroom window, he saw Kate beneath the car. He hadn't seen her for days. She was quiet, brought her food in a cooler, and carried out her own trash. She was under the Jeep, at war with the transmission, which she tried to remove. The Jeep quivered, but the transmission wouldn't budge. A second set of hands would help.

He rolled his hoodie into a ball, stuck in the ethical crisis. She hadn't asked for help. If he offered, would it seem like he'd been spying? He tossed the sweatshirt onto his desk on the way down the hall and poured two glasses of water on his way to the barn.

He took in the smell of warm wood and damp earth, pausing at the threshold, not wanting to startle her. She stood at the folding table that held her tools, cleaning her hands, and looking down at a book. He cleared his throat, and she jumped, removing a pair of earbuds.

"Jesus. You scared me half to death."

Alex winced. "I am so sorry. I wasn't trying to pry or spy on you or anything, but I went to get a sweatshirt from the room at the end of the hall here, and saw you fighting with the transmission. Thought you could use a break. Water?"

She returned to the book. "No thanks."

"More for me then."

Kate started to put her earbuds back in but stopped, dropped the iPod on the table, and flipped the page, tracing a line of instructions with her finger. She intimidated him, like an agile force of nature. It was her project, and he didn't want to intrude, but his mind saw a challenge, and he couldn't resist unwinding it.

"Do you want a second set of hands?"

"Nope. I'm good."

"Do you know what's wrong with it?"

"Transmission's stuck."

"Is the shaft bent?"

"I don't know."

"Maybe the transmission jack's at the wrong angle. A second set of hands might help. One person to adjust the jack and the other to free the transmission?"

She flipped the page with a snap. "No thanks."

"I didn't mean to intrude. You know much more about this than I do."

She made a noise. A short puff of air. As if she hadn't overlooked his unintended transgression. He stepped away from Kate and further into the barn, looking for an excuse to lighten her mood. He loved a good challenge. The dashboard sat off to the side. It was nothing more than a long flat piece of metal with holes drilled into it. In the Jeep, wires snaked through the firewall. A dozen or more were attached to the back of a gauge.

"It's such an elegant machine," Alex said.

Kate turned another page but didn't look up. "I guess."

"It's just form following function. Accessible, you know? Like an open book. It isn't difficult. It almost seems friendly."

"What's that supposed to mean?"

Alex shrugged. "It's approachable. It makes you want to be near it. You want to be nice to a car like this, because it deserves it."

"Maybe the car just wants to be left alone."

Alex got the hint. Maybe it was a bad day. She was frustrated with the car. Perhaps with herself. He shrugged it off instead of taking it personally and gave her the space she wanted.

In his office, his tugged on his hoodie. Sitting at the desk, he opened a new tab in the web browser. He entered her name into the search engine.

Something he should have done days before. Lennox Middle School. Teacher of the Year, 2002. Either this was a really bad day or Lennox had low standards.

* * *

Ancient gear oil that smelled like month old deviled eggs left in the sun dripped into a puddle beneath the Jeep. Kate tried to avoid it. Two days of lying in it, and she still wasn't used to it. If the jack was at the wrong angle, even a few millimeters could make a huge difference. She pulled down on the handle of the hydraulic jack. After every small adjustment, she tugged on the jack, hoping it would budge on its wheels and pull the transmission from the engine. Finally it gave way. The shaft came free. She didn't even care that her hair was lying in a pool of oil.

She inched from beneath the Jeep, her jeans and T-shirt stained. Her hands were slick with grease and oil. She took a red rag from the stack on a table and rubbed at her palm, her life line stained black. Her eyes wandered from the barn to the back yard, where morning dew lay on the grass like a billion diamonds scattered by the wind. Then Alex appeared, and she turned her back to the scene, picking up the chalkboard where she kept her list of work.

"I brought you a cup of coffee. Hope you don't mind."

She took in a deep breath. Metal and sulfur and damp wood. She held it in for a second, letting it baptize her, wash her clean. She turned to face him and accepted the coffee. His fingernails were neat and trim. Hers were caked with stubborn traces of grease and dirt.

City boys, she thought. *They never get dirty.* She thanked him for the coffee.

"You got it out."

"Were you watching me?"

"No. No, I saw your car and figured you got here early. I just woke up."

He was fully clothed and smelled like a soap. She didn't believe him.

Alex walked away from her, toward the car, and looked into the transmission. "How long did it take?"

"Half an hour, maybe."

"I thought you'd be more excited."

Kate pushed aside tubes of grease, making room to lay the chalkboard flat. "There's still a lot to do."

"Like what? What's next?"

She shrugged the stiffness from her shoulders. "Exhaust. Brakes. Wiring."

"How hard is the wiring?"

"Depends on how much of a fight the Jeep wants to put up."

"So, what's wrong with the transmission? Do you know yet?"

Kate opened the cover of the thick restoration manual and let it fall to the table. Knowing he couldn't see her face, she allowed herself to roll her eyes. It felt good to release some tension, but if he wasn't going to leave her alone, she was going to need thicker skin.

"I don't know, okay? I just got it out of the car." She didn't look up from the book.

"Sorry to bother you. I guess I just got a little excited. It looked like you were almost done and on your way out of here." Alex's footsteps on the hard concrete were soft, more like shuffles. He stopped at the door to the barn. "Sorry. That was mean of me."

Kate used a small piece of chalk, no bigger than a thumbtack, to cross removing the transmission from the list. Her hand shook and the line wavered. She should have been more friendly. He'd been so welcoming. Even his retort bordered on pleasant.

"No. I deserve it. It's been a rough few days. I'm not usually this grumpy."

When she looked up, she realized she was alone.

* * *

The hot air of summer grew thick and wet. Heavy raindrops tapped on the air conditioner in Alex's office. With a crack of thunder, the rain came fast, pounding on the roof. It hid the sound of the screen door but not the sound of water rushing in the kitchen sink. The power went out with a snap. Alex closed his laptop, took the small plastic flashlight from his desk drawer, and made his way down the hall to the kitchen. Kate hunched over the sink, her hand under a stream of water.

"Do you have any bandages?" she asked.

"As often as I cut myself? Of course. How bad is it?"

Kate's eyes were fixed on her feet. Blood flowed from a deep gash. Alex didn't want to alarm her.

"It might need stitches but maybe not. Let's clean it up." He dragged a kitchen chair to the sink. "Sit. Elevate it. What happened?"

"I was using a paint scraper to remove the gasket from the transfer case. Stupid thunder. I jumped, and it slipped."

"Looks painful." Alex wet the end of a clean dishrag and wrapped it around her hand, applying pressure. "Let's see if it'll stop bleeding on its own. Keep your hand up."

He dragged a second chair into the kitchen and sat across from her. Outside, the sky was barely light enough to see the wind toss the treetops. "Did you clean it out really well?"

She nodded. "It was pretty gross. Bits of gasket were stuck in there."

"Let's get your mind off of it for a second. Talk about something else." He looked around the kitchen. "What do you want for lunch?"

"What?"

"This storm should push out of here. There's not much here to eat, so I have to order out. There's a deli not far from here that will deliver. Thought I'd get a pastrami on rye. It's not New York, but it's pretty good. My treat.

Something you can eat with a fork, maybe?"

"I can pay my own way." Kate's jaw set, and her nose twitched, a flash of frustration or resistance. Maybe it was pain. "I do like pastrami on rye."

Alex tried to catch her eye, but she was fixated on the spot of blood that seeped through the dish towel. "I hope this wasn't new."

"Nah. It was old. My grandfather's. I have a bunch more." He peeled back the layers. The cut was deep, but the bleeding had slowed. "I think you're going to be okay. I don't think you need stitches."

He uncurled her fist and rubbed the tips of her fingers with his. "Do you feel that?"

Their eyes met. "Feel what?"

Her fingers were soft. Alex wasn't prepared for the lurch of his stomach, for the attraction. He swallowed, his mouth dry. "I'm checking for nerve damage. Do you feel anything?"

She pulled her hand away. "Yeah. I feel it."

She felt it, too. She had to. He knew he should get back to work, put back the distance between them. But her hand needed bandaging and she probably couldn't do it herself. "Do you trust me?"

"Why?"

"To bandage your cut? It'll be hard for you to do it with one hand."

* * *

Kate thought she had the upper hand when it came to Alex. She thought she had control of her emotions, but as she set her pastrami on rye on her plate, her good hand shook. She laced her fingers and put her hands in her lap to hide her clumsiness, willing herself to get it together and wishing she had an excuse to eat in the barn. She didn't want to like Alex. She didn't want to find him charming or kind. For all the cold shoulders she'd turned his way, he was nicer to her than she deserved. Not knowing where to look, her eyes darted from her plate to the print on the living room wall. "That print. What is that?"

"It's a section of a bridge. It was a gift from Eric. My boss. The first thing I ever designed."

"Where is it?"

"It runs over a creek in upstate New York."

"Is that where you're from?" Kate rescued a piece of cheese that fell from her sandwich. She swore that was the last personal question she'd ask. "I mean, you're not from here."

"That obvious, huh?"

"A little. Not in a bad way. You said you didn't know your grandfather very well and you don't seem…like you grew up in Buck Mountain."

"I grew up in New Haven. Then I moved to New York. I lived in Boston for a while and then Chicago, Seattle, then back to New York. I was thinking about moving to Philly before my grandfather died, then I inherited this place and thought I'd give the rural life a try for a while."

"So how is it? Rural life." Half of her didn't care if he liked Buck Mountain. She didn't care if he loved the scenery, the quaint towns, the hospitable people. But the other half of her was happy to sit with someone who didn't know how much she hurt. Someone who didn't know she was cold and unfeeling, that she expected the worst from people and usually got it. Someone who didn't know how hard she tried and how hard it was to heal.

"Jury's still out. There's a steep learning curve. Food shopping is strange. I used to be able to find food on every corner. Now I have to know what I'll want for dinner in four days. And knowing how to cook it is a whole new challenge. Foxes at night? Horrifying. And wasps. I don't know how to get rid of those. Also, are deer bad?"

Kate swallowed hard and stifled a laugh. "What do you mean?"

"Are they mean? Do they attack? I've seen them in the yard. Some of them are huge. Rabid deer. Is that a thing?"

"Um. No? They like to jump in front of cars, and they'll eat your plants. They can get protective, but mostly they're harmless. They just run away."

Alex nodded. "Good to know."

"My turn, again. How long ago did you move here?" She had been so cold to him, but he still treated her like a friend. She almost forgot that she wasn't in the market for a new one.

"About a year ago."

"Still new, then. Welcome. Around here, you're new until someone newer moves in. That could take a generation."

"Thanks. Feels like ten years, trying to get settled. Most of this stuff was his. It's been neat getting to know him while living in his shoes, but I want to replace most of it. I'm not really into antiques. My style is more modern, industrial. Although, the longer I live with some of it, the more I like it."

"Sounds like rural life is growing on you." He wasn't so bad. He didn't deserve her cold shoulder. "So why didn't you want to keep the Jeep? It was your grandfather's. You're out here in the woods. Why didn't you want to restore it yourself? It almost seems like a movie. A city-dwelling architect inherits a broken Jeep and a house in the woods. I can think of a thousand reasons for you to fix this car. Why not?"

Alex laid his sandwich on his plate and looked out the door. She followed his gaze. The sun had gone behind a cloud, shading the porch. Suddenly, the question seemed like a lot to ask. Of Alex and herself. Once they became friendly, there would be no going back without a fight. She rubbed the bandage on her hand and felt the sharp stab rush toward her elbow.

"I'm sorry." She shook her head. "I shouldn't have asked you such a personal question. That's none of my business."

"No. No, it's fine. It's a good question." He picked at the crust of his sandwich. "A lot of reasons, I guess. I can see the Jeep from my bedroom window. It haunted me for a while. The longer I looked at it, the more I knew I'd never do anything with it. Even if I did fix it up, I'd never drive it. It was just sitting there, rusting away."

"It's good to know when to walk away."

"It was hard. My grandfather left a note about it. He wanted my dad and me to restore it together, but my dad's not into stuff like that. That contributed to the guilt and regret, I guess."

"That's a lot of pressure."

"Tell me about it."

She looked down at her hands, at the grease and dirt that connected her to Alex and his grandfather and her father in a chain of stewardship. She felt bad for being cold to him. Her past, her problems, shouldn't be his. "I imagine those voices are pretty loud when you're out here in the quiet."

Alex laughed. "Oh, yeah. It's more than the lack of traffic and city sounds. I'm an introvert, and I'm used to working from home, but yeah, it's really isolating out here. That's why I offered for you to work on the Jeep here. It's been mutually beneficial."

"I can see why." Kate reclined, relaxed, glad that his motivation had nothing to do with attraction, but she reminded herself to keep her distance anyway. "I'm a teacher. I teach English to middle schoolers out in Lennox. I'm around kids all day until the summer comes. Then I'm alone in my little apartment while all of the other adults are at work. It's too quiet sometimes."

"What do you do with your summers out here in the wilderness, other than fix Jeeps and sit in your apartment?"

"I volunteer for a museum. Watch a lot of movies. Read. Hiking. There are so many beautiful lakes and creeks."

"That sounds nice." Something in Alex's demeanor, the way he rested

253

his arm on the table, the tilt of his head when he smiled, cemented for Kate the need for distance. She wiped her hands on her napkin and tossed it on her plate. "But there are also bugs. And bees. And animals. I'll make a list of great hiking spots for you and leave it on the counter."

"That would be great. Thanks." Alex reached across the table and took her plate, stacking them. "We should do lunch sometimes. Break up the day."

"Yeah, this wasn't bad," Kate replied. "The sandwich. It was good."

Kate wasn't sure how to hold Alex at arm's length when he drew her in. Her stomach gave a lurch, and she put a hand on it to calm her nerves. She forced herself into a relaxed position and hoped her mind would follow. He wasn't asking her for anything. He hadn't lied to her or pretended to be someone he wasn't. He wasn't manipulative. She told herself it was okay to ask.

"Hey, Alex? About the transmission. With my hand like this, maybe I could use a second set to remove these gaskets. Would you mind? Would you like to help?"

Alex gave her that look again, the one that made her insides turn to jelly. "Yeah, that might be fun. You want help now?"

"No, not now. Tomorrow? I think I'm going to clean up out there and head home. Elevate this thing. Put some ice on it or something and rest before I dig in again." *Make a little space before I make a big mistake.*

"Do you want some ice? I have an ice pack. You can take it with you."

Kate smiled and lined up her placemat with the edge of the table. "That's nice of you. No, it's okay. I think I'll just clean up and hit the road."

"Okay. Let it rest and heal a little." Alex took their plates to the sink. "Kate. *Psst.* Kate," he whispered. "Come here. Look."

She turned in her chair. Through the door she saw a deer walk through the yard, lifting its feet in a high step through the wet grass. It stopped and looked back. More deer would follow. Careful not to scrape her chair across the floor, she stood and joined Alex at the kitchen window.

"They always move after the rain," she said. A dozen deer joined the first, ears alert and heads high. "Looking for food."

"Look at the little one. It's so small. How long do they stay with their mothers?"

"A year or two, I think."

The deer moved along the row of arborvitae and into the empty field beyond. Someday, there would be houses there. Neighbors. Kids with bikes and vegetable gardens. For now, it was a sanctuary. Alex put his arm on Kate's shoulder and leaned forward. "And they're not mean?"

"They do get diseases. I don't know if they can get rabies or not. I'm not much of an expert on the dangers of wildlife."

His arm was warm. She let it stay.

* * *

The clock said three. Alex gave up on sleep. The television offered nothing but infomercials and old game shows. He tried to read, but Kate occupied too much space in his mind, and the words wouldn't stick.

Then Sarah. The feeling of trying so hard to please someone and never being good enough. He tossed the remote on the coffee table, pinched the bridge of his nose and squeezed his eyes tight.

He wasn't willing to travel that road again. Kate wasn't even kind half the time. She was grumpy and wanted nothing to do with him. Why did he gravitate toward people who didn't make him happy? The sooner she finished the car and moved on, the sooner he could find his balance and figure out how he fit into this new landscape. Maybe it wouldn't be too late to take the job in Philadelphia.

In dirty jeans and an old T-shirt, he opened the barn. He spread an old sweatshirt on the concrete floor and scraped gasket material from the machined surfaces. There was worth in the Jeep that he hadn't seen before. It was a simple machine, form following function. Elegant, in a way. He could identify with it. Something almost cast aside, no longer needed or valued. Unlovable, but being made new again. Finished with the transmission and finished with Kate, he wiped gear oil and rust into his jeans, staring down at the gears. He wished something would come along to mend his broken gears, replace his broken parts with good ones, and put him back on the road again.

CHAPTER TWENTY-SIX

Kate's predawn drive wound through patches of fog. Fitting weather for the feelings she'd passed through. She'd been mean to Alex, but she didn't intend to harm him. Keeping him at a distance kept him safe. She wanted to apologize, to explain, to be forgiven for the lapses of kindness. To be forgiven for years of misplaced anger. Michelle had been telling her all along that it wasn't her fault, that she had to forgive the men who'd done her wrong and love herself, but she'd wasted so much time, so much energy, doing it all backwards. It took quiet moments with the Jeep to hear the message through the mayhem. But even if he accepted her apology, it would only be a stepping stone. He would expect her to change. She would need new methods of protection. New ways to distance herself from him. In moments of clarity, she knew that wasn't the answer. That wasn't who she wanted to be.

She'd already pushed herself past the point of discomfort and toward a friendship. Now she needed to stop thinking about ways she could screw it up, stop counting ways to run if she did. She needed to tell Alex the truth.

Kate turned into his driveway. Light spilled from the open barn door, through the thin fog. Inside, Alex stood over the transmission, steam rising from the coffee cup between his hands, peering down at the gears like an oracle at the well. Wisps of fog followed her into the barn, and she stood across from him. The machined surfaces were clean. He had removed the gaskets while she slept.

Alex didn't look at her. He was cold and distant. She knew the look, because she wore it often.

She whispered, not wanting to disturb daybreak. "You've been up for a while."

"I've been doing a lot of thinking."

"Yeah? I know the feeling. Anything you want to talk about?"

"Nah, just personal stuff." He knelt over the transmission, moving the gears. "I got bored. Looks like just this one gear. It's pitted and gnawed up on the edges. Everything else looks good, though. I found the replacement you need. It's on the table."

"Thanks." Kate offered him a smile.

It broke something within Alex. Like a rubber band stretched past its limit, snapping with the release of tension. He looked at the toes of his sneakers and shrugged. "Wanna come inside and have some coffee with me? I was just about to make a second pot."

* * *

Alex sat on the floor of the barn next to his empty coffee cup, spinning the gears around the shaft, moving bearings back and forth and watching the gears engage. His mind was elsewhere, but he couldn't have told Kate where if she'd asked. He did wonder why he was still in the barn, considering how much work of his own he had to do. He knew the answer had something to do with Kate but wasn't sure he could accept it.

She sat next to him and laid a pair of latex gloves in his lap. "You might want these, if you're gonna help."

Was he still helping? He hadn't decided. "What's the next step?"

"For me to apologize."

Alex lined up the fingers of the stretchy blue gloves. "You don't have to apologize."

"I do. I've been grumpy and distant, and I intentionally tried to keep you away. I have a lot going on in my world, but none of it is your fault. I shouldn't be mean to you. You've been nothing but kind to me."

"I wouldn't say you were mean."

"I was mean, and I owe you an explanation."

"You really don't."

She waved her bandaged hand. "I do. I'm a bad judge of character. I grew up in this ideal little world where everybody could be trusted. Hard work and loyalty paid off, you know? But the real world isn't always that way. I've met my fair share of challenges. I started looking for this Jeep after a string of broken trust, and I'm learning that it isn't all or nothing. I can't stop trusting everyone because other people made bad choices."

It explained a lot. How she would reveal a bit of herself, let down her guard enough to laugh at a joke before shutting him down with a short comment or a biting phrase. It was the lighthearted Kate who kept him coming back for more. Alex wondered if revealing any of his own pain would bring her comfort, but he wasn't ready for her to know how unworthy he was. "We all go through that, at some point. Stop trusting for a while."

"Maybe for a little while, but I've been turning it into a personality trait. I'm trying to stop. Can this be a clean slate?"

Alex put his hand on her knee, a kind pat, a gentle gesture. "You got it. So what are these gloves for?"

"While the Jeep's in the air and the tires are off, I want to give it new brake cylinders. Then the exhaust. My hand should be better by then, and we can put the transmission in, if you still aren't sick of me."

Alex didn't hear half of what she said, because she lit up when she smiled. The whole barn lit up when she smiled. "I thought you wanted to do this on your own."

Kate shrugged. "Is it okay if I admit that I like having company?"

Alex considered his grandfather's old car. He'd enjoyed working on it, bringing something back to life instead of throwing it away. He decided to accept the invitation but warned his inner teenager to hold it together and not do anything stupid.

"It's a perfectly fine thing to admit," he said. But he couldn't bring himself to admit the same to her.

Morning wore into noon. The harsh rays of afternoon sun made their way into the barn as the sun took the apex toward the horizon, and the last of the brake cylinders were replaced. Alex's stomach grumbled, and he leaned around the car, trying get a good view of the clock.

"Does that clock tell the right time?" he asked.

She checked the time against her phone. "Seems to. I'm getting hungry, too. Lunch break." Rubbing her sore hand, she pulled their scattered tools into a pile. "This really is an awesome machine, isn't it? This whole car?"

"The result of designing a car that can be assembled from a crate, withstand a war, and be maintained in the middle of one." Alex rolled the last wheel to Kate, who lifted it onto the studs. It was easy, working together.

"Most people can spend their whole lives riding around, driving cars, and never know what makes them tick. They have no idea that it has a heartbeat." She finger-tightened the lugs.

Alex stepped beside her and tightened them with a lug wrench. "Did you ever notice how no two smell the same? There's a classic car get-together thing behind the firehall on Sundays. Went over there last weekend and noticed it. I'd never thought about it before."

"I never noticed that, but now that you mention it, you're right." Kate sat on a stool and wiped grime from a pair of spring pliers. "Cars amaze me. We had to accomplish so much to get here. Making glass. Refining oil. All this cork and grease and rubber. We had to build factories to refine raw materials and make sheets of metal and batteries. And all these details, like the little coiled choke cable. Just because we wanted to go forward. This mass of metal all because we wanted to go somewhere. Anywhere at all. And the thing we need most is usually right in front of us."

Alex wiped his hands on a rag that looked like part of an old T-shirt. His grandfather's, maybe. He had been attracted to the mysterious Kate who occupied his barn, but this thoughtful Kate was dangerous. And standing close. "I hadn't thought about it that way. To me it's just a machine, parts that fit together. This one is so simple that it's elegant. It's easy for engineers to overcomplicate things. Trust me. Architects do it, too." He dropped the rag on the table. It landed on a magnetic tray of bolts and screws. "Most people would say that the true genius is the modern car, but there's something beautiful about a straightforward network of parts like this. It gives so much and asks for so little in return."

Alex tidied the table, sorting tools into categories and folding clean rags. He lifted a small plastic package that held a cork gasket and turned it over in his hand, looking at the label with its faded lettering. "I wish people were like that. Like parts of a machine. I wish you could just take them out of their packaging and hold them up to the light, look up their part number in a catalog, see if they'll fit, you know."

"Wouldn't that take the fun out of getting to know people? I mean, for people who aren't afraid of people. I'm only guessing here."

He smiled at her. "I guess you're right."

Their eyes met for a little too long, and Alex looked away before she dragged something out of him he might regret.

"Hey, before you got your first car, where did you want to go?" she asked.

"I don't think it was as much about going somewhere as it was about leaving." He looked at Kate and wondered what it might be like to stop running.

* * *

Kate evicted spiders from the barn with a broom. It was the latest in a string of unnecessary tasks. Organizing shelves and condensing unused parts into fewer boxes. Tasks that required no thought, leaving her mind free to stumble its way through objections. No matter how she shaped them, Alex was the reason she lingered. She'd hoped to see him, but he hadn't emerged from his office since lunch.

She crossed the path to the house, lifted the sliding glass door, and left her shoes on the mat. She removed the bandage from her hand. It was starting to heal. Tender. She washed her hands with soap that smelled like grapefruit and filled a glass with water. Dishes were piled in the sink, cups from their morning coffee and plates from lunch. She did the dishes, put them away, and wrapped her hand in a new bandage. Alex was in his office. His typing had stopped. He was probably looking out the window, pondering some shiny new thing.

She dried her hands on a dishtowel and walked down the hall. Just outside his office door, Alex turned the corner and ran into her.

"Alex!" She put a hand on the wall to brace herself.

He put his hands on her shoulders to keep from stumbling over her. "I'm sorry. I was coming to tell you not to clean."

"It was no big deal. Just cups and plates. I washed my hands, and I just thought, why not? I was there and half of them were mine. I'm rambling, aren't I?" She willed herself to stop talking, or come up with something intelligent, but she couldn't remember why she'd walked into the house.

"A little. It's okay." Alex pushed his fists into his pockets.

The Jeep. The wiring harness. "I just. The wiring. It's still not here yet. I called, and they said it'll be a few more days. Anyway, I'm stuck. So I won't be here for a bit."

"No? Nothing else to do in the meantime?"

"We did the exhaust, the brakes. The transmission is done. The barn is clean. I've done all I can do out there. I didn't want you to think that I abandoned you." Kate scolded herself. Why couldn't she just say normal things? Why couldn't she put together a string of words that weren't embarrassing? "The Jeep. I didn't want you to think I abandoned the Jeep."

"Thanks for telling me. I would have worried."

"Yeah?"

"Bears. Ditches."

"Rabid deer?"

"Yeah. Rabid deer."

Kate stepped back, extracting herself from the awkward situation she'd created, wishing he'd give her an excuse to stay. "Okay, well. Hey, I don't know if you're interested, but when the wiring gets here, you could help if you want to." She turned and took a few steps down the hall. What if he didn't want to help? "I mean, if you thought it would be fun, you're welcome to." Did she sound like she was begging? "You know what I mean. Anyway, thanks. See you in a few days."

"Hey Kate?"

When she turned back, Alex was leaning against the wall. That smile. "Yeah?"

He didn't look at her like she was a victim. He didn't ask her why she was damaged or wonder if she'd let anyone in or healed a wound. He didn't tell her she was cold and unloving. She wanted to ask him to meet halfway, to go out for a hike, to have a drink. She lost her nerve.

"I'd love to help with the wiring," he said.

She nodded. "Great! It'll be fun. See you in a few days."

* * *

Mulch cut into Alex's knees. He pulled the price tag from a hand shovel and dug into the dirt, making piles of soil along the edge of the patio. He filled the voids with begonias and pansies until the porch was surrounded by hues of pink and white and purple. The little green Jeep watched from the barn. Kate was never far from his mind.

While the summer sun rose in the sky, Alex exhausted his distractions. The house was clean, the lawn was mowed. The sliding glass door was, at long last, repaired. He sat at the picnic table with a notepad and a pen and made lists. Lists of home improvements. Grocery lists. Two weeks of lunches for himself and Kate, and just in case, he included her in some dinner plans. He grew angry with himself, threw them away, and started again. He made pros and cons lists of reasons to build a sunroom on the back of the house, reasons to remodel the kitchen, and reasons never to date again.

Distance didn't have to make the heart grow fonder. He could use it to recharge his batteries, to figure out whether he was tumbling down an inherited spiral of negativity or if he really was as unworthy as he felt. He tapped his heel against the concrete patio and stared at his notepad.

He answered his Blackberry without looking, expecting Eric with revisions for his last design. "Alex, here."

"Alex!" It was Kate. "The wiring arrived today. I'll be back tomorrow, if that's okay..."

"Sure. That's more than okay." His stomach twisted into a knot. Distance had only confused things. He missed her voice, her presence in the house.

"I was going to come by this afternoon, but I need to lay it out on the floor and label the wires, so I know where they go. Unless..."

He looked down at his list of reasons to run. Expectations. Demands. Becoming an obstacle in someone else's life path. Shifting priorities. Being reminded that he was unlovable. He closed the cover. "No! I mean, yes. Bring it now. We can lay it out in the house or in the barn. I'd like to see it."

"Okay, that sounds great! I'll be there in about an hour."

Alex lifted the cover of the book and returned to his list. What if there was too much baggage? What if he carried around too much of the past to hold up his end of a relationship with Kate? What if he hurt her because he wasn't ready? What if her baggage was too heavy to lift? What if he simply found himself, yet again, unable to live up to the expectations of a partner? He read through the list again. The only battle he waged was with himself. And the only way to win the battle was to stop fighting it. He picked up his phone and sent a text message to Eric. "Re: Philly. Give me one more week to decide."

* * *

Kate followed streams and creeks, driving along the winding mountain roads, swatting at the butterflies in her stomach. Admitting to herself that she liked Alex was like escaping from a self-inflicted exile, but she didn't need him to know that. She collected boxes and bags from her car and entered his house through the sliding glass door in an animated blur. "You fixed the door!"

"I had some time on my hands." Alex joined her at the kitchen table, where she dropped everything in a pile.

"This is so neat. Have you ever seen a wiring harness before? Of course you have. Everybody has. Anyway, I bought a few connector sets." She dug through a plastic bag, lining up tubes and containers in a row. "Dielectric grease and shrink tubing and there's already a heat gun in the barn that we can use."

Alex shook a little box of connectors and lifted a flap of the cardboard

265

box to peek at the wiring. "Color coded. This looks fun."

They sat on the living room floor, uncoiling wires and matching them up to the diagram, labeling the ends with numbered slivers of masking tape. When they were done, Kate coiled the wires back into the box and carried it to the table. "Having everything numbered ahead of time will definitely make the job go faster."

"Anything to speed things up," he said.

Alex was inches away from her. The air between them grew warm. Her breath caught in her throat, and she wanted to get to the barn, where she felt confident and in control. It seemed strange to her, to think of the barn as her space, but once they began the task of rewiring the car, her hands would steady, and her mind would clear. She expected him to step back, to put space between them, but he froze, his eyes searching hers. She could tell he was searching for words or willing himself to speak. Or not to speak. Or maybe move closer. She wished he would move closer.

"How do you feel about a beer while we work?"

She exhaled. That's it? That's all he could come up with? "I thought you'd never ask. You don't happen to have any whiskey, do you?"

Alex stepped back toward the kitchen. "Absolutely."

CHAPTER TWENTY-SEVEN

The barn soaked up the red-orange glow of sunset. Kate sat on a barstool with a length of old wiring in her hand, its light brown fabric coating brittle, frayed. She bent it in half, and the outer fibers broke. Tiny puffs of dirt swirled into the air.

Alex pulled a stool close and sat next to her. "Whatcha thinking about?" His arm brushed against hers, but he didn't pull back this time like she expected.

She dangled the strand of wiring before him. "I wonder if this is the original wiring. Every mile this car has taken, every person it's ever known. Every night drive. Every trip to the store. This wiring would have lit up the brake lights every time. I almost wish we didn't have to replace it."

Alex bowed his head over the wire in his lap. "I didn't think about that. It's not very safe. It definitely has to go, but it does make you think about your place in its history."

There was enough electricity between them to start the car. Kate didn't want to leave. She didn't want to spend another night counting the ways she could screw it up before she even started. Counting the reasons to disconnect from how she felt. Stretching into the deepest, darkest corners for excuses.

Alex put the length of old wire in her hands, and she took it to the folding tables that served as a makeshift workbench. With her back to him, she let out a long, slow breath, closed her eyes, and reset her heart. She searched for words, for the strength to put them in the right order and the resilience to handle the consequences. She wiped her hands on her jeans and grabbed their whiskey glasses. "One sip left." His fingertips brushed her knuckles when he accepted the offering. "Toast to being off to a good start?"

"You bet." The clink of the glasses echoed in the barn. "It's nice out here at night. I've been thinking about making something out of this place." She willed Alex to meet her eyes, but he scanned the barn instead. "Put a little wood stove in the corner. String of lights. Some outdoor rugs and chairs. Maybe build a little bar out here? Hey, maybe we could invite your friends over when you're done with the Jeep. Celebrate."

We. She liked the way it sounded. "That would be beautiful in the winter, too. Great place to read a book and have a drink. Maybe I should drag out this project, so I can enjoy it." Kate swallowed hard, the strong, oaky finish lingering on her tongue, numbing the roof of her mouth.

"Maybe you should just come by."

"Maybe I should." The whiskey tasted smooth. Too smooth.

Alex took the last sip of his drink. "Right back at it tomorrow?"

"First thing in the morning." Kate swirled the last drop in the bottom of the glass, so thin that it covered the sides, colorless. It seemed to disappear. She watched it fall and form a puddle.

"You look sad," he said. "There's more, you know."

"Sad?" Her nose wrinkled when she grinned. "No. Not sad. I have to drive, anyway."

"There's a guest room. You're welcome to hang out. I like it when we hang out."

"Me, too." She took a sip and stepped closer to Alex, closing the distance. "Thank you."

"For what?"

"For letting me use your barn. Selling me your grandfather's Jeep. For forgiving me for being such a brat and accepting me the way I am, flaws and all."

"I have plenty of my own."

Their eyes met for an eternity, and her stomach burned with curiosity. She wanted to find the flaws. Every one of them. "Maybe it's the whiskey or the night air or the fun of working on the Jeep with you, but I'm really enjoying this night. I don't want it to end yet. I might take you up on that second drink and guest room offer." She tilted back the glass and took in the last of her drink. "I'm glad you're doing this with me. I missed you the last few days."

Alex reached out his hand. "Give me that glass, and I'll refill it."

Instead, she sat it on her empty seat. Slowly, gently, she removed the glass from Alex's hand and placed it next to hers. She wound her fingers in his. His hands were strong, and he pulled her in. She let go, falling into a kiss that was worth the wait.

* * *

The next morning, light spread its arms across the barn and embraced the house. It made its way between slats in the blinds, found every pinhole in the curtains. Kate woke. She rolled onto her side and reached out, touching a black line on Alex's arm, the edge of a tattoo.

"Are these city skylines?"

"They are." Alex twisted his arm and looked at them. Lines of color, traces of where buildings met the sky. "Every place I've ever lived."

"It looks like an erratic map of heartbeats." Kate traced the red horizon of New York. "You're really connected to the city, aren't you?"

Alex smiled. It was a wistful smile, derived from something far away. "I am. It's this constant churn of renewal. Everything is aging, being replaced. I get to make new things to fill the voids. I like to live as high up as I can, so I can sit on a fire escape and watch the lights."

"I need to keep my feet on the ground. I'd be terrified to live up that high." Kate traced a red line.

"Nah. You'd get used to it. What makes you feel small, like none of your problems matter?"

Kate rolled her pillow under her neck. "The sky at night. All those stars."

"The city's like that for me. I'm just one little atom in this giant molecule, and all those city lights remind me that I'm not alone."

Alone. The word brought a sour taste to her mouth. It was the last thing Brad said to her. That it was her fault he strayed, because she couldn't love, and she made him feel alone. She sat up in bed and reached for her shirt.

Alex traced her spine with his finger. "What's on your schedule for today?"

"Back to the wiring, I guess." Kate turned back to Alex. She grasped his hand, seeking comfort, reassurance that this wouldn't hurt, that she wouldn't turn him into a monster.

Alex squeezed back. "What's that look? What are you thinking?"

"I'm wondering if you have a spare toothbrush."

"Hall closet."

She gave him a quick kiss. "Thank you. Want to skip the car today? Go out for breakfast and hang out?"

"I thought you'd never ask."

Kate scampered down the hall for the toothbrush, and Alex called after her. "You could leave it in the holder on the sink if you want."

She called back, "I think I will."

Sunlight reached the foot of the bed, inching its way across the plaid duvet cover. Outside, birds took off in search of food, flapping wings and chirps breaking the silence.

Alex picked up his Blackberry and unplugged it from the charger. He opened a blank email to Eric. "Thanks for the offer on Philly. Give it to Kelsey. I'm gonna stay here for a while and see where the road leads."

Philadelphia would always be there.

* * *

Weeks went by. Happy weeks, lost in each other and the newness of discovery. For Kate, the new faded like old paint, etched by the claws Alex dug into her while trying to get to her emotional truths. She craved the silence with him, the stillness of his spirit. She wanted to be better, closer, open, but fear would consume her like a flow of lava when he got too close. It started at the source of her shame, at an unknowable core that drove people away, that made them cheat and lie and manipulate. And when the heat was too much to bear, old habits of distancing reached a boiling point. She turned back to the Jeep, a salve. Like bathing in exotic oils.

A few stray bits of wire were all that was left. After half a day of work, she waved one end of the battery cable at Alex. It was a big moment. Her Jeep. Her father's Jeep. Alex's grandfather's Jeep. Alive again.

"You want to do the honors?" Kate asked.

Alex waved his hand in protest. "No. You should. It's your Jeep."

"But it was your grandfather's, too. And we did the wiring together. Tell you what. You hook up the battery, and I'll start the engine."

Kate still hadn't told him that it wasn't hers to keep. That she was sending it home, back to her father, where it belonged. The time was never right. She couldn't find the words. Something else would come up. But those were just excuses. Maybe she wasn't ready for him to know yet. Maybe she was saving it for a surprise. All she knew was that every time she tried to form the words, anxiety would crackle and blister beneath her skin.

Kate scooted into the driver's seat and draped her left arm over the steering wheel. She waited for Alex's cue and turned the key. A little red light on the dash illuminated and she pulled a black knob with the word LIGHTS etched into it. The speedometer glowed. She beamed at Alex through the windscreen, and he gave her two thumbs up. So far, so good.

Eyes shut, she pulled on the choke and started the ignition. The engine sputtered to life. A puff of black smoke, thick with carbon that faded to gray then white. The smell of gasoline and burning grease stung her nose. She listened to the rise and fall of the valves and cut the engine. She hopped from the Jeep. "We did it! I can't believe it. I've never done anything like this before. Taking apart a transmission and rewiring a car has to be one of the coolest things I've ever done."

Alex gripped her in a bear hug and brushed her hair from her face.

Her excitement faded in the sour squeeze of intimacy, and she pulled away. She wasn't in the mood. Something shadowed Alex's face. Disappointment. Hurt, maybe. She turned her back to him and tugged the key from the ignition.

She owed him something to compensate for the chill. "There's not much left to do. Want to celebrate? We can pick up some stuff from my apartment and stop at the market on the way back. Make a nice dinner and eat on the patio?"

"Yeah." Behind her, Alex shoved his hands in his pockets. "Dinner would be nice. Maybe we could talk."

"Sure. If you want." The talk. She was surprised it had taken that long. Kate hopped back into the Jeep and started the engine again. It sputtered to life and stalled.

* * *

Alex sprinkled cinnamon onto a sweet potato and dug at it with a fork.

Across from him, Kate did the same. Her hands moved gracefully, and he smiled at his peas and carrots, remembering how clumsy he used to be around her.

The start of school was approaching. Alex wanted to ask her where they were headed, but he hesitated. She would let him in but only so far before she would change the subject or shut down, like a music box with its lid slammed shut. He decided to tackle a tangible matter, to ease into the topic of her distance and their future.

"With school starting, will you spend weeknights here? I'd love it if you were here all the time, but I don't want our relationship to make things hard for you. We can stay at your place, too, if it's more convenient."

"Are you only saying that because I work forty-five minutes away? That's no big deal."

"Okay." Good. But that didn't explain her distance. "You're welcome to come here every night. I would miss you if you weren't here, but we can go to your place, too. I just don't want to you feel like you're the only one who has to make an effort."

"I don't mind if you come to my place. It's a little noisy sometimes with the neighbors and all. It's just nicer being here. I know what you mean, though. I don't want anything to change, either."

If school wasn't what troubled her, maybe it was the Jeep. Maybe it was him. Maybe he wasn't enough. As they cleared the table, Alex took aim, hoping for an answer he could bear. "Hey, didn't you want to finish the Jeep before the end of summer? Is that still the goal?"

Kate scraped their plates into the trash can, dropping sweet potato skins, peas and carrots into the can. The lid slammed when she took her foot from the lever. "You're really worried about school, aren't you?"

"Not school. Not exactly. Maybe it's the changing of the seasons. Your schedule. The end of you working on the Jeep."

"If it makes you feel any better, there's still stuff to do." Her voice trailed off, and she sounded disinterested. She seemed disinterested in everything. The Jeep. Him.

"You're not giving up on it, are you?"

"Definitely not. I just lost motivation for a while, I guess. A little distracted."

"Yeah?" That much he knew. If it wasn't school or the Jeep, then that left him. He had to find a way to make her happy. If he could make her happy, then he'd know that he was good enough. "Do you want help with the Jeep? What's left?"

She waved a hand, brushing it off. "I feel like it's my mess to clean up. Something is wrong with the timing or the carburetor or both. The engine keeps shutting down. Maybe the timing. I'm not even sure if that's really the problem."

"I don't want to take over your project. I know you were looking forward to finishing it." Alex tugged her into a stiff hug. She returned it, but it felt like obligation. Like the departing hug from a visiting friend. He felt the familiar pain of anticipated loss spread through him. He wanted to stop the clock, to hold everything together until he could figure it out. Maybe a shower would clear his head, help him come up with the words to her closer before she fell away. "Tell you what, I'm going to hop in the shower, and when I get out, we can figure out what's next and make a plan? Maybe you can get it running before school starts. If you want."

"Sounds good. I know how much you love a list."

Alex accepted a kiss and went down the hall.

* * *

Water rushed through the pipes to the shower. Kate poured a finger of whiskey into two glasses and flipped on the television. News anchors were fixated on subprime mortgages and hedge funds. She turned it off and went to Alex's office, stretched across his desk to take a pen from a glass jelly jar. From the top of a stack of magazines, she lifted the composition notebook in which Alex made lists and notes. Settled on the sofa, she opened to the middle, flipping forward to find the first blank page and her eyes fell on two columns of neat handwriting. The Kate List. There were far more cons than pros.

CHAPTER TWENTY-EIGHT

Head rush. Kate gripped the edge of the sofa cushion. The cover of the composition book was cool against her knees. She opened one eye and peeked at the list. Still there.

She slammed the book closed, refusing to read it. She didn't need to. She already knew. She didn't know how to be intimate. She pulled away too often. She was cold. Always somewhere else. She didn't give him a reason to stick around, so he'd find someone prettier, funnier, more girly. Someone who would wear the right thing and laugh at the right times. Even if the lyrics were different, the song was the same. She didn't need to waste her time with someone who could find more reasons to be without her than with her. She hadn't wanted to know Alex four months ago, and she wouldn't want to know him tomorrow.

Her shoes sat by the door. She wanted to run, to slip them on and be gone before he got out of the shower, but that would be letting him off too easy. She prepared like a prize fighter. Shoulders back. Back straight. She waited.

When the water stopped and Alex entered the living room in a pair of blue pajama bottoms and smelling like the aftershave she liked so much, she didn't move. The book rested, open, on the table on front of her.

Alex came to a halt. "What happened, Kate?"

"That's a good question. I've been trying to figure that out. Let's see…things were going fine. We had dinner, and you asked me if we'd still see each other as much once school started. Then you asked me when I would be done with the Jeep." Kate cracked her knuckles. "I wonder about that. Are you trying to give me some kind of hint? Get me to leave? Maybe if I go on my own, you won't have to break up with me. I don't even know what this is to you. This thing we have. Well, that's not true. I know, at the very least, it's a pros and cons list."

"Oh God. Kate, that list…"

"Wait. I want to get comfortable." Everything that ate her from the inside out about being cheated on by a coward and a failed fiancé boiled to the surface. She grabbed her drink from the table and sat back on the sofa. "Before you start, you should know that I've seen some really good performances by some expert manipulators. It's gonna take a lot to get a rave review. Go ahead."

Alex approached slowly, cautiously, like a lion tamer aware of the risk, but intent on breaching the divide. "I'm sure you have been through some insanity. I have, too. That's what this list was. I promise, it has nothing to do with you and everything to do with me battling my own demons."

"Cliché. I can't believe you went for the 'it's not you it's me' line. I'm feeling sympathetic, so I'll give you another try."

Alex put the list in her lap. "Read it, Kate. Read it."

She threw it on the floor. "It doesn't matter what your reasons are. You can't come up with more than one to be with me, but you sure could fill a page with reasons not to. I'm just curious, for the sake of closure, what made you change your mind? If I was just a summer fling, now's a good time to let me know."

Alex winced. It was enough of an admission for Kate. She moved to the door and shoved her feet into her sneakers.

"Summer fling? You were anything but convenient. I've been down my own long road. The last thing I wanted was for…"

The door closed, and she was gone.

"For you to show up on my doorstep and become my everything." Alex wanted to run after her, to stand in front of her car, to hug her, to stop her from hurting, to tell her that it wasn't what she thought. He wanted to make her listen to all the ways he didn't deserve her. All the ways he knew he wasn't good enough. All the ways that she was right, and he didn't deserve her because he was careless and thoughtless and stupid. But he let her go.

* * *

Kate pulled into an abandoned gas station at the edge of town and wiped her eyes with her sleeve. She dug her phone from the bottom of her purse, but her shaking hands wouldn't scroll through her contacts to find Michelle. She threw her Blackberry on the passenger seat, angry with herself for trusting when she knew she shouldn't, disappointed in herself for not restoring the Jeep before she ruined the relationship. Kate cried angry tears and drove home in the rain.

The devastation of loss arrived like an old acquaintance. The kind who remembers the worst of you and reminds you of every fault, every mistake. She wound the window down and let the night air whisk her feelings away, leaving her raw and numb. Burned skin and dead nerves.

* * *

Alex faced the door that Kate closed in his face. She had pulled night air into the room like a vacuum. He let it fill the wound in his chest. The ache turned into searing pain as he listened to her car fade into the mountains and bored a hole through the door with his stare. He couldn't blame her for being angry or for bringing baggage into their relationship. He'd been worried enough about his own to make a list, and it became a self-fulfilling prophecy.

The depression she'd made in the sofa remained. Her seat was probably still warm. Alex knocked back both of their drinks, smoothed the fabric over the cushion, and paced. When sunlight inched over the horizon, he pulled the blinds, and when it seeped around the edges, he decided to reclaim it.

He drove for hours in his bedroom slippers, winding through the mountains, immersed in the smell of earth and pine after the rain. In his search for distraction or clarity, he only found that he didn't know himself at all. He didn't yearn for the changing skyline of a bustling city and the dissonance of humanity, of a billion individuals melting into mob that craved validation in the tumult. He no longer sought comfort among people, all seeking the same relief from themselves. He knew the answer was within, but out of reach. Hungry and tired, he navigated home. There was nowhere to run to and nothing worth running from.

* * *

Kate climbed the stairs to her apartment and slipped into a grimy pair of oversized orange sweatpants and a housecoat. She turned to the old standbys. Ice cream. Chardonnay. Bad movies. Food wrappers, take-out containers, delivery menus piled on tables and counters. She turned off her phone, removed the battery, and let the laundry pile up until she was forced to kick her laundry bag down three flights of stairs and back up again, risking being seen by a neighbor.

She shook her clean laundry out of the bag and onto her bed. Clean socks and T-shirts, some permanently stained with grease and oil, tumbled out and formed a mountain she didn't intend to fold. With one last shake, a washcloth and a set of keys fell onto the bed. It unlocked a fear, irrational as it was, that gripped the numbness by the throat. She backed out of the room and closed the door, sealing the key away like a plague.

Days later, in need of clean clothes, she faced her bedroom door with a glass of whiskey. Liquid resolve. She pushed open the door, took the rusted keyring in her hand, and tucked it in the pocket of her housecoat.

Car parts haunted her. She found a bolt from the floor pan on the kitchen windowsill. A grease fitting in the bathroom. Stray electrical connectors in the hall closet. She scoured the apartment, collecting parts in the pocket of her housecoat. She stood above the kitchen sink and wondered how much damage they would do to the garbage disposal. She threw them into the trash instead, carried the bag to the dumpster, and slammed the door. She erased every memory of the Jeep from her apartment.

* * *

In the forest, in his home in the woods, days passed. Alone, Alex faced down the man who repeated the same mistakes for comfort and security. The man who walked away because it was easier than digging deep into a real human connection. The man who created his own shame and wore it like a status symbol. In the bathroom mirror, he came face-to-face with his unlovable self and rejected that man. He decided to stop shaving.

Cereal bowls piled in the sink. Mail sat unread on the coffee table. Dust piled on baseboards and picture frames. On the fifth day without Kate, a work deadline called to him, but his office felt like a crime scene, the place where his relationship had died. If Kate hadn't picked up that composition book, she'd still be here. If it weren't for that list, she never would have left.

Seated at his kitchen table, he surrounded himself with bound volumes of paper. He ripped out page after page, purging the goals and ambitions of the old Alex, of the one who wanted to run and replace. Except for that list. He tucked that list into his desk drawer and fed the rest into the shredder. He carried grocery bags stuffed with strips of paper outside to the trash cans and stopped on the patio, transfixed at the sight of the Jeep peering out of the barn like a judgmental old man who'd seen it all and had no time for his nonsense.

He climbed into the driver's seat, baptized by the smell. The same smell his grandfather knew. The Jeep knew his grandfather better than he did. He let the car and all its memories, those who came before, give him comfort.

But the Jeep wasn't his, it was Kate's. So was the barn. He remembered wanting to string up lights, make it a useful space. A restorative space. The old Alex had one aspiration worth pursuing, so the new Alex started to clean. Everything seemed to hinge on reclaiming the barn, making it his, removing the memory of her. Boxes of unused car parts, rusty tools, and old rakes were pushed into a heap in the furthest empty bay of the barn. He smeared rust and dirt from his hands to his housecoat as he dug his Blackberry from the pocket and scrolled through his contacts in search of the scrap metal guy.

Hours passed. On his hand and knees, he scrubbed the house, starting at the bottom. Every baseboard. Every inch of grout in the bathroom floor. When the doorbell rang, Alex jumped like hunted prey. He peered through a gap in the curtain and relaxed at the sight of the scrap metal guy on his porch.

"It's just that pile in the barn, right?" The man motioned toward the barn and his idling truck.

"Yeah. Not the stuff on the other side or against the wall." Alex started to close the door.

"What's the deal with that old Jeep?"

Alex stepped onto the front porch and tied his stained and tattered housecoat tight, looking toward the barn, at the closed door that hid it from view.

"Wish I knew."

"I got a lot of old cars out at the junkyard, and there's a market for parts. I'd be happy to take it off your hands. I'd pay ya for it."

It was tempting, just to see it gone. But it wasn't his Jeep. Alex waved it off. "I don't know what the deal is. It's not mine anymore. I sold it."

The man dug a business card from his pocket. "You've got my number, but pass this on to whoever owns it. If they're interested. Have 'em call me."

"Will do." Alex took the card and closed the door. He pushed the sharp corner of the thick paper into his thumb, where it left a dent. He went down the hall to his office and propped the card against his monitor. She hadn't returned any of his messages, but in a last-ditch effort, he dug the phone from his pocket and left one more, offering to buy back the Jeep so he could sell it for scrap and get his barn back.

Her voice. The voicemail greeting pulled melancholy to the surface again. His eyelids grew warm, his eyes wet. He blinked it away. He left one last message. Too bruised for the barn, he pushed open the window, letting cool air fill his lungs. Papers rustled on his desk and fluttered to the floor. In a restorative purge, he gathered them into a pile and tossed them in a filing cabinet drawer, leaving his desk bare. In its place, he piled the contents of the shelves, a blend of his books and his grandfather's records. A thesaurus. A dictionary. A black binder.

He threw open the cover and a pen fell out, yellowed plastic with red lettering. The first page was a bill of sale, something or other that his grandfather had owned and loved. Receipts. A note in unfamiliar handwriting about a headlight bulb. Receipt for ice cream and oil. And photographs.

Alex laid the notebook on his desk and read every note, examined every photograph. It was the Jeep.

CHAPTER TWENTY-NINE

Alex closed the belt to his housecoat in the door, cursed, and dropped his keys while trying to free himself. He drove an hour in his pajamas to Kate's apartment complex and stood in the parking lot, looking at the tall, arched entrances. All the buildings looked the same. He couldn't remember which was Kate's. He tried to retrace the last steps he took there and ended up at a nameless door that looked like all the others.

"I don't know, son, but she doesn't live here." A woman his mother's age peeked through the crack in the door, her face obscured by the door chain.

"She's about this tall. Brown hair. Beautiful. And she sings in the shower."

"I can promise you I know nothing about how my neighbors sing in the shower. Are you sure that you're okay, honey? You don't look so good."

"I'm fine. I'll be better when I find her."

She closed the door. He returned to the parking lot and tried again. Two buildings down and two flights up, he faced a familiar door, her name barely visible on a faded slip of paper beneath the peephole. He knocked and waited, looking down at his shoes. He had no idea what he would say when she opened the door. If she opened the door.

"Alex."

"Unchain the door. Please. You don't have to let me in. You can talk to me out here. I don't care. Please. I need to talk to you."

"You need to shave. You should go home and do that." She pushed the door closed, and he blocked it with his hand.

"I probably should, but I can't. I have something for you, and I need to talk to you. Please."

"Move your hand." She closed the door enough to unhook the chain and stepped to the side. "Come in, then. You're scaring my neighbors."

"Can you please do both of us a favor and read this damn list." Alex dangled the paper before her, but she crossed her arms in icy defiance.

"Why not?"

"Because I don't need you."

"Ouch." He looked around her apartment. She wasn't doing much better than him by the looks of the food wrappers. He had been focused on getting her to listen and hadn't noticed she was wearing his orange sweatpants. They were a contrast to her green flip flops and purple housecoat. "Why are you being irrational? This isn't you. I don't know what's going on, but it isn't you. I get that you're really pissed at me, but has it occurred to you that you're mad for the wrong reason? When you look back on this in a year, don't you want to know the real reason you ended a relationship with someone who really cared about you? Because I think you're just trying to protect yourself before you get hurt by something that isn't even real."

"Maybe. But it doesn't matter because I'm already over you."

"Yeah, it looks like it. No signs of grief in this apartment."

"Are you done?"

"No. That Jeep is still sitting there. I don't know why you wanted it so bad, but you had something to prove to yourself, and you haven't finished yet. You need to finish that Jeep."

"You're right, I was proving something to myself, but I already learned my lesson the hard way. And don't use the Jeep as a pry bar to get in here and try to make me change my mind."

"Again. Ouch. You're not the only one in this relationship, and you don't get to throw in the towel without letting me have my say. That's not fair. I'm not leaving until you read this. Call the cops if you want, but they'll only charge you with being a hoarder, and once they read this, they'll think you're crazy, too."

The look she gave him was probably the same look she gave to her middle schoolers when they were out of control. "You've already had your say. It was all there in your list of cons."

"How would you know? You won't even read it. Do you honestly think that I'm trying to justify something I can't prove? I'm only guilty of adding an insensitive title to a list of my baggage. I have proof. It's right here. Why would I lie to you?"

"I don't care. I really don't care why you'd lie to me."

"Here! I'll read it to you. I've destroyed every relationship I've ever been in."

"Get out."

"I can't meet anyone's high standards. I'm never enough."

"I'm serious, Alex. Stop." She pulled her Blackberry from the pocket of her sweatpants, a hollow in the back where the battery once fit. "I will call the cops. I swear."

"It doesn't even have a battery in it. Here. Read it on your own time." Alex brushed food wrappers from her coffee table and slapped the list down. "You're using this as an excuse so you don't get hurt. If you were over me, you wouldn't need a way out. So let me ask you this: are you in love with me?"

"Are you insane? No."

"I think you are."

"How arrogant. I'm not. Stop saying that."

"I know you want to finish this Jeep. If you were over me, you'd be finishing that car not hiding from me."

"No."

"Okay, hiding from yourself. I'm right, aren't I?"

"I do not love you, Alex. I don't." She flinched when she said it.

"That wince? You lied. You do love me."

"Get out. Please."

"God, you're good at denial. Fine. I'll go, but I'm gonna leave that list here. You'll read it eventually." He took a step closer, still clutching the binder, and she took a step back. "I want you to know that I don't want anything from you, Kate. You owe me nothing. I'll even give you your money back for the Jeep, and you can pretend none of this ever happened if that makes you happy, but I don't think it would. I came here because …because I love you, too. I am absolutely terrified, because this isn't predictable. It isn't the kind of pain that I'm used to. I don't know how this is going to end, but I know that it can't end here."

"Stop. Stop." Tears pooled in her eyes.

Was she giving in?

He bit his tongue and swallowed hard to hide his flinch. He didn't want to hurt her, but he needed to speak his truth. She needed to find her own. "I don't want to keep making the same mistakes. You are not a mistake." He turned toward the door, his hand on the cool metal latch. "Let me know what you want to do about the Jeep."

"I need it. I'll figure it out. I'll send a tow truck or something."

The latch clicked, and the door released from the jamb. She wasn't calling his bluff, and he was running out of chances. "When? I don't think you want to finish the Jeep. If you did, you'd have finished it already. That car's just an excuse to you. It was an excuse to avoid me, then it was an excuse to be near me, and now you're hiding behind it so you don't have to admit something to yourself. I don't know why you wanted it, why a suburban teacher needs a forty-year-old Jeep, but I hope you find out someday."

He opened the door and a commingled swirl of cooking smells from outside entered the room.

"Wait." Kate's eyes begged him not to go.

He closed the door and leaned against it, clutching the notebook to his chest like a shield, waiting for her to break down her defenses.

"Okay." She sat and tucked her hands between her knees. "Okay. I've been lost. I was numb for a while. I tried to untangle this spider web, like plucking at the strings. Shutting you out is the easy road, but you're right, it isn't fair. And I can't untangle this without doing the work. Maybe I have been hiding behind the Jeep. I've been hiding behind things my whole life, because it's easier than trying to figure out why I keep making the same mistakes. I finally make a different choice, maybe even the right choice, and I don't know how to prepare for the fallout. It's easy to stay mad at you about that list, because at least I know what to expect. If I read it, and I'm wrong, I have to forgive you and accept that I'm terrified, stupid, irrational. I can't resist the urge to protect myself from another depressing surprise at the bottom of the cereal box. I thought I could handle being in a relationship again. Liking you was one thing, but I'm afraid that I'll lose control the second I admit that I love you."

Silence. A door slammed down the hall and laughing children left the building. Alex closed the door and stepped closer. "Kate, I can't make any guarantees, and you wouldn't want me to. We've all been through our share of shit. We're all rusty. I'm not judging you by your rust any more than I want you to judge me by mine. That's what that list was. It was me, chipping away at layers of rust. It's me trying to prove to myself that I'm lovable, that I'm worthy of whatever this might become. I'm not the horrible person other people made me feel like I am. Why do we do this to ourselves, carrying around so much hurt from people who never loved us that we can't see the love from the people who do?"

Kate took the paper from the table and folded it in half. She tore it in two, again and again, until she was left with confetti. It fell from her hand and scattered on the floor. "Can we start over?"

He laid the binder on the table and sat next to her.

"What's that?" she asked, her eyes locked on his.

"What's what?"

"That notebook."

"It's yours. It's about the Jeep. It was in my office with my grandfather's things."

She pulled it onto her lap and ran her hand over the cover. "Oh my God. It survived." She opened it and slammed it closed again, her eyes wide. "My dad."

"What survived? Your dad?"

"I get it."

"You get what?"

"I'm so stupid. My dad. My mom died when I was young. Very young. I never knew her, and my dad never moved on. He clung to the grieving process. Some people might say he was stuck there, but I think he did it on purpose. My mom was everywhere in our house. Pictures and the stories he would tell. Most girls had fairy tales, but I had a real fairy godmother. He made her so vibrant that it felt like she was there, you know? She's in all these memories I have, but she wasn't even there.

"Anyway, when my mom died, my dad gave up everything to pay the bills. He never cared much for material things, but the one thing he regretted giving up was his Jeep."

She put the notebook on his lap, opened to the sixth page, and pointed to a photograph of a couple. They stood on a porch, the man holding a baby. In the driveway sat the Jeep. "That's my dad."

"I've been looking for this Jeep off and on for years, but when Brad cheated on me, and I had to cancel all the wedding plans, I looked even harder. I figured the money I saved by not having a wedding could help me get my dad's Jeep back. It could have moved away from here or been totaled years ago, but my gut told me it was out there somewhere, so I kept looking. You had it."

"Are you kidding?" Alex's mouth went dry. He took the notebook from her and flipped through the pages. Similar noses. She had her mother's eyes. "This is your father's Jeep. Why didn't you tell me?"

"It was so deeply personal. At first, I didn't want you to know me that well and later—"

"Later, you were too busy putting up walls to keep me out."

"It isn't like that, Alex."

"Then what is it like, Kate? You're like the tide sometimes. You get close to me, then you pull away."

Kate turned her face.

"No, Kate. Talk to me. Where do you go when you run off like that?"

"I don't know. I don't know how to do this. I'm afraid to get hurt again, and it's not like a have a toolbox of inherited perspectives on relationships that I can fall back on."

"What is that supposed to mean?"

"I grew up in a house where love and loss were the same thing. I had a great childhood, and my dad is the best, but I didn't grow up at the intersection of love and happiness. I never saw people argue and make up or express their affection. All I saw was hurt and grief."

Alex looked down at the notebook, at the black and white photos of the smiling family, and the hint of something metal between the sofa cushions caught his eye. He dug between them, fishing out a rusty key ring with two small keys and dropped them into her palm.

She closed them in her fist. "I thought I threw these away. I kept finding things around here. Bolts and screws and random parts. I went on a rampage and threw them all out, but then I couldn't find the key. It must have fallen out of my pocket."

Alex closed his hand around hers. "I think this Jeep is trying to tell you something."

"I think this Jeep is trying to take me home."

CHAPTER THIRTY

Kate filled one of Walter's mugs with coffee and stepped onto the patio. Her eyes were slow to adjust in the dark, and her bare feet stung on the cold pavement. She inched her way to the Jeep, lowered the tailgate, and secured it with its chains. Sitting on a wheel well, she let the coffee warm her hands. The sky lightened, separating from the trees, bringing to light the red and orange and golden yellow shades of autumn that were beginning to stake their claim on the landscape.

The day was well established when Alex crept into the barn with the notebook and an envelope of photos. The Jeep bobbed on its leaf springs while he settled into place across from her, their knees touching.

"You're up early. Everything okay?"

"Yeah, I just couldn't sleep. I guess I'm nervous. And a little sad."

"Yeah, I know the feeling. It's been a great few days. I can't believe today's the day we take him to Elk River. I'm really gonna miss this little guy. What time did you get up?"

"Maybe an hour ago. Just before sunrise. I wanted to spend time with it alone, you know? The way it smells. Like metal and earth."

"I get that. I have a feeling you'll see it again, though."

"Oh, yeah. Any time I like, I imagine. I'll probably inherit it along with the farm someday."

A flock of geese moved south, honking overhead. "I always wondered what it would be like to live on a farm. It's the complete opposite of everything I've ever known."

Kate laughed. "It smells bad. It's a lot of hard work, and there's not much money in it."

"Good thing I'm an architect, then." Alex lifted the notebook to his lap and handed the envelope to Kate. "Wanna pick out which pictures to put in here? You hand them to me, and I'll find a place for them."

"Sure." Kate sifted through photographs they'd asked strangers to take. They posed with the Jeep by lakes and covered bridges and beside rocky streams. She held out one, the two of them by the Jeep in the barn. It was the only one that wasn't blurry, taken after Alex learned to use the timer on his grandfather's old camera. "This one. I love this one."

Alex was careful not to damage the brittle clear cover when he put the picture in place. He held the notebook out to her. "Full circle, then," he said.

"Full circle." Kate dropped the notebook to the floor of the Jeep. The thud echoed in the barn.

"There's a lot of history in there," Alex said. "You could probably turn it into a movie."

Kate looked down at it. "Or a book. Maybe after it's full. There are still blank pages in there." She leaned forward and smiled. "This car's been on a heck of a journey. I owe it a lot. And you. Thank you. For everything. I love you, Alex. I really do."

He believed her.

CHAPTER THIRTY-ONE

James peeked at the last page of his novel. Six pages left. He squeezed in every last word while his hand searched the drum table for his glasses. He pushed aside the television remote, a picture frame, a drink coaster. He shook the glasses open and squinted through them to look at the clock. It was too early to leave, but he hated to be late for things.

He uncoiled a small piece of leather and used it to mark his place. From the back of the kitchen chair, he collected his jacket and hat. Keys and wallet were in his pocket. He stepped onto the porch, and the screen door slammed behind him. It carried a lot of memories, some he clung to and some he'd forgotten. He was used to them now, like old acquaintances. He even chose not to replace the door when he had the chance.

He locked the back door and crossed the gravel drive to his truck, which sat outside under Claire's old veterinary clinic sign.

The drive to the bar was longer than it used to be. A few red lights. Ten-year-old stop signs that most Elk River residents still considered new. He parked in front of the bar at the curb and pushed open the heavy wood door.

Either he was early, or she was late.

* * *

Kate stepped out of the Jeep and into the street. She took Alex's hand and led the way to the bar. She turned to tell him the trick to closing the heavy wooden door, but he managed it without effort, and it closed without a sound.

The bartender lifted his chin in greeting. "Long time, no see, kid. You good?"

"Great. How about you, Tom?"

"Same. Nothing ever changes in here. What'll ya have?"

Kate took in the earthy, oaky, sweet smell of alcohol soaked into wood. She chose the stool beside a tall man in a plaid flannel shirt. Gray hair tumbled from beneath his hat, and he hunched over a newspaper, nursing a small glass of amber liquid.

"What he's having." She rested her forearms on the bar. "Beam, neat."

"Same," said Alex.

Beside her, her father lowered his paper. "Kiddo! You're late."

"No, Dad. You're early. You're always early. I wondered how long it would take you to look up." She reclined and looked between the two men. "Dad, this is my boyfriend, Alex. Alex, my dad."

Kate knew her father's handshake was crushing, and it lingered. She hoped he let up fast, because the anticipation was eating at her insides.

"So this is the boyfriend. The architect from the city. How are you adjusting to life out here?"

"Pretty well. It took a while to get used to the quiet."

"Mmm. I can imagine. I could never live with all that sound." He folded his newspaper neatly and laid it on the bar. "What is this surprise?"

Kate took the notebook from Alex and laid it on the bar in front of her father. "Let's start with this."

* * *

James ran his hand over the black cover. The light seemed to fade in the bar, like a cloud passed before the sun. The tiny nick in the bottom corner felt familiar. It couldn't possibly be the same notebook.

The pen was still in the front pocket, where it had stretched the plastic over the years. It had yellowed, and the red lettering faded, but the pen was the same. Blue ink from his signature had bled into the bill of sale, widening and blurring the letters. The plastic covers had yellowed, but they still held the memories to the pages. He traced the corner of the first photo. It was like seeing old friends. Claire, standing in the creek, taken the day after they painted her bathroom. He had been so nervous that he would say the wrong thing. That he wouldn't be able to make her happy. That the monster caged within him would consume them both. It never did. It wasn't real. She had shown him that.

It had been years since James looked at photographs of Claire. After Kate went to college, he took down her pictures. He had never moved on from her. Never wanted to. He would miss her forever, but he didn't need her photos. He had memories and her daughter.

Blinking back tears, he skipped ahead, turning two and three pages at a time. He stopped at a photo of a couple in caps and gowns labeled "William and Rebecca."

"William. Right. I remember this guy. I forgot his name, though. I didn't think he'd keep up with this." James looked past Alex to the end of the bar. "I sat right over there and sold him my Jeep. I can't believe this notebook survived this long. Where did you find this?"

"Keep going, Dad. There's more."

"This was your mother's idea." James thumbed forward, past photos of the Jeep inside a service station and by a water tower. "I was using it to keep track of receipts. Stuff like that. She wanted to fill it with pictures. Said they were building that highway, and all this would change. That we should take photos to remember it all by. She was right. I thought it was silly, but that was your mother. She was sentimental. And smart. In case you wondered where you got it from."

Page after page of notes and receipts and photographs told the story of his Jeep. Ben and Olivia in front of a college dorm. Mark and Olivia in the snow. Peter and his parents at the general store outside Buck Mountain. Walter with the Jeep by an old barn. Teddy bears. Kate and Alex.

"No..." James looked up from the notebook, his breath stuck somewhere in his chest. "How?"

"I found the Jeep. Your Jeep. I bought it from Alex. His grandfather had it. That's how we met. We've been working on it for months. It's been hard not to tell you, but I really wanted it to be a surprise."

His daughter took the notebook from him. She closed the cover, handed it to her boyfriend and stood, stepping toward the door.

"Come on, Dad. Come look," she said.

He willed his feet to follow his daughter out the door and into the sun, unable to put into words the sense of shock. His Jeep stood at the curb. He ran his hand along the curled metal edge of the tailgate and down the side of the car. He looked across the driver's seat and along the dash. "This is my Jeep. I can't believe you found my Jeep."

"I know how much you loved it. You talked about it all the time. It was in pictures all over the house, and I wanted you to have it. I needed to give it back to you. I need for you to have this car." Kate reached into the back pocket of her jeans and handed him the key, a simple little key that could have belonged to a filing cabinet. It dangled from a new keyring.

"I can't believe you did this. But why do you need me to have it?"

"You gave up a lot of things for me when I was little. You were my dad and my mom. You taught me how to bake cupcakes and repair broken tractors. I don't think I'll ever know how hard it was for you when Mom died. My tiny little shares of heartache broke me more than I knew until recently, and they were nothing compared to what you went through. I think—if I could give Mom back to you, I would, of course. This doesn't come close, but it's the best I can do. Giving it to you means patching a hole in the heart of my family."

James watched his daughter wipe her nose on her sleeve, and he put a hand on her shoulder. "Peanut, there's no hole in the heart of your family."

"But you never moved on. You never loved again."

"I didn't need to. I had everything I needed. I still do. Your mom has been there the whole time. She was there when you were eleven and buried your dog. She was there when you came running in the house with that envelope, yelling because you got into college. She kept me company while you danced at your prom. She sat next to you when that piece of…when that guy cheated on you and broke your heart. And she's gonna be there when you marry whatever guy is lucky enough to be chosen by you. Sure, I miss giving her a hug sometimes. But she's always here. And she's really proud of you."

James left his daughter's side and let his words sink in before the memories pulled him to pieces. He gripped the tailgate and looked into the back. He recalled a time when his life with Claire was new. When they watched the rains move across the fields, and she changed his life.

The climb into the driver's seat wasn't as easy or as graceful as it used to be. He wrapped his hands around the cool black wheel. It had been replaced. He pulled in his stomach and swore it was closer than it used to be. With the heel of his left foot, he tapped the gas tank. Three quarters full. His eyes moved along the dashboard to the yellowed numbers of the gauge face. He ran his thumb over the lettering that was embossed into the choke knob, and his feet found their place above the pedals.

The key felt the same in his fingers. Older, duller, less shiny but smooth. Like him, it was a little more experienced but none the worse for wear. He could still fit it into the ignition without looking, but he didn't start the car. Not yet. He tilted his head back to look beyond the sky.

James drifted back to a rainy day with Claire and petrichor. After all those years, his CJ-5 still smelled the same. It was an evocative tonic that transported him to a time before Kate. To a survivor in the making. Oils and grease and rubber fusing together. If there was a word for that smell, he didn't need to know. The smell didn't need a name. It was the smell of metal and earth.

ABOUT THE AUTHOR

A Maryland native and Pennsylvanian at heart, Jennifer M. Lane is a resident of East Norriton, PA. She holds a bachelor's degree in philosophy from Barton College where she served as editor of the newspaper. She also holds a master's in liberal arts with a focus on museum studies from the University of Delaware, where she wrote her thesis on the material culture of roadside memorials. She once co-hosted a daily automotive blog and served as the president of a large car club. She enjoys coffee, whiskey, Earl Grey tea, and spending time with her partner Matthew and their own 1964 Jeep CJ-5.

Printed in Great Britain
by Amazon